In White Raiment

William Le Queux

Prologue.

Yes; it was utterly inexplicable.

So strange, indeed, were all the circumstances, and so startling the adventures that befell me in my search after truth, that until to-day I have hesitated to relate the narrative, which is as extraordinary as it is unique in the history of any living man.

If it were not for the fact that a certain person actively associated with this curious drama of our latter day civilisation, has recently passed to the land that lies beyond the human ken, my lips would have perforce still remained sealed.

Hitherto, my literary efforts have been confined to the writing of half-illegible prescriptions or an occasioned contribution to one or other of the medical journals; but at the suggestion of the one who is dearest to me on earth, I have now resolved to narrate the whole of the astonishing facts in their due sequence, without seeking to disguise anything, but to lay bare my secret, and to place the whole matter unreservedly before the reader.

Every doctor has a skeleton in his cupboard. I am no exception.

Any dark or mysterious incident, however trivial, in the life of a medical man, is regarded as detrimental by his patients. It is solely because of that I am compelled to conceal one single fact—my true name.

For the rest, reader, I shall be quite straightforward and open in my confession, without the affectation of academic phrases, even though I may be a physician whose consulting-room in Harley Street is invariably full, whose fees are heavy, and whose name figures in the public prints as the medical adviser of certain leaders of society. As Richard Colkirk, M.D., M.R.C.S., M.R.C.P., F.R.S., specialist on nervous disorders, I am compelled to keep up appearances and impress, with a sense of superior attainments, the fashionable world who seek my advice; but as Dick Colkirk, the narrator of this remarkable romance, I can at all times be frank and sometimes confidential.

In the wild whirl of social London there occur daily incidents which, when written down in black and white, appear absolutely incredible. Amid the fevered rush of daily life in this, our giant city of violent contrasts, the city where one is oftentimes so lonely among millions, and where people starve and die in the very midst of reckless extravagance and waste, one sometimes meets with adventures quite as astounding as those related by the pioneers of civilisation—adventures which, if recounted by the professional novelist, must of necessity be accepted with considerable reserve.

Reader, I am about to take you into my confidence. Think for a moment. Have you not read, in your daily paper, true statements of fact far stranger than any ever conceived by the writer of fiction? Have you not sat in a dull, dispiriting London police-court and witnessed that phantasmagoria of comedy, tragedy, and mystery as presented to that long-suffering public servant, the Metropolitan Stipendiary?

If you have, then you will agree that romance is equally distributed over Greater London. Love is as honest and hearts beat as true in Peckham, Paddington, or Plaistow as in that fashionable half-mile area around Hyde-park Corner; life is as full of bitterness and broken idols in Kensington as it is in Kentish Town, Kennington, or the Old Kent Road. The two worlds rub shoulders. All that is most high and noble mingles with all that is basest and most criminal; therefore it is not surprising that the unwary frequently fall into the cunningly-devised traps prepared for them, and even then most prosaic persons meet with queer and exciting adventures.

Chapter One.

Mainly about People.

My worst enemy—and, alas! I have many—would not accuse me of being of a romantic disposition.

In the profession of medicine any romance, acquired in one's youth or college days, is quickly knocked out of one by the first term at the hospital. The medical student quickly becomes, in a manner, callous to human suffering, and by the time he obtains his degree he is generally a shrewd and sympathetic observer, but with every spark of romance crushed dead within his heart. Thus, there is no bachelor more confirmed than the celibate doctor.

I had left Guy's a year. It is not so very long ago, for I am still under forty—young, they say, to have made my mark. True, success has come to me suddenly, and very unworthily, I think, for I confess that my advancement has been more by good luck than by actual worth.

At Guy's I had been under Lister and other great men whose names will ever remain as medical landmarks, and when I left with my degree I quickly discovered that the doctor's calling was anything but lucrative.

My first engagement was as assistant to a country practitioner at Woodbridge, in Suffolk; a man who had a large but very poor practice, most of his patients being club ones. Upon the latter I was allowed to exercise my maiden efforts in pills and mixtures, while my principal indulged freely in whisky in his own room over the surgery. He was a hard drinker, who treated his wife as badly as he did his patients, and whose habit it was to enter the cottages of poor people who could not pay him, and seize whatever piece of family china, bric-à-brac, or old oak which he fancied, and forcibly carry it away as payment of the debt owing. By this means he had, in the course of ten years, made quite a presentable collection of curios, although he had more than once very narrowly escaped getting into serious trouble over it.

I spent a miserable year driving, by day and by night, in sunshine and rain, far afield over the Suffolk plains, for owing to my principal's penchant for drink, the greater part of the work devolved upon myself. The crisis occurred, however, when I had been with him some eighteen months. While in a state of intoxication he was called out to treat a man who had met with a serious accident in a neighbouring village. On his return he gave me certain instructions, and sent me back to visit the patient. The instructions—technical ones, with which it is useless to puzzle the reader—I carried out to the letter, with the result that the poor fellow's life was lost. Then followed an inquest, exposure, censure from the coroner, a rider from the jury, and my employer, with perfect sang froid, succeeded in fastening the blame upon myself in order to save the scanty reputation he still enjoyed over the countryside.

The jury were, of course, unaware that he was intoxicated when he attended the man and committed the fatal blunder, while I, in perfect innocence, had obeyed his injunctions. It is useless, however, to protest before a coroner; therefore I at once resigned my position, and that same night returned to London, full of indignation at the treatment I had received.

My next practice was as an assistant to a man at Hull, who proved an impossible person, and through the five years that followed I did my best to alleviate human ills in Carlisle, Derby, Cheltenham, and Leeds respectively.

The knowledge I obtained by such general and varied practice, being always compelled to dispense my own prescriptions, was of course invaluable. But it was terribly uphill work, and a doctor's drudge, as I was, can save no money. Appearances have always to be kept up, and one cannot put by very much on eighty or one hundred pounds a year. Indeed, one night, seven years after leaving Guy's, I found myself again in London, wandering idly along the Strand, without prospects, and with only a single sovereign between myself and starvation.

I have often reflected upon that memorable night. How different the world seemed then! In those days I was content to pocket a single shilling as a fee; now they are guineas, ten or more, for as many minutes of consultation. It was an unusually hot June, and the night was quite stifling for so early in summer. Although eight o'clock, it was not yet dark; but, as I strolled westward past the Adelphi, there was in the sky that dull purple haze with which Londoners are familiar, the harbinger of a storm. I had sought several old friends of hospital days, but all were out of town. June was running out, and the season was at an end.

London may be declared empty, and half a million persons may have left to disport themselves in the country or by the sea, yet the ebb and flow in that most wonderful thoroughfare in the world—the Strand—is ever the same, the tide in the dog-days being the same as in December. It is the one highway in London that never changes.

I had strolled along to the corner of Bedford Street, down-hearted and low-spirited, I must confess. Ah! to know how absolutely lonely a man can be amid those hurrying millions, one must be penniless. In the seven years that had passed, most of my friends had dispersed, and those who still remained cared little for a ne'er-do-well such as myself. In that walk I calmly reviewed the situation. Away in quiet old Shrewsbury my white-haired, widowed mother lived frugally, full of fond thoughts of her only boy. She had brought herself to the verge of poverty that I might complete my studies and become a doctor. Poor mother! She believed, like so many believe, that every doctor makes a comfortable income. And I had worked—nay, slaved—night and day, through seven whole years, for less wage than an average artisan.

I had not dined, for, truth to tell, I had hesitated to change my last sovereign; but the pangs of hunger reminded me that nothing had passed my lips since the breakfast in my dingy lodgings, and knowing of a cheap eating-house in Covent Garden, I had paused for a moment at the corner.

Next instant I felt a hearty slap on the back, and a cheery voice cried—

"Why, Colkirk, old fellow, what's up? You look as though you're going to a funeral?"

I turned quickly and saw a round, fresh-coloured, familiar face before me.

"By Jove!" I exclaimed in pleasant surprise. "Raymond! is it really you?" And we grasped hands heartily.

"I fancy so," he laughed. "At least, it's what there is left of me. I went out to Accra, you know, got a sharp touch of fever, and they only sent back my skeleton and skin."

Bob Raymond was always merry and amusing. He had been the humourist of Guy's, in my time: the foremost in practical joking, and the most backward in learning. The despair of more than one eminent lecturer, he had, nevertheless, been one of the most popular fellows in our set, and had occupied diggings in the next house to where I lodged in a mean street off Newington Butts.

"Well," I laughed, "if you left your flesh behind you on the West Coast, you've filled out since. Why, you're fatter than ever. What's your beverage? Cod-liver oil?"

"No; just now it's whisky-and-seltzer with a big chunk of ice. Come into Romano's and have one. You look as though you want cheering up."

I accepted his invitation, and we strolled back to the bar he had mentioned.

He was a short, fair-haired, sturdily-built fellow with a round face which gave him the appearance of an overgrown boy, a pair of blue eyes that twinkled with good fellowship, cheeks that struck me as just a trifle too ruddy to be altogether healthy, a small mouth, and a tiny, drooping, yellow moustache. He wore a silk hat of brilliant gloss, a frock-coat, as became one of "the profession," and carried in his hand a smart ebony cane with a silver crook. I noticed, as we stood at the bar, that his hat bulged slightly on either side, and knew that in it was concealed his stethoscope. He was therefore in practice.

Over our drinks we briefly related our experiences, for we had both left the hospital at the same term, and had never met or heard of each other since. I told him of my drudgery, disappointment, and despair, to which he listened with sympathetic ear. Then he told me of himself. He had gone out to Accra, had a narrow squeak with a bad attack of fever, returned to London to recover, and became assistant to a well-known man at Plymouth.

"And what are you doing now?" I inquired.

"I've started a little practice over in Hammersmith," he answered. "I've been there a year; but Hammersmith seems such a confoundedly healthy spot."

"You haven't got many patients—eh?" I said, smiling.

"Unfortunately, no. The red lamp doesn't seem to attract them any more than the blue lamp before the police-station. If there was only a bit of zymotic disease, I might make a pound or two; but as it is, gout, indigestion, and drink seem to be the principal ailments at present." Then he added, "But if you're not doing anything, why don't you come down and stay a day or two with me? I'm alone, and we'd be mutual company. In the meantime you might hear of something from the Lancet. Where's your diggings?"

I told him.

"Then let's go over there now and get your traps. Afterwards we can go home together. I've got cold mutton for supper. Hope you don't object."

"Very digestible," I remarked. And, after some persuasion, he at length prevailed upon me to accept his hospitality.

He had established himself, I found, in the Rowan Road—a turning off the Hammersmith Road—in an ordinary-looking, ten-roomed house: one of those stereotyped ones with four hearth-stoned steps leading to the front door, and a couple of yards of unhealthy-looking, ill-kept grass between the bay window and the iron railings.

The interior was comfortably furnished, for Bob was not wholly dependent upon his practice. His people were brewers at Bristol, and his allowance was ample. The dining-room was in front, while the room behind it was converted into a surgery with the regulation invalid's couch, a case of secondhand books to lend the place an imposing air, and a small writing-table whereat my hospital chum wrote his rather erratic ordinances.

Bob was a good fellow, and I spent a pleasant time with him. Old Mrs Bishop, his housekeeper, made me comfortable, and the whole day long my host would keep me laughing at his droll witticisms.

Patients, however, were very few and far between.

"You see, I'm like the men in Harley Street, my dear old chap," he observed one day, "I'm only consulted as a last resource."

I did not feel quite comfortable in accepting his hospitality for more than a week; but when I announced my intention of departing he would not hear of it, and therefore I remained, each week eager for the publication of the Lancet with its lists of assistants wanted.

I had been with him three weeks, and assisted him in his extremely small practice, for he sometimes sought my advice as to treatment. Poor old Bob! he was never a very brilliant one in his diagnoses. He always made it a rule to sound everybody, feel their pulses, press down their tongues and make them say, "Ah?"

"Must do something for your money," he would say when the patient had gone. "They like to be looked at in the mouth."

One afternoon, while we were sitting together smoking in his little den above the surgery, he made a sudden suggestion.

"Do you know, Dick—I scarcely like to ask you—but I wonder whether you'd do me a favour?"

"Most certainly, old chap," I responded.

"Even though you incur a great responsibility?"

"What is the responsibility?"

"A very grave one. To take charge of this extensive practice while I go down to Bristol and see my people. I haven't been homesick a week."

"Why, of course," I responded. "I'll look after things with pleasure."

"Thanks. You're a brick. I won't be away for more than a week. You won't find it very laborious. There's a couple of kids with the croup round in Angel Road, a bedridden old girl in Bridge Road, and a man in Beadon Road who seems to have a perpetual stomach-ache. That's about all."

I smiled. He had not attempted to diagnose the stomach-ache, I supposed. He was, indeed, a careless fellow.

"Of course you'll pocket all the fees," he added, with a touch of grim humour. "They're not very heavy—bobs and half-crowns—but they may keep you in tobacco till I come back."

And thus I became the locum tenens of the not too extensive practice of Robert Raymond, surgeon, for he departed for Paddington on the following evening, and I entered upon my somewhat lonely duties.

The first couple of days passed without incident. I visited the two children with the croup, looked in upon the bedridden relict of a bibulous furniture-dealer, and examined the stomach with the perpetual pain. The latter proved a much more serious case than I had supposed, and from the first I saw that the poor fellow was suffering from an incurable disease. My visits only took an hour, and the rest of the day I spent in the little den upstairs, smoking furiously and reading.

On the third morning, shortly before midday, just as I was thinking of going out to make my round of visits, an unusual incident occurred.

I heard a cab stop outside, and a moment later the surgery bell was violently rung. I started, for that sound was synonymous with half a crown.

A middle-aged woman, in black, evidently a domestic servant, stood in the surgery, and, as I confronted her, asked breathlessly—

"Are you the doctor, sir?"

I replied in the affirmative, and asked her to be seated.

"I'm sorry to trouble you, sir," she said, "but would you come round with me? My mistress has been taken worse."

"What's the matter with her?" I inquired.

"I don't know, sir," answered the woman, in deep distress, "But I do beg of you to come at once."

"Certainly I will," I said. And leaving her, ascended, put on my boots, and placing my case of instruments in my pocket, quickly rejoined her, and entered the cab in waiting.

On our drive along Hammersmith Road, and through several thoroughfares lying on the right, I endeavoured to obtain from her some idea of the nature of the lady's ailment; but she was either stupidly ignorant, or else had received instructions to remain silent.

The cab at last pulled up before a fine grey house with a wide portico, supported by four immense columns, before which we alighted. The place, standing close to the entrance to a large square, was a handsome one, with bright flowers in boxes before the windows, and a striped sun-blind over the balcony formed by the roof of the portico. The quilted blinds were down because of the strong sun, but our ring was instantly answered by a grave-looking footman, who showed me into a cosy library at the end of the hall.

"I'll tell my master at once that you are here, sir," the man said. And he closed the door, leaving me alone.

Chapter Two.

The Third Finger.

The house was one of no mean order, and a glance at the rows of books showed them to be well chosen—evidently the valued treasures of a studious man. Upon the writing-table was an electric reading-lamp with green shade, and a fine, pale photograph of a handsome woman in a heavy silver frame. In the stationery rack upon the table the note-paper bore an embossed cipher surmounted by a coronet.

After a few moments the door re-opened, and there entered a very thin, pale-faced, slightly-built man of perhaps sixty, carefully dressed in clothes of rather antique cut. He threw out his chest in walking, and carried himself with stiff, unbending hauteur. His dark eyes were small and sharp, and his clean-shaven face rendered his aquiline features the more pronounced.

"Good morning," he said, greeting me in a thin, squeaky voice. "I am very glad my servant found you at home."

"And I, too, am glad to be of service, if possible," I responded.

He motioned me to be seated, at the same time taking a chair behind his writing-table. Was it, I wondered, by design or by accident that in the position he had assumed his face remained in the deep shadow, while my countenance was within the broad ray of sunlight that came in between the blind and the window-sash? There was something curious in his attitude, but what it was I could not determine.

"I called you in to-day, doctor," he explained, resting his thin, almost waxen hands upon the table, "not so much for medical advice as to have a chat with you."

"But the patient?" I observed. "Had I not better see her first, and chat afterwards?"

"No," he responded. "It is necessary that we should first understand one another perfectly."

I glanced at him, but his face was only a grey blotch in the deep shadow. Of its expression I could observe nothing. Who, I wondered, was this man?

"Then the patient is better, I presume?"

"Better, but still in a precarious condition," he replied, in a snapping voice. Then, after a moment's pause, he added, in a more conciliatory tone, "I don't know, doctor, whether you will agree with me, but I have a theory that, just as every medical man and lawyer has his fee, so has every man his price!"

"I scarcely follow you," I said, somewhat puzzled. "I mean that every man, no matter what his station in life, is ready to perform services for another, providing the sum is sufficient in payment."

I smiled at his philosophy. "There is a good deal of truth in that," I remarked; "but of course there are exceptions."

"Are you one?" he inquired sharply, in a strange voice.

I hesitated. His question was curious. I could not see his object in such observations.

"I ask you a plain question," he repeated. "Are you so rich as to be beyond the necessity of money?"

"No," I answered frankly. "I'm not rich."

"Then you admit that, for a certain price, you would be willing to perform a service?" he said bluntly.

"I don't admit anything of the kind," I laughed, not, however, without a feeling of indignation.

"Well," he said after a few moments hesitation, during which time his pair of small black eyes were, I knew, fixed upon me, "I'll speak more plainly. Would you object, for instance, to taking a fee of five figures to-day?"

"A fee of five figures?" I repeated, puzzled. "I don't quite follow you."

"Five figures equal to ten thousand pounds," he said slowly, in a strange voice.

"A fee of five figures," I repeated, puzzled. "For what?"

In an instant it flashed across my mind that the thin, grey-faced man before me was trying to suborn me to commit murder—that crime so easily committed by a doctor. The thought staggered me.

"The service I require of you is not a very difficult one," he answered, bending across the table in his earnestness. "You are young—a bachelor, I presume—and enthusiastic in your honourable calling. Would not ten thousand pounds be of great use to you at this moment?"

I admitted that it would. What could I not do with such a sum?

Again I asked him the nature of the service he demanded, but he cleverly evaded my inquiries.

"My suggestion will, I fear, strike you as curious," he added. "But in this matter there must be no hesitation on our part; it must be accomplished to-day."

"Then it is, I take it, a matter of life or death?"

There was a brief silence, broken only by the low ticking of the marble clock upon the mantelshelf.

"Of death," he answered in a low, strained tone. "Of death, rather than of life."

I held my breath. My countenance must have undergone a change, and this did not escape his observant eyes, for he added—

"Before we go further, I would ask you, doctor, to regard this interview as strictly confidential."

"It shall be entirely as you wish," I stammered.

The atmosphere of the room seemed suddenly oppressive, my head was in a whirl, and I wanted to get away from the presence of my tempter.

"Good," he said, apparently reassured. "Then we can advance a step further. I observed just now that you were a bachelor, and you did not contradict me."

"I am a bachelor, and have no intention of marrying."

"Not for ten thousand pounds?" he inquired.

"I've never yet met a woman whom I could love sufficiently," I told him quite plainly.

"But is your name so very valuable to you that you would hesitate to bestow it upon a woman for a single hour—even though you were a widower before sunset?"

"A widower before sunset?" I echoed. "You speak in enigmas. If you were plainer in your words I might comprehend your meaning."

"Briefly, my meaning is this," he said, in a firmer voice, after pausing, as though to gauge my strength of character. "Upstairs in this house my daughter is ill—she is not confined to her bed, but she is nevertheless dying. Two doctors have attended her for several weeks, and to-day in consultation have pronounced her beyond hope of recovery. Before being struck down by disease, she was hopelessly in love with a man whom I believed to be worthless—a man whose name they told me was synonymous with all that is evil in human nature. She was passionately fond of him, and her love very nearly resulted in a terrible tragedy. Through the weeks of her delirium she has constantly called his name. Her every thought has been of him; and now, in these her last moments, I am filled with remorse that I did not endeavour to reclaim him and allow them to marry. He is no longer in England, otherwise I would unite them. The suggestion I have to make to you is that you should assume that man's place and marry my daughter."

"Marry her!" I gasped.

"Yes. Not being in possession of all her faculties, she will, therefore, not distinguish between her true lover and yourself. She will believe herself married to him, and her last moments will be rendered happy."

I did not reply. The suggestion held me dumbfounded.

"I know that the proposal is a very extraordinary one," he went on, his voice trembling in deep earnestness, "but I make it to you in desperation. By my own ill-advised action and interference, Beryl, my only child, is dying, and I am determined, if possible, to bring peace to her poor unbalanced mind in these the last hours of her existence. My remorse is bitter, God knows! It is little that I can do in the way of atonement, save to convince her of my forgiveness."

His face, as he bent forward to me at that moment, came, for the first time, within the broad bar of sunlight that fell between us, and I saw how white and haggard it was. The countenance was no longer that of a haughty man, but of one rendered desperate.

"I fear that in this matter it is beyond my power to assist you," I said, stirring myself at last. Truth to tell, his proposal was so staggering that I inclined to the belief that he himself was not quite right in his mind. The curious light in his eyes strengthened this suspicion.

"You will not help me?" he cried starting up.

"You will not assist in bringing happiness to my poor girl in her dying hour?"

"I will be no party to such a flagrant fraud as you propose," I responded quietly.

"The sum insufficient—eh! Well, I'll double it. Let us say twenty thousand."

"And the marriage you suggest is, I presume, to be a mock one?"

"A mock one? No, a real and binding one—entirely legal," he responded. "A marriage in church."

"Would not a mock one be just as effective in the mind of the unfortunate young lady?" I suggested.

"No, there are reasons why a legal marriage should take place," he answered distinctly.

"And they are?"

"Ah! upon that point I regret that I cannot satisfy you," he answered. "Is not twenty thousand pounds sufficient to satisfy you, without asking questions?"

"But I cannot see how a legal marriage can take place," I queried. "There are surely formalities to be observed."

"Leave them all to me," he answered quickly. "Rest assured that I have overlooked no detail in this affair. A mock marriage would, of course, have been easy enough; but I intend that Beryl shall be legally wedded, and for the service rendered me by becoming her husband I am prepared to pay you twenty thousand pounds the instant the ceremony is concluded."

Then, unlocking a drawer in his writing-table, he drew forth a large bundle of notes secured by an elastic band, which he held towards me, saying—

"These are yours if you care to accept my offer."

I glanced at the thick square packet of crisp notes, and saw that each was for one hundred pounds. My eyes wandered to the Tempter's face. The look I saw there startled me. Was he actually the devil in human guise?

He noticed the quick start I gave, and instantly his features relaxed into a smile.

"I cannot see what possible ground you can have for scruples," he said. "To deceive a dying girl in order to render her last moments happy is surely admissible. Come, render me this trifling service."

And thus he persuaded and cajoled me, tempting me with the money in his hand to sell my name. Reader, place yourself in my position for a moment. I might, I reflected, slave through all my life, and never become possessed of such a sum. I was not avaricious, far from it; yet with twenty thousand pounds I could gain the zenith of my ambition, and lead the quiet, even life that had so long been my ideal. I strove to shut my ears to the persuasive words of the Tempter, but could not. The service was not a very great one, after all. The woman who was to be my wife was dying. In a few hours, at most, I should be free again, and our contract would remain for ever a secret.

The sight of that money—money with a curse upon it, money that, had I known the truth, I would have flung into the grate and burned rather than suffer its contact with my hand—decided me. Reader, can you wonder at it? I was desperately in want of money, and, throwing my natural caution and discretion to the winds, I yielded. Yes, I yielded.

The Tempter drew a distinct sigh of relief. His sinister face, so thin that I could trace the bones beneath the white, tightly-stretched skin, grinned in satisfaction, for he was now confident of his power over me. He had me irretrievably in his toils. He tossed the notes carelessly back into the drawer and locked it with the key upon his chain, then, glancing at the clock and rising, said—

"We must lose no time. All is prepared. Come with me."

My heart at that instant beat so loudly that its pulsations were audible. I was to sacrifice myself and wed an unknown bride in order to gain that packet of banknotes. Mine was indeed a strange position, but, held beneath the spell of this man's presence, I obeyed him and followed him, curious to see the face of the woman to whom I was to give my name.

Together we went out into the hall where stood the man-servant who had admitted me.

"Is everything ready, Davies?" his master inquired. "Everything, sir. The carriage is at the door."

"I would ask of you one favour," the Tempter said, in a low voice; "do not express any surprise. All will be afterwards explained."

From the inner pocket of his frock-coat he produced a pair of white kid gloves, which he handed me, observing, with a smile—

"They are large for you, I fear; but that will not much matter. You will meet my daughter at the church; it looks better."

Then, as I commenced putting on the gloves, we went out together, and entered the smart brougham awaiting us. All preparations had evidently been made for my marriage.

Our drive was not a long one; but so bewildered was I by my singular situation, that I took little notice of the direction in which we were travelling. Indeed, I was utterly unfamiliar with that part of London, and I only know that we crossed Sloane Street, and, after traversing a number of back streets, suddenly stopped before a church standing in a small cul-de-sac.

The strip of faded red baize upon the steps showed that we were expected; but the church was empty save for a wheezy, unshaken old verger, who, greeting us, preceded us to a pew in front.

Scarcely had we seated ourselves, conversing in whispers, when we heard a second carriage stop; and, turning, I saw in the entrance the silhouette of my unknown bride in her white satin gown. She advanced up the aisle leaning heavily upon the arm of a smartly-dressed man, who wore a monocle with foppish air. Her progress was slow—due, no doubt, to extreme weakness. Her veil was handsome, but so thick that, in the dim gloom of the church, I was quite unable to distinguish her features.

As she passed where I sat, silent, anxious, and wondering, the Tempter prompted me, and I rose and took my place beside her, while at the same moment the officiating clergyman himself appeared from the vestry. His face was red and pimply, showing him to be of intemperate habits; but at his order I took my unknown companion's slim, soft hand in mine, and the scent of the orange blossom in her corsage filled my nostrils. I stood like a man in a dream.

At that instant the Tempter bent tenderly to her, saying—

"Beryl, my child, this is your wedding day. You are to be married to the man you love. Listen!" Then in a nasal tone, which sounded weirdly in the silence of the place, the clergyman began to drone the first words of the Marriage Service, "Dearly beloved, we are gathered together," until he came to the first question to which I responded in a voice which sounded strange and cavernous.

I was selling myself for twenty thousand pounds. The thought caused me a slight twinge of conscience. Turning to the woman at my side, he asked—

"Wilt thou have this man to thy wedded husband, to live together after God's ordinance in the holy estate of matrimony? Wilt thou obey him, and serve him, love, honour, and keep him in sickness and in health; and, forsaking all other, keep ye only unto him as long as ye both shall live?"

A silence fell, deep and complete.

Two ordinary-looking men, who had entered the church to serve as witnesses, exchanged glances. Then a slight sound escaped my unknown bride, like a low sigh, and we could just distinguish the reply—

"I will."

The remainder of the service was gabbled through. A ring which the Tempter had slipped into my hand I placed upon her finger, and ten minutes later I had signed the register, and was the husband of a woman upon whose face I had never looked.

The name which she signed with mine was "Beryl Wynd"; beyond that I knew nothing. Utterly bewildered at my position, I sat beside my bride on the drive back, but she preserved silence, and I exchanged no word with her. She shuddered once, as though cold. Her father accompanied us, keeping up a lively conversation during the whole distance.

Arrived at the house, the woman who had sought me at Rowan Road came forward to meet my bride, and at once accompanied her upstairs, while we entered the dining-room. The two witnesses, who had followed in the second carriage, quickly joined us. The butler Davies opened champagne, and my health, with that of the bride, was drunk in solemn silence. The man with the monocle was absent. Truly my nuptial feast was a strange one.

A few minutes later, however, I was again alone in the library with the Tempter, whose eyes had grown brighter, and whose face had assumed an even more demoniacal expression. The door was closed, the silence unbroken.

"So far all has been perfectly satisfactory," he said, halting upon the hearthrug suddenly and facing me. "There is, however, still one condition to be fulfilled, before I place the money in your hands."

"And what is that?" I inquired.

"That your wife must die before sunset," he answered, in a hoarse, earnest whisper. "She must die—you understand! It is now half-past twelve."

"What?" I cried, starting forward. "You would bribe me to murder your own daughter?"

He shrugged his thin shoulders, made an impatient movement, his small eyes glittered, and in a cold hard voice, he exclaimed—

"I said that it is imperative she should die before the money is yours—that is all."

Chapter Three.

Concerning a Compact.

"Then you make murder one of the conditions of payment?" I said, facing him.

"I have only said she must die before sunset," he answered. "She cannot live, in any case, longer than a few hours. It is easy for you, a doctor, to render her agony brief."

"To speak plainly," I said, with rising indignation, "you wish me to kill her! You offer me twenty thousand pounds, not for marriage, but for the committal of the capital sin."

His thin lips twitched nervously and his brows contracted.

"Ah!" he responded, still quite cool. "I think you view the matter in a wrong light. There are various grades of murder. Surely it is no great crime, but rather a humane action, to put a dying girl out of her agony."

"To shorten her life a single minute would be a foul assassination," I replied, regarding him with loathing. "And further, sir, you do not appear to fully realise your own position, or that it is a penal offence to attempt to bribe a person to take another's life."

He laughed a short, defiant laugh.

"No, no," he said. "Please do not waste valuable time by idle chatter of that kind. I assure you that I have no fear whatever of the result of my action. There is no witness here, and if you endeavoured to bring me before a judge, who, pray, would believe you?" There was some truth in those defiant words, and I saw by his attitude that he was not to be trifled with.

"I take it that you have objects in both your propositions—in your daughter's marriage, and in her death?" I said, in a more conciliatory tone, hoping to learn something further of the motive of his dastardly proposal.

"My object is my own affair," he snapped.

"And my conscience is my own," I said. "I certainly do not intend that it shall be burdened by the crime for which you offer me this payment."

He fixed me with flaming eyes. "Then you refuse?" he cried.

"Most certainly I refuse," I responded. "Moreover, I intend to visit your daughter upstairs, and strive, if possible, to save her."

"Save her?" he echoed. "You can't do that, unless you can perform miracles. But perhaps," he added with a sneer, "such a virtuous person as yourself may be able to work marvels."

"I may be able to save her from assassination," I answered meaningly.

"You intend to oppose me?"

"I intend to prevent you from murdering your own daughter," I said warmly. "Further, I forbid you to enter her room again. I am a medical man, and have been called in by you to attend her. Therefore, if you attempt to approach her I shall summon the police."

"Rubbish!" he laughed, his sinister face now ashen pale. "You cannot prevent me from approaching her bedside."

"I can, and I will," I said. "You have expressed a desire that she should, for some mysterious reasons, die before sunset. You would kill her with your own hand, only you fear that when the doctor came to give his certificate he might discover evidence of foul play."

"Exactly," he responded with perfect coolness, thrusting his hands into his pockets. "It is because of that I offer you twenty thousand pounds. I am prepared to pay for your scientific knowledge."

"And for a death certificate?"

"Of course."

"Well, to speak plainly, I consider you an inhuman scoundrel," I said. "If your daughter's dying hour is not sacred to you, then no man's honour or reputation is safe in your hands."

"I thank you for your compliment," he replied with a stiff bow. "But I might reply that you yourself are not very remarkable for honour, having in view the fact that, in the hope of gaining a sufficient price, you have married a woman upon whom you have never set eyes."

"You tempted me!" I cried furiously. "You held the money before my gaze and fascinated me with it until I was helpless in your power. Fortunately, however, the spell is broken by this inhuman suggestion of yours, and I wash my hands clean of the whole affair."

"Ah, my dear sir, that is not possible. Remember you are my daughter's husband."

"And yet you ask me to kill her."

"Who has greater right to curtail her sufferings than her husband?"

"And who has greater right to endeavour to save her life?"

"But you cannot. It is impossible."

"Why impossible?"

"She is doomed."

"By you. You have resolved that she shall not live till morning," I said, adding: "If, as you tell me, her mysterious illness must prove fatal, I see no reason why you should offer me a bribe to encompass her death. Surely a few hours more or less are of no consequence."

"But they are," he protested quickly. "She must die before sundown, I tell you."

"Not if I can prevent it."

"Then you will forgo the money I have offered you," he inquired seriously.

"I have no intention of touching a single farthing of it."

"Until you are forced to."

"Forced to!" I exclaimed. "I don't understand your meaning."

"You will understand one day," he answered with a grin—"one day when it may, perhaps, be too late. It would be best for us to act in unison, I assure you."

"For you, possibly; not for me."

"No—for you," he said, fixing his crafty, evil-looking eyes upon me. "You have taken one step towards the goal, and you cannot now draw back. You have already accepted your price—twenty thousand pounds."

"Enough!" I cried indignantly. "If I were to give information to the police regarding this conversation, you would find yourself arrested within an hour."

"As I have already told you, my dear sir, I am not at all afraid of such a contretemps; I am no blunderer, I assure you."

"Neither am I," I answered quickly, resolving to remain there no longer discussing such a subject. From the first moment of our meeting I had entertained a suspicion of him. Several facts were evident. He had some strong motive, first in marrying his daughter Beryl, secondly in encompassing her death before sundown, and thirdly in implicating me so deeply that I should be unable to extricate myself from the net which he set to entrap me.

A fourth fact, apparently small in itself, had caused me considerable reflection: the hand that I had held and on the finger of which I had placed the bond of matrimony, was in no sense chilly or clammy. It was not the wasted hand of a moribund invalid, but rather that of a healthy person. While I had held it I felt and counted the pulsations. The latter had told me that my mysterious bride was without fever, and was apparently in a normal state of health. It was curious that she should have walked and acted involuntarily, if only half-conscious of her surroundings.

The Tempter was endeavouring to deceive me in this particular. But it was in vain.

"Cannot we come to terms?" he asked in a low, earnest voice. "There is surely no object to be gained in our being enemies; rather let us act together in our mutual interests. Recollect that by your marriage you have become my son-in-law and heir."

"Your heir!" I echoed. I had not thought of that before. His house betokened that he was wealthy. "You are very generous," I added, not without some sarcasm. "But I do not feel inclined to accept any such responsibility from one whose name even I do not know."

"Of course," he said easily. "I was stupid not to introduce myself. In the excitement it quite slipped my memory. Pray forgive me. My name is Wynd—Wyndham Wynd."

"Well, Mr Wynd," I said with some forced politeness, "I think we may as well conclude this interview. I wish to make the acquaintance of my wife."

"Quite natural," he answered, smiling good-humouredly. "Quite natural that you should wish to see her; only I beg you, doctor, to prepare for disappointment."

"Your warning is unnecessary," I responded as carelessly as I could.

My curiosity had been aroused by the healthfulness of that small, well-formed hand, and I intended to investigate for myself. That house was, I felt certain, a house of mystery.

I had turned towards the door, but in an instant he had reached it and stood facing me with his back to it resolutely, saying—

"You will go to her on one condition—the condition I have already explained."

"That I take her life seriously, and give a certificate of death from natural causes," I said. "No, Mr Wynd, I am no murderer."

"Not if we add to the sum an extra five thousand?"

"I will not harm her for an extra fifty thousand. Let me pass!" I cried with fierce resolution.

"When you have promised to accede to my request."

"I will never promise that."

"Then you will not enter her room again."

Almost as the words left his lips there was a low tap at the door, and it opened, disclosing Davies, who announced—

"The Major, sir."

"Show him in."

The visitor, who entered jauntily with his silk hat still set at a slight angle on his head, was the well-groomed man who had led my bride up the aisle of the church. I judged him to be about forty-five, dark-complexioned, good-looking, but foppish in appearance, carrying his monocle with ease acquired by long practice.

"Well, Wynd," he said, greeting his friend, cheerily, "all serene?"

"Entirely," answered the other. And then, turning to me, introduced the new-comer as "Major Tattersett."

"This, Major, is Dr Colkirk, my new son-in-law," he explained. "Permit me to present him."

"Congratulate you, my dear sir," he responded laughing good-humouredly, while the Tempter remarked—

"The Major is, of course, fully aware of the circumstances of your marriage. He is our nearest friend."

"Marriage rather unconventional, eh?" the other remarked to me. "Poor Beryl! It is a thousand pities that she has been struck down like that. Six months ago down at Wyndhurst she was the very soul of the house-parties—and here to-day she is dying."

"Extremely sad," I remarked. "As a medical man I see too vividly the uncertainty of human life."

"How is she now?" inquired the Major of her father. "The same, alas!" answered the Tempter with well-assumed sorrow. "She will, we fear, not live till midnight."

"Poor girl! Poor girl!" the new-comer ejaculated with a sigh, while the Tempter, excusing himself for an instant left the room.

I would have risen and followed, but the Major, addressing me confidentially, said—

"This is a strange whim of my old friend's, marrying his daughter in this manner. There seems no motive for it, as far as I can gather."

"No, none," I responded. "Mr Wynd has struck me as being somewhat eccentric."

"He's a very good fellow—an excellent fellow. Entirely loyal to his friends. You are fortunate, my dear fellow, in having him as a father-in-law. He's amazingly well off, and generosity itself."

I recollected his dastardly suggestion that my wife should not live longer than sundown, and smiled within myself. This friend of his evidently did not know his real character.

Besides, being an observant man by nature, I noticed as I sat there one thing which filled me with curiosity. The tops of the Major's fingers and thumb of his right hand were thick and slightly deformed, while the skin was hardened and the nails worn down to the quick.

While the left hand was of normal appearance, the other had undoubtedly performed hard manual labour. A major holding her Majesty's commission does not usually bear such evident traces of toil. The hand was out of keeping with the fine diamond ring that flashed upon it.

"The incident of to-day," I said, "has been to me most unusual. It hardly seems possible that I am a bridegroom, for, truth to tell, I fancied myself the most confirmed of bachelors. Early marriage always hampers the professional man."

"But I don't suppose you will have any cause for regret on that score," he observed. "You will have been a bridegroom and a widower in a single day."

I was silent. His words betrayed him. He knew of the plot conceived by his friend to bribe me to kill the woman to whom I had been so strangely wedded!

But successfully concealing my surprise at his incautious words, I answered—

"Yes, mine will certainly have been a unique experience."

He courteously offered me a cigarette, and lighting one himself, held the match to me. Then we sat chatting, he telling me what a charming girl Beryl had been until stricken down by disease.

"What was her ailment?" I inquired.

"I am not aware of the name by which you doctors know it. It is, I believe, a complication of ailments. Half a dozen specialists have seen her, and all are agreed that her life cannot be saved. Wynd has spared no expense in the matter, for he is perfectly devoted to her."

His words, hardly coincided with the truth, I reflected. So far from being devoted to her, he was anxious, for some mysterious reason, that she should not live after midnight.

"To lose her will, I suppose, be a great blow to him?" I observed, with feigned sympathy.

"Most certainly. She has been his constant friend and companion ever since his wife died, six years ago. I'm awfully sorry for both poor Beryl and Wynd."

I was about to reply, but his words froze upon my lips, for at that instant there rang through the house a shrill scream—the agonised scream of a woman.

"Listen!" I cried. "What's that?"

But my companion's jaw had dropped, and he sat immovable, listening intently.

Again the scream rang out, but seemed stifled and weaker.

The Tempter was with his daughter whom he had determined should die. The thought decided me, and turning, without further word, I dashed from the room, and with quickly-beating heart ran up the wide thickly-carpeted staircase.

Chapter Four.

The Note of Interrogation.

On reaching the corridor I was confronted by the thin, spare figure of the Tempter standing resolutely before a closed door—that of Beryl's chamber.

His black eyes seemed to flash upon me defiantly, and his face had reassumed that expression which was sufficient index to the unscrupulousness of his character.

"Let me pass!" I cried roughly, in my headlong haste. "I desire to see my wife."

"You shall not enter?" he answered, in a voice tremulous with an excitement which he strove in vain to control.

"She is in distress. I heard her scream. It is my duty, both as a doctor and as her husband, to be at her side."

"Duty?" he sneered. "My dear sir, what is duty to a man who will sell himself for a handful of banknotes?"

"I yielded to your accursed temptation, it is true!" I cried fiercely. "But human feeling is not entirely dead in my heart, as it is in yours. Thank God that my hands are still unsullied!"

He laughed—the same harsh, discordant laugh that had escaped him when, below in the library, I had refused to accept the vile condition of the compact.

He stood there barring my passage to that room wherein lay the unknown woman who had been so strangely united to me. Whoever she was, I was resolved to rescue her. Mystery surrounded her—mystery that I resolved at all hazards to penetrate.

"You were in want of money, and I offered it to you," the Tempter answered coldly. "You have refused, and the matter is ended."

"I think not," I said warmly. "You will hear something more of this night's work."

He laughed again, displaying an uneven row of discoloured teeth. To argue with him further was useless.

"Come, stand aside?" I cried, making a movement forward.

He receded a couple of paces, until he stood with his back against the door, and as I faced him I looked down the shining barrel of a revolver.

I do not know what possessed me at that instant. I did not fully realise my danger, that is certain. My mind was too full of the mystery surrounding the unknown woman who was lying within, and whose hand had showed me that she was no invalid. Physically I am a muscular man, and without a second's hesitation I sprang upon my adversary and closed with him. His strength was marvellous. I had under-calculated it, for he was wiry, with muscles like iron.

For a few moments we swayed to and fro in deadly embrace, until I felt that he had turned the weapon until the barrel touched my neck. Next instant there was a loud report. The flash burned my face, but fortunately the bullet only grazed my cheek.

I was unharmed, but his deliberate attempt to take my life urged me to desperation, and with an almost superhuman effort I tripped him by a trick, and kneeling upon him, wrenched the weapon from his grasp. Then, leaving him, I dashed towards the door and turned the handle, but in vain. It was locked. Without more ado I stepped back, and taking a run, flung myself against the door, bursting the lock from its socket and falling headlong into the chamber.

The light was insufficient in that great chamber; therefore I drew up one of the blinds partially and crossed to the bed, full of curiosity.

My wife was lying there, silent and still. Her wealth of dishevelled hair strayed across the lace-edged pillow, and the hand with the wedding-ring I had placed upon it was raised above her head and tightly clenched in that attitude often assumed by children in their sleep.

She had screamed. That sound I had heard, so shrill and plain, was undoubtedly the voice of a young woman, and it had come from this room, which was directly above the library. Yet, as far as I could see, there was nothing to indicate the cause of her alarm.

Utterly bewildered, I stood there gazing at the form hidden beneath the silken coverlet of pale blue. The face was turned away towards the wall, so that I could not see it.

Why, I wondered, had the Tempter barred my entrance there with such determination, endeavouring to take my life rather than allow me to enter there?

The small ormolu clock chimed the hour upon its silver bell. It was one o'clock.

Attentively I bent and listened. Her breathing seemed very low. I touched her hand and found it chilly.

For a moment I hesitated to disturb her, for she was lying in such a position that I could not see her face without turning her over. Suddenly, however, it occurred to me that I might draw out the bed from the wall and get behind it.

This I did, but the bed, being very heavy, required all my effort to move it.

Strangely enough at that moment I felt a curious sensation in my mouth and throat, and an unaccountable dizziness seized me. It seemed as though my mouth and lips were swelling, and the thought occurred to me that I might have ruptured a blood-vessel in my exertions in moving the bed.

Eager, however, to look upon the face of the woman who was my wife, I slipped between the wall and the bed, and, bending down, drew back the embroidered sheet which half concealed the features.

I stood dumb-stricken. The face was the most beautiful, the most perfect in contour and in natural sweetness of expression, that I had ever gazed upon. It was the face of a healthful and vigorous girl of twenty, rather than of an invalid—a face about the beauty of which there could be no two opinions. The great blue eyes were wide open, looking curiously into mine, while about the mouth was a half-smile which rendered the features additionally attractive.

"You are ill," I whispered in a low, intense voice, bending to her. "Cannot you tell me what is the matter? I am a doctor, and will do all in my power to make you better."

There was no response. The great blue eyes stared at me fixedly, the smile did not relax, the features seemed strangely rigid. Next second a terrible suspicion flashed across my mind, and I bent closer down. The eyes did not waver in the light as eyes must do when a light shines straight into them. I touched her cheek with my hand, and its thrilling contact told me the truth only too plainly.

My wife was dead. She had died before sunset, as the Tempter had intended.

The discovery held me immovable. Hers was a face such as I had never seen before. She was a woman before whom, had I met her in life, I should have fallen down and worshipped. Indeed, strange as it may seem, I confess that, as I stood there, I fell in love with her—even though she was a corpse.

Yet, as my eyes fixed themselves lovingly upon her features, as sweet, tender, and innocent in expression as a child's, I could not imagine the cause of death. There was no sign of disease or unhealthiness there.

Why had she uttered those screams? Why, indeed, had the door of the death-chamber been afterwards locked? Had she, after all, fallen a victim to foul play?

I drew down the bed-clothes and exposed her neck in order to make an examination. She wore, suspended by a thin gold chain, a small amulet shaped like a note of interrogation and encrusted with diamonds. My observations told me that she had not worn it very long, for the edges of the stones were sharp, yet the delicate skin remained unscratched. A desire possessed me to have some souvenir of her, and without further ado, I unclasped the chain from her neck, and placed it and the little charm in my pocket.

Then, in continuation of my examination, I placed my hand upon her heart, but could detect no cause of death.

Upon her breast, however, I found a curious tattoo-mark—a strange device representing three hearts entwined. Now in my medical experience, I have found that very few women are tattooed. A woman usually shrinks from the operation—which is not unaccompanied by pain—and, on careful examination of this mark, I came to the conclusion that it had been pricked some years ago by a practised hand; further, that it had some distinct and mysterious signification.

It was in the exact centre of the breast, and just sufficiently low to remain concealed when she had worn a décolleté dress. The light was dim and unsatisfactory, but all my efforts to trace the hand of an assassin were futile.

Suddenly, however, as I examined her eyes, the left one, nearest the pillow, bore an expression which struck me as unusual. Both organs of sight seemed to have lost their clearness in the moments I had been standing there, and were glazing as rigor mortis set in, but the left eye was becoming more blurred than its fellow—an unusual circumstance which attracted me. The bright blue which I had seen in its unfathomable depths had contracted in a manner altogether unaccountable until it was now only the size of a pin's head. I bent again closely and peered into it. Next instant the awful truth was revealed.

She had been foully murdered.

With quick heart-beating I examined the eye carefully, finding symptoms of death from some deliriant—a neurotic acting on the brain and producing delirium, presbyopia, and coma. Certain it was that if this were actually the Tempter's work, he was a veritable artist in crime, for the manner in which death had been caused was extremely difficult to determine.

Finding myself undisturbed there, I made further and more searching examination, until I held the opinion that death must have been almost, if not quite, instantaneous.

But such theory did not coincide with the screams that had escaped her. On reviewing the whole of the circumstances, I felt confident that she must have been fully conscious at the time, and that those shrieks were shrieks of terror. She had divined the intention of her enemies.

About the vicinity of the bed I searched for any bottle of medicine that might be there, but in vain. If she had really been ill previously, as the Tempter had alleged, the medicine prescribed might give me some clue to the nature of her disease.

Upon a chair close by, her bridal veil of Brussels lace was lying crumpled in a heap, while her gown of white satin was hanging upon the door-knob of the handsome wardrobe. The orange-blossoms diffused their perfume over the room, but to me it was a sickly odour emblematic of the grave.

My wife, the most beautiful woman upon whom my eyes had ever fallen, was lifeless—struck down by the hand of a murderer.

As I bent, looking full into the contracted pupil, I suddenly detected something half concealed in the lace edging of the pillow. I drew it forth, and found it to be a crumpled letter, which I spread out and read. It had evidently been treasured there, just as invalids treasure beneath the bolster all the correspondence they receive.

In an angular hand, evidently masculine, was written the simple words, without address or signature, "I have seen La Gioia!"

Who, I wondered, was "La Gioia"? Was it a happy meeting or a disconcerting one? The announcement was bare enough, without comment and without detail. Significant, no doubt, it had been received by her and kept secret beneath her pillow.

I started across the room to investigate my dead wife's surroundings and to learn, if possible, by observation, something concerning her life. A room is often indicative of a woman's character, and always of her habits. The apartment was, I found, artistic and luxurious, while the few books lying about showed her to be a woman of education, culture, and refinement. Upon a little side-table, concealed behind a pile of books, I found a small blue bottle which, taking up, I held to the light, and afterwards uncorked and smelt, wondering whether its odour would give me any clue to its composition. The bottle contained pure chloroform.

Once more I crossed to the bed when, of a sudden, I again felt that strange sensation in my mouth and throat, both of which seemed to contract until my breathing became difficult. I felt half strangled. I fought against the curious feeling that crept over me, but a dizziness seized me, and I was compelled to clutch the foot of the bed in order to steady myself.

My mouth was burning, my head reeling, while my lower limbs seemed to have, in that moment, become cold, benumbed, and devoid of all feeling. I held my breath, determined to battle against the faintness; but all was useless. Sharp, acute pains shot through my legs as though red-hot wires were being thrust through my muscles, and a second later I became seized by a kind of paralysis which held my jaws immovable.

I placed my hands to my parched lips, and found that they had swollen to an enormous size. My tongue seemed too large for my mouth, and my throat so small that I could not swallow.

My head was swimming, but nevertheless I strove to calmly consider my situation. The symptoms were plain enough, and could not be mistaken. The Egyptian cigarette which the Major had given me had been strongly impregnated with some deleterious and poisonous substance.

I had, after all, fallen a hapless victim to my enemies, for by moistening the cigarette I had absorbed the poison, and, by the rapidity with which my mouth was swelling.

I knew that I had been given a fatal dose. With set teeth I stood trying to bear up against the sudden paroxysm of agony, but so excruciating was it that it proved too much. A loud cry escaped me. Writhing in the awful pains that gripped me from head to foot, I grew so weak that my legs refused to support me. Then, out of sheer exhaustion, I sank upon the floor, and the rest became blotted out in unconsciousness.

Chapter Five.

Outward Bound.

Strange noises aroused me slowly to a sense of my helplessness. My head seemed heavy as lead, my brain incapable of receiving any impression, my throat contracted as though by a diphtheritic swelling.

A low continued roaring sounded in my ears, accompanied by a curious unusual jarring. Slow to fully realise my position, it was some moments before I became convinced that the regular throbbing beneath my head was caused by machinery, and that the steady motion to and fro was the rocking of the waves.

I opened my eyes and found that it was broad daylight. To the left was a round opening closed by glass—a porthole through which the summer sun was shining, its rays being shut out now and then by the bright green water that rose against it as the waves hissed past. I was on board a ship at sea. The cabin was a narrow, rather dirty place, and the mattress on which I was lying was hard, being filled with straw. It was not a passenger cabin, that was certain, for the beams across were black and dirty, and swinging on a nail were a set of unclean yellow oil-skins and a sou'-wester.

So sudden and unaccountable had been my transition from the bed-chamber in that mysterious house of the Wynds', wherein my wife had been murdered, to that narrow pallet out at sea, that at first I could not believe it possible. I raised myself and looked around in wonder, half inclined to believe that the past events had been but a dream.

In that instant all the curious circumstances which had followed my call to the house with the big portico came vividly before me in rapid succession, the crafty actions of the Tempter and my wife's marvellous beauty most of all. With her, I had fallen a victim to the two ingenious conspirators, her father and the Major. It had, no doubt, been intended that I should die; yet certain of the Tempter's actions seemed out of keeping with the others, thus rendering the enigma more complete.

The pains in my head and the swelling in my mouth and throat were sufficient, however, to prove that the past was no chimera of the imagination. I had met with an adventure stranger, perhaps, than that experienced by any other man, for I had been both bridegroom and widower within an hour.

With some little difficulty I rose, but my legs were weak and cramped, and this, combined with the rolling of the ship, caused me to quickly seat myself on the edge of the narrow berth. My nerves were unstrung, my brain dulled, and the giddiness that seized me was such as I had never before experienced. It was not mal de mer, for I had travelled much by sea and had never experienced nausea, even in roughest weather. No; I had, by moistening the cigarette with the saliva, absorbed a strong dose of some anaesthetic, and its effect had been to a great extent irritant as well. Only my robust constitution had succeeded in throwing it off; the dose must, I felt confident, have killed a weaker man.

In a few minutes I succeeded in standing erect, and struggled to the cabin door. I turned the handle, but could not open it. I was locked in.

Again I seated myself upon my mattress and tried to calmly review the situation. Of a sudden I bethought myself of the amulet I had taken from the neck of my dead wife, and thrusting my hand into my pocket, was gratified to find it still there, together with a pair of white gloves that the Tempter had given me.

I took it out and carefully examined it. The chain was a very fine but strong one, and the curious little charm of plain gold on that side that would lay against the skin, was beautifully set with diamonds which now sparkled and flashed with a thousand fires in the brilliant sunset. About an inch and a half long, it was of most delicate workmanship. I had seen in jewellers' windows in Bond Street and Regent Street many articles of jewellery—brooches, breast-pins, and the like—in the form of a note of interrogation, but never one made in this manner. It was different to all the others, a costly ornament without doubt, for all the stones were well matched, and, as far as I could judge, not being an expert, of the first water.

What was its significance, I wondered, as it lay in the palm of my hand. It was a souvenir of her—a souvenir of the woman who was my legal wife, and who had fallen a victim beneath the cruel hand of an assassin.

The crumpled scrap of paper I had also secured I brought from my pocket and likewise examined. The words upon it were in a man's hand without a doubt—an educated hand which, by its angularity and the formation of the letters might possibly have been acquired on the Continent.

"I have seen La Gioia!"

The words conveyed some distinct message or warning which I could not determine. One fact was, however, plain; if I could discover this mysterious "La Gioia," be she a woman or an object, I might perhaps ascertain the true meaning of the words, the reason they were penned, and the motive Beryl had in thus treasuring them beneath her pillow.

A desire possessed me to escape from that narrow place wherein the air was stifling. The porthole was screwed down so tightly that I could not move it without a wrench, and the place seemed hermetically sealed.

By the terrible racket of the machinery and the strong smell of tar and oil I felt certain that it was no passenger steamer by which I was travelling. Everywhere were traces of black dust. I dipped my finger in some of it, examining it closely; it was coal dust. The ship was a collier.

I rose again, and taking up a stout piece of wood lying on the floor, battered heavily at the door, demanding release. But the clash and roar of the rickety engines drowned my voice, and I feared that no one could hear me above the din.

A strong sea was running, although the sun shone brightly. We were evidently somewhere in the Channel, but from my porthole I could see no land.

Again and again I battered furiously, until of a sudden I heard gruff voices, and the door was unlocked and opened cautiously, disclosing two rough-looking bronzed seamen, dark-bearded and dressed in patched and faded dungareen.

"Well, mister," exclaimed the elder of the two, "what's the fuss?"

"No fuss at all," I responded. "I only want to be let out."

"No doubt," he responded, with a grin at his companion. "You'd like a breath of fresh air—eh?"

"Yes, I should."

"But sea-air ain't good for your constitution mister, so you'll have to stop here. You've got a cabin all to yourself, so what more do you want? Perhaps you'd like a bloomin' saloon?"

"Look here, my man," I said, as calmly as I could, "just do me a favour and ask your captain to step down here. I'd like to speak to him before the farce proceeds further. You're only obeying orders by locking me up here, of that I'm sure. But just tell the captain that I'm better, and want to have a word with him."

Both men looked somewhat surprised.

"We were goin' to have a look at you in a few minutes, and see whether you'd come to, if you hadn't have kicked up such a confounded row."

"Well, go and tell the captain I want to see him," I said, endeavouring to smile.

"All right, sir, I will," answered the man; "but I'll have to lock the door again."

"Very well," I laughed. "Only don't starve me, remember." The situation seemed humorous.

Both men grinned broadly; the door was closed, and I heard one remark to the other in true cockney English—

"'E ain't such a vi'lent fellow, after all, Bill." Five minutes later the door was again opened, and a burly, full-bearded, black-eyed man in a pea-jacket and peaked cap entered the cabin.

"You are the captain, I presume?" I said.

"That's me," he answered, leaning against the wooden partition opposite my bunk.

"Well," I said, "I'd like to know by what right you lock me up here? I've been unconscious for a long time, and on coming to myself, I find I'm here onboard your ship at sea, imprisoned, and not allowed out."

"You're in here for the benefit of your health," he answered roughly. "A sea voyage'll do you good."

"Then perhaps you'll tell me the name of the ship on board which I'm taking this pleasure trip?" I said sarcastically.

"Better find that out."

"No very difficult matter, I suppose," I answered quite coolly. "Only I should like to point out that even though you may be skipper of this coal hulk, you have no right to imprison me here."

"I shall do just as I like, cocky," he responded. "And further, you'd best be quiet and keep a still tongue, or perhaps you won't see land again."

"That's certainly a very genteel speech," I said; "and perhaps the British Consul at your port of destination will have something to say regarding your conduct."

"I don't care a brass button for all the blanked consuls in the whole Consular Service," he replied, with a coarse laugh. "You are on board my ship, and I'll give you to understand now, once and for all, that I'm master here."

"Perhaps you'll pipe to a different tune when your master's certificate is suspended for a year or two."

"It 'ud take a better man than you to suspend it. While you're on board this craft, it'll be a wise policy to keep a still tongue in your head."

"And it will be wiser if you allow me my liberty, and just tell me how and why I came aboard here."

"You were brought here, but for what reason I don't know."

"And who brought me here?"

"I don't know. I wasn't on board when you arrived."

"The ship was lying in the Thames, wasn't it?"

"Yes," he answered. "It wasn't on Clapham Common, that's a certainty."

"And where are we now?"

"At sea."

"I'm aware of that, but in what sea—the Channel, the North Sea, or the Atlantic?"

"You'll know soon enough. Just breathe the ozone, and make

yourself comfortable. That's all you have to do," he responded, with his bearded chin thrust forward, in an air of unconcern.

"Well, you haven't provided many creature comforts for me," I remarked, with a glance round the stuffy little place.

"No, this isn't exactly a Cunarder," he admitted. "But I'll tell the men to bring you some grub, at any rate. Like some duff?"

"You're very kind; but I'd rather take a walk on deck in order to get an appetite."

"No; the sun's a bit too strong," he answered waggishly. "You might get sunstroke, you know."

"I shall be asphyxiated if I remain here."

"Well, that's a comfortable death, I believe. More than one chap has died for want o' breath in the hold of this ship when we've been trimmin' coal."

"Then you refuse me my liberty?" I said, feeling that to argue pleasantly was useless.

"Yes, you've got to stay 'ere."

"By whose orders?"

"That's my own business," he growled.

"And mine also," I responded firmly. "You may be skipper of this craft, but you are not a gaoler, you know."

"I'm your gaoler, at any rate."

"That remains to be seen," I answered. "I suppose you've been paid to take me out of the country, like this; but I may as well warn you that you are aiding and abetting a murder, and that when you get ashore you'll find yourself in a very nasty position."

"With the Consul, eh?" he laughed. "Well, they're a decent lot, as a rule. We don't get much trouble with 'em if we deposit our papers in order."

"But if I demanded your arrest for illegal imprisonment?"

"I don't fancy you'd do that, mister," he responded with sarcasm. "It might be a bit of a bother for me in England, but the foreign police are a bit chary of touching a British capt'n."

There was, I knew, some truth in that. Yet I did not intend to remain cooped up there, a prisoner, for the remainder of the voyage.

"Well, now, look here," I said, in a more conciliatory tone. "Why are you not frank with me?"

"Because you ain't responsible for your actions."

"And that's why you won't allow me on deck?" He nodded.

"Then I suppose when I was handed over to your tender charge they told you I was a lunatic?"

"Well, they said you'd better be kept under restraint. I was told that you'd had a bad touch of the blues, it seems."

"And yet you took me aboard while I was unconscious," I said. "That was scarcely a wise proceeding was it?"

"You were here when I returned; I've told you I found you here."

"Then you mean to tell me that you don't know who paid you to take me on this pleasure trip?"

"No, I don't. I've only received orders, and just observed them."

"Orders from whom?"

"From my owners."

"Your owners! What possible interest could your owners have in shipping me aboard while I was unconscious? Who are they?"

"Hanways, of Newcastle."

"And what ship is this?"

"The Petrel, of Newcastle."

"Bound for where?"

"No," he replied. "I've strict orders to keep you confined in the cabin, to treat you as well as your behaviour will allow, and to tell you nothing."

"Well, captain, you're a sensible man, and surely you'll listen to reason."

"What reason? I've got my orders. That's enough for me."

"But I tell you that by this action you are aiding in the concealment of a terrible crime—the dastardly murder of a lady in London," I burst forth.

"Of course. That's the yarn they said you'd spin. Well, you can stow that for the present. I'll come down and hear it over a pipe, when I want a bit of relaxation. For the time being, just you sniff the ozone, and fancy yourself in a drawin'-room."

Then, without more ado, the burly fellow made his exit, slammed the heavy door and bolted it, leaving me still a prisoner within that tiny cabin.

Chapter Six.

Captain Banfield Explains.

The hours passed but slowly. The man who had first answered my summons brought me some food but to all my arguments he remained obdurate.

"The cap'n says you're to stay 'ere," he responded, "and if I let you out he'd put me in irons. Old Banfield ain't a skipper to be trifled with, I can tell yer."

So I remained there, filled with gloomy thoughts, and wondering where I was being taken, and what possible interest Messrs Hanway, the owners of the Petrel, could have in my forcible abduction.

I sat there, helpless and puzzled, until it grew quite dark, then my head feeling heavy, and my limbs exhausted on account of the drug that had been so ingeniously administered to me, I threw myself down, and the motion of the vessel soon lulled me to sleep.

The long green waves were sweeping past in the sunlight when I again opened my eyes, and from the porthole I could see a large steamer with a pair of red and black funnels in the distance, leaving a long trail of smoke behind her. Soon, however, she was beyond the range of my vision, and I could do nothing except sit there and review the whole situation.

The beautiful face of my murdered wife arose ever before me. It seemed to cry to me for vengeance. I was her husband, and I alone knew the truth.

Yet it was evident that I was still in the hands of enemies, and, imprisoned there, I could do nothing.

The day passed, and fortunately I found myself feeling better. The effect of the noxious drug was slowly wearing off; yet the strain upon my nerves was terrible, and the imprisonment, coupled with uncertainty as to the future, was driving me to desperation.

A third day passed, much as the second. The only person I saw was the sailor who brought me food from the cook's galley in the morning and at evening—badly cooked sailors' fare that I could scarcely touch. As the sun was sinking, we suddenly approached a blue line of coast, and continued to skirt it until it became swallowed up in the night mists. Then, wearied, I again lay down to sleep.

I was awakened by the sudden stoppage of the engines, and found that it was already day again, and that we were in calm water. Outside my porthole was a flat stone wall which shut out everything.

Much shouting and tramping sounded above, and I knew that we were being made fast at a quay.

My opportunity for escape had arrived. If only I could break open the door, and slip up on deck unobserved, I might regain my freedom.

Now, I had during the past two days made a most careful

examination of my cabin and of the door, during which I had noticed that, supporting the box-like berth beneath, was an iron stay, the lower end of which was flattened out so that it could be more easily screwed down to the floor. The screws were loose, like most of the fittings of the badly kept craft; therefore, after some little trouble, I managed to remove it, and found that I held in my hand a capital crowbar.

Presently I managed to work the thin end between the door and the lintel, and then, throwing my whole weight against it, endeavoured to force the outer bolt from its fastenings.

My first attempt was abortive, but I saw that the screws were giving away; therefore I continued my efforts carefully so as not to attract attention, until, of a sudden, the socket of the bolt flew off, and the door was burst open. Then, holding my iron bar in self-defence, I stepped along to the foot of a ladder, by which I climbed on deck.

The vessel, it seemed, was not a large one, and of a particularly dirty and forbidding appearance. With care I crept round the deck-house unobserved, until I reached the gangway, and just as my presence was discovered by the captain, I slipped across it nimbly, and was on the quay amid a crowd of labourers, custom officers, and the usual motley assemblage which gathers to watch an arriving vessel.

I heard the skipper shouting violently, and a couple of the crew started in pursuit; but, taking to my heels I soon outdistanced them, and after some little time found myself walking in a large handsome street lined with fine shops and showy cafés. I was in Christiania.

I inquired in French of several persons the whereabouts of the British Consulate, and about an hour later found myself in the private office of the representative of her Majesty, a tall, good-looking man in a cool suit of white linen.

To him I related the whole circumstances. He listened, but smiled now and then with an air of incredulity. I told him of the murder, of the manner in which my life had been twice attempted, and of the remarkable circumstances of my abduction.

"And you say that you were taken on board the Petrel," he said reflectively. "I know Captain Banfield quite well. He is a strict disciplinarian, an excellent sailor, and is held in high esteem by his men. We must hear his explanation of the affair at once. If what you have said is true, it is certainly most remarkable."

I drew the trinket with the golden chain from my pocket, together with the crumpled note, and showed them to him.

"Strange," he remarked. "Most extraordinary! I'll send down to the docks for Banfield at once;" and, calling a clerk, he dispatched him in a cab.

In the meantime, in response to his questions, I gave him the most minute details of the startling affairs, as well as the ingenious manner in which Beryl Wynd had been murdered. I knew that the story when related sounded absolutely incredible; but it was equally certain that the Consul, at first inclined to doubt my statement, had now become highly interested in it.

I remarked upon the extraordinary mystery, and its features which seemed to stagger belief.

"But you are a medical man of considerable attainment, I notice from your card," he resumed. "I have no reason to doubt your story. It is rather a matter which should be strictly inquired into. Any person abducted from England, in the manner you have been, has a right to seek protection and advice of his consul."

And we continued chatting until, after a lapse of nearly half an hour, the captain of the Petrel, wearing his shore-going clothes, was ushered in.

"Good morning, sir!" he exclaimed, addressing the representative of the Foreign Office, but taking no notice of my presence. "You've sent for me?"

"Yes, Captain," the Consul responded rather severely. "Kindly sit down. There is a little matter upon which you can throw some light. You know this gentleman?"—and he indicated myself.

"Yes, sir. I know 'im."

"Well, he has lodged a very serious complaint against you, namely, that you have held him a prisoner on board your ship without any just cause; and, further, that contrary to the regulations of the Board of Trade, you carried him from port while in an unconscious condition." The skipper remained quite unabashed.

"Well, sir," he answered, "as I've already told the gentleman, I've only acted under strict orders from my owners. I suppose they'll take all the responsibility?"

"No; the responsibility rests upon yourself. You've held a master's certificate a good many years, and you are fully acquainted with the Board of Trade regulations."

"Of course, I don't deny that," the other responded.

"But my orders were quite precise."

"And now, tell me, how came this gentleman on board your ship?"

"To tell the truth, sir, I don't know exactly. We were lying in the St.

Katherine Docks, and my last evening ashore I spent at home with my wife, over at Victoria Park. We were to sail at four o'clock in the morning, but I didn't get aboard before about ten past four. When I did so, orders from the owners were put into my hand, and I was told that there was a passenger who'd been brought aboard, lying asleep below. 'Ere's the letter;" and he drew it from his pocket and handed it to the Consul.

The latter read it through, then, with an exclamation of surprise, handed it over to me.

It certainly increased the mystery, for it was from the office of the owners, Messrs Hanway Brothers, in Leadenhall Street, ordering that I should be taken on the round voyage to the Baltic, well cared for, but kept looked in a cabin, as I had developed homicidal tendencies.

"The gentleman, whose name is Doctor Colkirk," continued the letter, "is subject to fits, in which he remains unconscious for some hours; therefore there is no cause for alarm if he is not conscious when he reaches you. He is under an hallucination that he has been witness of some remarkable crime, and will, no doubt, impress upon you the urgent necessity of returning to London for the prosecution of inquiries. If he does this, humour him, but on no account allow him to go on deck, or to hold conversation with any one. The gentleman is a source of the greatest anxiety to his friends, and, we may add, that if the present orders are strictly carried out, the gentleman's friends have promised the payment of a handsome bonus to yourself. We therefore place him on board the Petrel, in preference to any other vessel of our fleet, because of the confidence we entertain that you will strictly carry out your orders."

The letter was signed by the firm.

"It seems very much as though the owners had some object in sending you aboard," observed the Consul.

Then, turning to the skipper, he asked, "How was the gentleman brought on board?"

"He was brought in a private carriage about six o'clock in the evening, my men say. Two gentlemen carried him on board. The dock police stopped them, but they told the constable that the gentleman was drunk."

"And when you received this letter, what did you do?"

"Well, I put him in the second mate's cabin, and left him alone till two days later, when he came to. Then I just carried out my orders."

"Where are you bound for?"

"The round trip—Stockholm, Riga, St. Petersburg, Drammen, Christiansund, and home."

"That means a month."

"More—six weeks."

"Your owners, therefore, were anxious that the doctor should be absent from England during that time. There is some mystery here, on the face of it. Doctor Colkirk has related to me a very remarkable story, and the most searching inquiry should be instituted."

"Well, sir," Banfield said apologetically, "I hope you don't consider my conduct bad. I've only carried out my orders to the letter. You see I didn't know that the gentleman was on board until we'd actually left the quay; and the letter says, quite distinctly, that he's subject to fits, therefore I let him remain quiet until he regained consciousness." Then, turning to me, he added, "I trust, sir, that you'll accept my apology."

"That's all very well," interposed the Consul; "but you know that you did entirely wrong in sailing with an unconscious stranger on board."

"I admit that. But you see I had my orders, sir."

"Who delivered them to you?" I inquired.

"The two gentlemen who brought you on board," he responded.

"Have any of your men described them to you?"

"They only said that they were both well dressed, and about middle age."

They were, without doubt, the Tempter and his accomplice. The conspiracy had been conceived and carried out with amazing ingenuity.

"And they brought the doctor on board and delivered this letter?"

"Yes, sir. They afterwards re-entered the carriage and drove away."

"Well," said the Consul, "the only course I see is for the doctor to take this letter, return to London, and seek an explanation of your owners."

"No, sir, I shan't give up the letter. It's written to me," demurred the captain.

"But it is in my hands," responded the Consul. "I am making inquiries into this affair, and I shall act as I think best in the interest of all parties concerned. The letter is your property, certainly; but recollect that this affair may prove very awkward for your owners. Therefore, take my advice, Captain, and assist this gentleman in his inquiries."

"I protest against you keeping the letter."

"Very well, I will see that your protest is forwarded to your owners," replied the Consul; and he handed me the letter, saying—

"Your best course. Doctor, is to return by the Wilson boat to Hull. She sails this afternoon at four. Then go down to Leadenhall Street and, make inquiries—it seems a strange affair, to say the least."

"It is entirely unaccountable," I said. "There seems to have been a widespread plot against me, with a single motive—the concealment of the murder of Beryl Wynd."

"But in that case why not let me telegraph to Scotland Yard?" suggested the Consul, as the sudden idea occurred to him. "They would watch the house until your return. To-day is Tuesday. You'll be in London on Thursday night, or early on Friday morning."

The proposal was an excellent one, and I gladly acceded. Next instant, however, the bewildering truth flashed across my mind. I had not hitherto realised my position. My heart sank within me.

"Would that your suggestion could be carried out," I replied. "But, truth to tell, I don't know the house, for I took no notice of its situation, and am unable to tell the name of the road."

"Ah! how extremely unfortunate. London is a big place, and there are thousands of houses that are outwardly the same. Didn't the servant who called at your surgery give you the address?"

"No; she gave it to the cabman, but I did not catch it. Men of my profession take little heed of the exterior of houses. We make a note of the number in our visiting-books—that's all."

"Then you really haven't any idea of the situation of the house in which the tragedy occurred?"

"None whatever," I replied. A moment later a further thought occurred to me, and I added, "But would not the registry of marriages give the address of my bride?"

"Why, of course it would!" cried the Consul excitedly. "An excellent idea. Return to London as quickly as you can, and search the marriage register. From that I'm certain you'll obtain a clue."

Chapter Seven.

My New Patient.

On Friday morning I entered the office of Messrs Hanway Brothers in Leadenhall Street, and after a short wait was accorded an interview with the manager.

I demanded, of course, an explanation why I had been shipped away from London in such a summary manner, whereupon he apparently regarded me as a lunatic.

"I really had no knowledge of the affair," he replied, smiling incredulously. "Do you actually allege you were taken on board the Petrel and kept imprisoned in a cabin by Captain Banfield? A most extraordinary story, to say the least."

I told him of the inquiries made by the British Consul in Christiania, and added—

"I have here the captain's written orders from your firm, signed by yourself." And I produced the letter.

He glanced it through eagerly, and then carefully scrutinised the signature.

"This renders the affair far more mysterious," he exclaimed with increased interest. "The letter-paper is certainly ours, but the whole thing is a forgery."

"It is not your signature?"

"No, certainly not—only a clumsy imitation;" and taking up a pen, he wrote his signature and handed them both to me for comparison. At once I saw that several of the peculiarities of his handwriting were absent from Banfield's orders.

"The type-writing is done by a different machine to ours. We use Bar-Locks, while this has probably been written by a Remington," he went on. "Besides, look at the edge of the paper, and you'll see that it is badly cut. It is, without doubt, a sheet out of several reams, that were delivered by the stationers some months ago, and were rejected by me because of the careless manner in which the edges had been cut."

Then he touched his bell and the chief clerk appeared. To him he showed the letter, and without a moment's hesitation he declared it to be a forgery.

Without going into details of the events of that memorable night, I described how I had recovered consciousness to find myself at sea, and the strict obedience, of the captain to the orders he had received.

"Well, all I can conjecture is," declared the manager, much puzzled, "that you have fallen the victim of some clever conspiracy. The details show that there was some strong motive for your abduction, and that the conspirators well knew that Banfield remained at home until almost the last moment before sailing. They were, therefore, enabled to put you on board during his absence. The forged orders, too, were brief and well to the point—in fact, worded just as they might be if sent from this house. No; depend upon it there has been some very ingenious plotting somewhere."

I remained with him a short time longer, then, realising the uselessness of occupying his time, I withdrew, and in further prosecution of my inquiries drove to Doctors' Commons.

Here, after certain formalities, I gained knowledge which seemed of distinct advantage. Of the official there I learned that the special licence by which I had been married had been applied for by Beryl herself, and was shown a copy of the application signed by her, "Beryl Wynd."

I read the document through, and its contents held me in amazement, for it prayed "that a licence might be issued for the solemnisation of marriage in the church of St. Ann's, Wilton Place, between herself and Richard Dawes Colkirk, bachelor, Doctor of Medicine, of 114, Rowan Road, Hammersmith." Besides, it was dated nearly a fortnight before—soon after I had accepted Raymond's invitation to be his guest.

But my main object in making inquiries at the registry was to discover my wife's address, and in this I was successful, for in the same document I found that she was described as "Beryl Grace Wynd, spinster, of 46, Earl's-court Road, Kensington."

I had, at least, gained knowledge of the house in which the tragedy had been enacted.

"When the young lady called to make this application, were you present?" I inquired eagerly.

"Yes. I saw her."

"What was she like? Could you give me a description of her?"

"She was good-looking, elegantly dressed, and about middle height, if I remember aright."

"And her hair?"

"It was of a colour rather unusual," answered the man, peering at me through his spectacles. "A kind of golden-brown."

The description was exact. Beryl had been there, and of her own accord applied for a licence to marry me. The mystery increased each moment.

"Was she alone?" I inquired.

"No. Her father was with her."

"How did you know he was her father?"

"He introduced himself to me as such—Major Wynd."

"Major Wynd!" I ejaculated. "But Mr Wynd is not an officer. What kind of man is he?"

"Of military appearance, round-faced, and good-humoured."

"Old?"

"Certainly not—scarcely fifty. He wore a single eyeglass."

The description did not answer to that of the Tempter, but rather to that of Tattersett. The truth seemed plain: the Major had posed as Beryl's father, and had given his consent to the marriage.

The registry official, a little dry-as-dust individual who wore steel-rimmed spectacles poised far down his thin nose, endeavoured to learn who and what I was; but I merely replied that I was making inquiries on behalf of certain friends of the lady, and having satisfied myself by another glance at the signatures, I bade him good afternoon.

After a hasty lunch in a bar at the foot of Ludgate Hill, I set forth by the underground railway to Earl's Court, and experienced but little difficulty in discovering Number 46. It stood on the right, between Park Terrace and Scarsdale Villas; but at a single glance I saw that it was not the house to which I had been conducted. The latter had been a big, substantial mansion with a spacious portico supported by four huge pillars, whereas this was a small, old-fashioned house of perhaps ten rooms.

Nevertheless, I walked up the garden path and rang the bell. My summons was answered by a neat maid, who called her mistress, an elderly lady, and the latter declared that she had lived there five years and had never heard the name of Wynd.

"Have you ever let your house furnished?" I inquired.

"Never," She responded. "But the name is somewhat uncommon, and you ought to have no difficulty in finding the address."

"I hope sincerely that I shall," I answered, and, apologising for disturbing her, went down the steps, feeling that my mysterious wife had purposely given a false address in order to place any inquirer on a wrong scent.

Along to the corner of Kensington Road I strolled slowly, debating in my mind the best course to pursue. I turned into a public-house at the corner, and asked to see a London Directory, which I searched eagerly. But there was no such name as Wynd among the residents, neither could I find it among those of people living in the suburbs.

I called upon the Vicar of St. Ann's, Wilton Place, and saw the register I had signed, but the officiating clergyman had been a friend of Wynd's, and he did not know his address.

It seemed suspiciously as though the name of Wynd was an assumed one. If a false address had been given by the Major at Doctors' Commons, then in all probability the surname was likewise false.

Fatigued, hungry, and dusty, I at last found myself once again in Rowan Road before the door of Bob Raymond's house, and entered with my latch-key.

Old Mrs Bishop came forward excitedly to meet me.

"Oh, Doctor," she cried, "wherever had you been all this week? I felt certain that something had happened to you, and yesterday I got my daughter to write a line to Dr Raymond. But I'm so glad you are back again sir. It's given my daughter and me such a fright. We imagined all sorts of horrible things like those we read of in Lloyd's and Reynolds'."

"Well, I'm back again, Mrs Bishop," I answered as carelessly as I could. "And I'm confoundedly hungry and tired. Get me a cup of tea and a chop, there's a good woman." And I ascended to Bob's cosy little den from which I had been so suddenly called seven days before.

So Mrs Bishop had written to Bob, and no doubt he would be very surprised that I had disappeared and left the practice to take care of itself. He would certainly consider that my gratitude took a curious form. Therefore, I decided to send him a wire, telling him of my return and promising explanations later.

I cast myself wearily into the big leather armchair, and sat plunged in thought until the old housekeeper entered fussily with my tea.

"Well," I asked, "I suppose there have been no new patients during my absence?"

"Oh, yes. One, sir."

"Who was it?"

"A lady, sir. She came about noon on the second day of your absence, and said she wished to consult you. I told her that you'd been called out two days ago, and that you had not returned. She asked when you'd be in, and I said I didn't know for certain. So she called again later, and seemed very disappointed and anxious. She came next day; but as you were still absent, she left her card. Here it is." And Mrs Bishop took a card from the tray on a side-table and handed it to me. Upon it was the name, "Lady Pierrepoint-Lane."

"Was she young or old?"

"Rather young, sir—not more than thirty, I think. She was dressed in deep mourning."

"And you have seen nothing more of her?" I inquired interestedly.

"There's no address on the card."

"She came again two days ago, and finding that you had not returned, left this note, telling me to give it to you on arrival." And the woman fumbled behind the mirror on the mantelshelf and handed me a dainty note, the envelope of which bore a neat coat-of-arms.

The heading was "88, Gloucester Square, Hyde Park," and the brief note ran—

"Lady Pierrepoint-Lane would esteem it a favour if Dr Colkirk could make it convenient to call upon her at his earliest opportunity."

Curiosity prompted me to turn to Debrett's Baronetage, in Raymond's bookcase, and from it I discovered that her ladyship was the wife of Sir Henry Pierrepoint-Lane, Bart., a wealthy landowner and the patron of several livings in Yorkshire and Shropshire whose principal seat was Atworth, in Wiltshire. His wife was the eldest daughter of General Sir Charles Naylon, late of the Indian army.

Having re-read the short paragraph in the Baronetage, which gave a facsimile of the coat-of-arms upon the envelope, I sipped my tea and then wrote a short note regretting my absence from home, and stating my intention to call upon the following morning at eleven o'clock. This I dispatched by boy-messenger.

Hence it was that next morning, when I passed down Stanhope Street and turned into Gloucester Gardens, I felt in no mood to humour and sympathise with the whims and imaginary maladies of a fashionable patient.

With a feeling of irritation and low spirits, I mounted the steps of the house in Gloucester Square and inquired for my new patient.

I was ushered into a pretty morning-room, and shortly afterwards there entered a slim, youngish-looking woman, not exactly handsome, but of refined appearance, dark, with hair well coiled by an expert maid, and wearing a simple dress of pearl-grey cashmere, which clung about her form and showed it to distinct advantage. Before she had greeted me I saw that she was a type subject to nerve-storms, perhaps with a craving for stimulants after the reaction.

"Good morning, Doctor," she exclaimed, crossing the room and greeting me pleasantly. "I received your note last night. You were absent each time I called."

"Yes," I responded. "I was called out to an urgent case, and compelled to remain."

"Does that happen often in your profession?" she asked, sinking into a chair opposite me. "If it does, I fear that doctors' wives must have an uncomfortable time. Your housekeeper was quite concerned about you."

"But when one is a bachelor, as I am, absence is not of any great moment," I laughed.

At that moment her dark, brilliant eyes met mine, and I fancied I detected a strange look in them.

"Well," she said with some hesitation, "I am very glad you have come at last, Doctor, for I want to consult you upon a secret and very serious matter concerning myself, and to obtain your opinion."

"I shall be most happy to give you whatever advice lies in my power," I responded, assuming an air of professional gravity, and preparing myself to listen to her symptoms. "What is the nature of your ailment?" I inquired.

"Well," she answered, "I can scarcely describe it: I seem in perpetually low spirits, although I have no cause whatever to be sad, and, further, there is a matter which troubles me exceedingly. I hardly like to confess it, but of late I have developed a terrible craving for stimulants."

I put to her a number of questions which it is unnecessary here to recount, and found her exactly as I had supposed—a bundle of nerves.

"But this unaccountable craving for stimulants is most remarkable," she went on. "I am naturally a most temperate woman, but nowadays I feel that I cannot live without having recourse to brandy or some other spirit."

"Sometimes you feel quite well and strong, then suddenly you experience a sensation of being extremely ill?" I suggested.

"Exactly. How do you account for it?"

"The feeling of strength and vigour is not necessarily the outcome of actual strength, any more than is the feeling of weakness the necessary outcome of actual weakness," I responded. "A person may be weak to a degree, and the sands of life be almost run out, and yet feel overwhelmingly strong and exuberantly happy, and, on the other hand, when in sound and vigorous health, he may feel exhausted and depressed. Feelings, especially so with women of the better class, rise into being in connexion with the nervous system. Whether a person feels well or ill depends upon the structure of his nervous system and the way in which it is played upon, for, like a musical instrument, it may be made to give forth gay music or sad."

"But is not my case remarkable?" she asked.

"Not at all," I responded.

"Then you think that you can treat me, and prevent me from becoming a dipsomaniac?" she said eagerly.

"Certainly," I replied. "I have no doubt that this craving can be removed by proper treatment. I will write you a prescription."

"Ah?" she exclaimed, with a sigh. "You doctors, with your serums and the like, can nowadays inoculate against almost every disease. Would that you could give us women an immune from that deadly ailment so common among my sex, and so very often fatal."

"What ailment?" I asked, rather surprised at her sudden and impetuous speech.

"That of love!" she responded in a low, strained voice—the voice of a woman desperate.

Chapter Eight.

What Happened to me.

"Do you consider love an ailment?" I asked, looking at her in quick surprise.

"In many cases," she responded in a serious tone. "I fear I am no exception to the general rule," she added meaningly.

Those words amounted to the admission that she had a lover, and I regarded her with considerable astonishment. She was a smart woman. I could only suppose that she and her husband were an ill-assorted pair. Possibly she had married for money, and was now filled with regret, as, alas! is so frequently the case.

"You appear unhappy," I observed in a sympathetic tone, for my curiosity had been aroused by her words.

"Yes, Doctor," she answered in a low, intense voice, toying nervously with her fine rings. "To tell the truth, I am most unhappy. I have come up to town to consult you, unknown to my husband, for I have heard that you make the treatment of nervous disorders your speciality."

"And by whom was I recommended to you?" I inquired, somewhat interested in this new and entirely undeserved fame which I had apparently achieved.

"By an old patient of yours—a lady whom I met at a house-party a month ago, in Yorkshire."

"But I understood that you were consulting me regarding your craving for stimulants," I said, as her dark, serious eyes met mine again.

She was a decidedly attractive woman, with the easy air and manner of one brought up in good society.

"The craving for drink is the least dangerous of my ailments," she responded. "It is the craving for love which is driving me to despair."

I remained silent for a moment, my eyes fixed upon her.

"Pardon my remark," I said, at last, in a low tone, "but I gather from your words that some man has come between yourself and your husband."

"Between myself and my husband!" she echoed in surprise. "Why, no, Doctor. You don't understand me. I love my husband, and he has no love for me!" Her statement was certainly a most unusual one. She was by no means a simple-minded woman, but, on the contrary, clever and intelligent, with a thorough knowledge of the world. It therefore seemed astounding that she should make this remarkable confession. But I controlled my surprise, and responded—

"You are, unfortunately, but one wife among thousands in exactly the same position. If we only knew the composition of the ancient love-philtre it would be in daily requisition. But, unfortunately, medical science is unable to influence the passion of the heart."

"Of course," she sighed. Then, with her eyes cast down upon the small table beside which she was sitting, she added, "I suppose, if the truth were known, you consider me very foolish in making this confession to you, a comparative stranger?"

"I do not consider it foolishness at all," I hastened to assure her. "A neglected wife must always excite sympathy."

"And have I yours?"

"Most assuredly," I answered. "It is evident, from my diagnosis, that you are suffering from sudden and abrupt alterations in the feelings. You are more especially subject to a feeling of malaise, accompanied by mental depression, as at this moment. Therefore, I must endeavour to remove the cause. As regards the affection you bear your husband, I would presume to remind you of the very true adage which declares that 'Love begets love.'"

"Ah," she interrupted, "that is untrue in my case."

"Am I, then, to understand that your husband is attracted by some other person?"

"I really don't know; I do not know what to think. He is indifferent—that is all."

"What difference is there in your ages?"

"I am thirty. He is fifty-eight."

"Ah!" I exclaimed. "And am I to presume that your marriage was a loveless one?"

"Not at all," she answered quickly. "I was very fond of him, and he made some pretence of affection."

"And how many years have you been married?"

"Three," she responded.

According to "Debrett" she had married five years ago, but for such small untruths a woman may always be forgiven.

I looked at her, unable to entirely satisfy myself regarding her. She seemed suffering from an agitation which she was striving with all her might to control. That her nervous organisation was impaired was no doubt correct, but it struck me that the cause of it all was some sudden and terrible shock to the system.

"I assure you that you have my sympathy in your mental distress," I said at length. "There have always been fatalists who have argued that we must accept without question what is sent us, that we must bow in submission to a 'will' without really seeking to find out what the 'will' is."

"Yes," she said thoughtfully. "It is quite impossible not to admit that the increased knowledge of the laws which regulate the visible universe has increased our living faith and added to the glory of the Almighty, while it has made it more difficult for men to make gods after their own image and use them for their own purposes."

"Exactly," I said. "Modern medicine is teaching us every day that much bodily suffering is due to man's wilful neglect of the beneficent laws of Nature. That diseases are due to ignorance and disregard of law, and are not 'sent' as scourges by a petulant and capricious deity, is clearly a doctrine which in no way dims the glory of God."

"I quite agree," she responded. Then, in a low tone, more confidential than before, she added, "You, Doctor, have expressed sympathy for me in my distress, and I look to you for assistance. Curious though it may seem, I have scarcely a single friend in whom I can confide."

"I shall respect your confidence, as is my duty," I answered, "and will do my best to stifle your craving for stimuli."

"But the love of my husband?"

"Endeavour to live uprightly and honestly, and show him your true worth above all other women," I said. "It is the only way."

"I have done so," she answered sadly, "but have failed."

"Do not give up. A man is never wholly proof against a good woman, especially if that woman be his wife."

A silence fell between us.

"And may I count upon your aid in all this, Doctor?" she asked, with some hesitation.

"Certainly," I responded. "If I can give you any advice, I shall always be pleased to do so."

"But my husband must know nothing. Recollect I have consulted you unknown to him."

"As you wish, of course."

"And, in future, if I wish to see you, may I call at your surgery?"

"If you desire," I replied. "But I am only locum tenens for my friend, Doctor Raymond, who is in the country. Perhaps I may go into practice in the country afterwards."

"And leave me!" she exclaimed anxiously. "I hope not."

"I shall still consider you my patient," I said.

"No," she said. "I trust that you will regard me as more than a mere patient—as your friend."

"I am honoured by your friendship," I replied. "And if I can, at any time, do anything to assist you in this mental trouble of yours, I will do it with pleasure."

I had, during our conversation, been attracted by her frankness of manner and the evident sorrow which weighed so heavily upon her. She had confessed to me, and we had now become friends. My position was a curious one: the adviser of a woman who was wearing out her heart for her husband's love. It was not altogether devoid of danger either, for her ladyship was an exceedingly attractive woman.

I had written the prescription and handed it to her, but, apparently in no mood to allow me to go, she did not rise.

While I had been busily writing at the little escritoire her manner had apparently changed, for she was no longer the serious, nervous woman of ten minutes before, but quite gay and vivacious, with a look of triumph in her fine, dark eyes.

"I am very glad, Doctor Colkirk, that you have promised to assist me," she said, laughing merrily and stretching out her tiny foot from beneath the hem of her skirt with a distinct air of coquetry. "I feel sure that we shall be excellent friends."

"I hope so," I replied. "But you must be careful of your general health, and persevere with the treatment."

"I don't care much for chemists' concoctions," she laughed. "It's very good of you to have given me this prescription, but I don't propose to make use of it."

"Why not?" I inquired in quick surprise.

"Because I only described to you imaginary symptoms," she laughed mischievously. "I enjoy a glass of port immensely after dinner, but further than that never touch stimulants, nor have any inclination for them."

"So you have deceived me," I said severely, for it seemed as though she wished to poke fun at me.

"Yes. But I hope you will forgive me," she answered, laughing.

"I cannot see what motive you can have in calling me in to describe a malady from which you are not suffering. A doctor's time is valuable."

"I had a motive."

"And pray what was it?"

"Well, I wished to make your acquaintance," she answered boldly, without hesitation.

"You adopted a rather unusual course," I remarked, somewhat annoyed.

"I think, under the circumstances, this little ruse of mine may possibly be forgiven," she answered. "I am not the first woman who has called in a doctor professionally merely in order to make his acquaintance."

"And for what reason did you wish to know me?"

"I trust you are not annoyed with me?" she exclaimed. "You must admit that I acted the part of the nervous woman so well that even you, a medical man, were, deceived."

"I admit that you have taken an unfair advantage of me," I answered calmly, wondering why she should thus have sought my acquaintance.

"But you will forgive me, Doctor, won't you?" she urged.

"If you will tell me the reason you were so desirous of meeting me."

"I wanted to know you."

"Why?"

"I had seen you in the distance many times, and desired to become personally acquainted with you."

"For what reason?"

She hesitated, and I thought I detected a faint blush upon her cheek.

"I—well, I wished to number you among my friends."

"Then I presume that the story regarding your husband is also a fiction?" I said, surprised that I had previously formed such an entirely wrong impression of her.

"No, not exactly," she responded. "I hope to have the pleasure of introducing you to him some day ere long."

"I shall of course be delighted," I answered in a tone which I fear did not convey any desire on my part to be honoured by the baronet's acquaintance. "But, having deceived me as you have to-day, I confess that my confidence is somewhat shaken."

She laughed and raised her hand to her hair.

"Ah! it is always best to commence by being enemies and to end by being friends."

"You intend, then, that we shall be friends?"

"Of course. That is the reason why I asked you to call on me."

"But where have you seen me?"

"Oh, in lots of places," she answered vaguely. Her attitude was very strange. Could it be possible that she had seen me, and, becoming attracted by my personal appearance, had found out who and what I was? Was it possible that she intended that I should be her lover?

The thought flashed across my mind as she sat there smiling upon me, displaying an even row of pearly teeth, while her face was radiant with triumph and happiness. I had promised friendship to this woman, who had so cleverly formed my acquaintance.

"Tell me one place where we have met," I asked, for, to my knowledge, I had never set eyes upon her before that morning.

"You were having supper at the Savoy with your friend, Doctor Raymond, one night three weeks ago," she answered. "On the following evening you both dined together at the exhibition at Earl's Court."

"And you saw us at both places?" I exclaimed, surprised.

"Yes," she laughed. "You see how well acquainted I have been with your recent movements."

"I had no idea that any lady had been taking an interest in my unimportant self," I laughed.

Yes, it was true, this woman was seeking to fascinate me by those wiles so purely feminine. But I laughed within myself, for I was fortunately proof against it all. The incident was decidedly amusing. Of a verity the doctor is bound to steel his heart against many feminine blandishments.

Ere the words had left my lips, however, our conversation was interrupted by a woman's voice outside the room, crying merrily—

"Nora! Nora! Where are you? We shall be so awfully late!"

And an instant later a young girl, dressed to go out, burst gaily into the room. She drew back with a quick word of apology when she recognised that her ladyship was not alone, but at sight of her I sat there dumb-stricken and rigid as a statue.

Was I dreaming? Could it be, after all, only a mere chimera of an excited imagination? No; I knew myself to be in full possession of all my faculties. The mystery was inscrutable. There before me, somewhat abashed by her own unceremonious intrusion, her soft cheeks slightly flushed, radiant and in perfect health, stood my dead wife in the flesh!

Chapter Nine.

A Maze of Mystery.

I sat erect in my chair, open-mouthed, unable to move. My eyes were riveted upon the slim graceful form before me. I held my breath in wonder. She wore a smart tailor-made gown of pale fawn, with a large black hat which suited her admirably, while across the face—every feature of which had been so indelibly photographed upon my memory—was a thin gauzy veil which only served to heighten, rather than to conceal, her striking beauty.

"I'm so sorry to have disturbed you," she exclaimed, turning to her ladyship. "But I hadn't any idea that you had a visitor."

"Oh," laughed the other, "our conversation is not at all of a private character. Let me introduce you." Then, turning to me, she said—

"This is my cousin, Feo Ashwicke—Doctor Colkirk."

My wife turned to me and bowed, a sweet smile upon her lips.

"I hope, Doctor, you will forgive me for bounding into the room like this," she said.

"Certainly," I answered, still gazing at her like a man in a dream.

She had been introduced to me as Feo Ashwicke, the cousin of this rather curious woman, Lady Pierrepoint-Lane. Yet there could be no doubt that she was actually Beryl Wynd, the sweet-faced girl whom I had seen lying dead in that house of mystery eight days before.

Neither our introduction nor the mention of my name had in the least disconcerted her. She remained perfectly frank and natural, betraying not the slightest surprise. Could it be possible that she was not aware of her marriage with me?

I looked straight into her clear blue eyes. Neither appeared affected. Nevertheless, had I not, on that fatal night, seen the strange contraction of the pupil, which had rendered one—the left eye—sightless and so strange-looking?

She was talking to her cousin, and thus I had opportunity of regarding her critically. Her hands were gloved, therefore I could not see whether she still wore the ring I had placed upon her finger. Still, if she were really Feo Ashwicke, what motive had she in masquerading as the daughter of that crafty scoundrel Wyndham Wynd?

I longed to speak plainly to her and seek some explanation, yet at that moment it was impossible. Her frank and open manner rendered it quite evident that to her I was an utter stranger.

It was this failure on her part to recognise my name that aroused within my mind a doubt whether, after all, her personal appearance only bore a very striking resemblance to that of my mysterious wife.

"Nora always forgets her engagements," she laughed, turning to me. "This morning we've got quite a host of places to go to and things to buy, for we leave town again to-night. After breakfast we arranged to go out together at eleven, and she's actually forgotten all about it!"

"Short memories are sometimes useful," I remarked with a smile.

"I hope that is not meant for sarcasm, Doctor," protested the baronet's wife.

"I am never sarcastic at the expense of my patients," I responded.

"But I presume I am a friend. Do your friends fare any better?"

"With my friends it is quite different. I myself am generally the object of their sarcasm."

They both laughed.

"How hot it is this morning," observed the mysterious Feo. "I've only been in town three days, and shall be very glad to get back again into the country."

"To what part are you going?" I inquired.

"Only to Whitton, near Hounslow, to visit the Chetwodes. Do you know them?"

"No," I replied. "Are you staying there long?"

"Oh, a fortnight or so," she replied. "The Chetwode girls were at school with me near Paris, and we are very good friends. They always have a big house-party at this time of the year, and there is usually lots of fun."

"You're quite right, dear," exclaimed her cousin, rising. "We must really make haste if we are to do all our shopping and catch the five o'clock from Waterloo. In Maud's letter, this morning, she says she will send the carriage to meet that train."

I rose also. I was loth to leave the presence of this charming girl, who was undoubtedly my bride, but who, it appeared, was entirely unconscious of the fact. Yet the woman who had called me in for consultation, and had acted so strangely that it almost seemed as though she had fallen in love with me, had pointedly dismissed me; therefore I was compelled to take my leave.

"I hope, Doctor, that we shall see something more of you on our return to town," her ladyship said, as we shook hands. "Recollect our conversation of this morning," she added meaningly.

"Of course I shall be most delighted to call and see how you have progressed," I responded. "You have the prescription, and I hope you will persevere with it."

"If I feel worse." She laughed, and I knew that she did not mean to have the mixture made up. She had shammed illness very cleverly. I was amused and annoyed at the same moment.

"I hope Doctor Colkirk will dine with us here one evening," said the woman who was my bride. "I'm sure Sir Henry would be charmed to meet him."

"Yes," answered her cousin; "only he must not know that I have consulted him professionally. That must be kept a secret."

"All women love secrets," I remarked.

"And men also," responded Feo. "Some appear to think that a little mystery adds an additional zest to life."

Her words were strange ones, and seemed to have been uttered with some abstruse meaning.

"Do you yourself think so?" I inquired, looking earnestly into those bright eyes of clear, childlike blue, that were so plainly indicative of a purity of soul.

"Well, I scarcely know," she responded, returning my glance unflinchingly. "We all of us have some little mystery or other in our lives, I suppose."

I had taken her hand in adieu, and was still holding it.

"And are you no exception?"

"Ah! now, Doctor, you're really too inquisitive." And she laughed, just a trifle unnaturally I thought, as though I had approached an unwelcome topic.

"Well," I said smiling, "I won't press you further; it isn't fair. Good-bye, and I trust I shall meet both your cousin and yourself at a date not far distant—that is, if I am still in town."

"Oh, I hope you will be!" exclaimed her ladyship; "I can't think why doctors go and bury themselves in the country."

"There are just as many patients in the country districts as in the towns," I responded. "And in the country one carries on one's profession amid more congenial surroundings."

I repeated my farewells, and, with a final and longing glance at my mysterious wife, went forth into the hall, and was let out by the liveried servant.

To approach my wife boldly and demand the truth was, I saw, useless. First I must, by my own careful observation, establish her identity with Beryl Wynd, and, secondly, clear up the mystery of how a woman could be dead and yet still live.

The expression of those clear, honest eyes, the form of the beautiful face, as flawless as that of Titian's "Flora" in the Tribune of the Uffizzi, the unusual tint of that gold-brown hair were all unmistakable. They set at rest any doubt which arose within me that the woman whose hand I had held was not the same upon whose finger I had placed the wedding-ring. Incredible though it seemed, I had that morning spoken with my unknown wife, and she had not known me. We were strangers, yet united in matrimony.

Mechanically I walked towards Kensington Church in order to take the omnibus back to Hammersmith. My mind was filled with the mystery of my marriage and the reason why the sum of twenty-five thousand pounds had been offered me if I would consent to secretly kill my bride.

Certain it was that I had been the victim of a cunningly devised plot, and further, that the fact of my return to London was known to those who had conspired against me. Therefore, it behoved me to exercise considerable care and caution in the prosecution of my inquiries. The two scoundrels, Wyndham Wynd and Major Tattersett, must, I resolved, be discovered at all hazards, while I must also leave no stone unturned to find out the house in which the marriage had taken place.

The man Wynd had intended that my wife should die, but it was plain that, by some good fortune, she had escaped him. Yet the most curious phase of the affair was that she appeared utterly unconscious of it all.

It struck me that I might, by dint of careful questioning, learn something from Sir Henry's wife. But she was, I knew, a clever, intelligent woman; and if she held a secret, it would be exceedingly difficult to obtain knowledge of it.

I returned to Rowan Road, and, on entering with my latch-key, found Bob standing in the hall.

"Why, my dear fellow?" he cried; "I had a wire to say you were missing, and so came up to look after you. Where, in the name of fortune, have you been?"

"I've been abroad," I responded vaguely.

"Abroad!" he cried incredulously. "Why? What made you go abroad?"

"I'll tell you all when we get upstairs," I answered; and we ascended together to the little den.

Then, over our pipes, I related to him the curious story.

"Well," he declared, in profound amazement. "I've never heard of a stranger adventure than that! Do you mean to say that you're actually married?"

"Without a doubt. A special licence was obtained and the marriage is, therefore, quite legal. The most remarkable fact of all is, that while I know my wife, she doesn't know me. To her I'm a perfect stranger."

"But the fellow, Wynd, whoever he is, is evidently no novice in crime," Bob declared thoughtfully. "The contraction of the eye was a curious symptom."

"Yes. It was in the pupil of the left eye."

"And yet the girl you have met to-day is perfectly sound in both eyes?" he remarked.

"Perfectly."

"But, my dear fellow, it can't be! If she were dead, as you say, she can't, as you yourself know, be still alive."

"That's just where the mystery becomes so inscrutable?" I cried. "The woman whom I married evidently died. Indeed, I'd have given a certificate of death and backed it by my professional reputation. Yet she's alive and well, and I have, only an hour ago, spoken with her."

"Bless my soul?" cried Bob. "Most extraordinary thing I've ever heard of! There must have been some very strong reason why you should marry her, or that scoundrel Wynd would not have offered such a sum. He evidently wished to get her married, and then do away with her for reasons which I hope we shall, some day, be able to discover. The thing's a complete enigma," he went on, "and if I can help you to solve it, Dick, I'll do so willingly. In my opinion there's a great deal more in this affair than we dream of. The whole thing seems to have been most carefully worked out, and I shouldn't wonder if her ladyship has not had a hand in the affair. She seems too bold; and therefore I have suspicions of her."

"So have I, old fellow," I said. "The strongest suspicions. Her very words have betrayed her."

"Unless"—he hesitated—"unless she saw you at the Savoy when we fed together in honour of my birth, and was struck by your appearance—in fact, to put it plainly, unless she has fallen in love with you."

"But why?" I demanded. "I've never met the woman before, to my knowledge."

"But you're a good-looking Johnnie, my dear Dick," my friend declared, laughing; "and she's certainly not the first woman who has fallen over head and ears in love with you."

"You're devilish complimentary, old chap," I answered; "but if she is, as you think, really attracted towards me, then she'll have a cruel awakening when she finds that I'm actually the husband of her cousin Feo."

"That's just what I've been thinking," he replied, with a serious expression on his face. "Your position is an exceedingly difficult one, and the inquiries must be made with the utmost tact and care. At all hazards you must humour her ladyship, and retain her as your friend. Indeed if, as you say, your wife is not aware that you are actually her husband, then it might not be a bad plan to flatter her ladyship by making violent love to her."

"I can't, Bob," I declared. "In this matter I must at least act straightforwardly. Feo has fallen a victim, just as I myself have—that's evident."

"You were entrapped, it's true; but I take it that you really admire this mysterious Feo?"

"Admire her!" I cried with enthusiasm. "That's the most curious feature of the whole affair. I freely confess to you, my dear fellow, that not only do I admire her, but I'm madly in love with her! She's the most graceful and beautiful woman I've ever beheld."

"Well, Dick," he observed after a pause, during which time he puffed vigorously at his big briar, "you are about the last man I should have suspected of having a romance. Every detail of it is, however, bewildering. It's a perfect maze of mystery—a mystery absolutely incredible!"

Chapter Ten.

The Major.

On the following day I was seized by a burning desire to again see the woman whom I had so strangely grown to love. Time after time I discussed the matter with Bob, and he was full of my opinion that I might, by watching my wife's movements, discover some fact which might give me a clue.

I proposed to Bob that I should go straight to her and make a full explanation, but he urged patience and diplomacy.

"Go down to Whitton and watch her at a distance, if you like," he answered. "But be very careful that you are not recognised. No man cares to be spied upon. In this matter you must exercise the greatest discretion, if you really intend to get to the bottom of this puzzling affair."

"I do intend to solve the enigma," I declared. "If I'm ten years over it, I mean to claim Feo as my wife."

"You can't do that until you've obtained absolute proof."

"And, in the meantime, Wynd and his accomplice may make another attempt upon her life," I observed dubiously.

"Forewarned is forearmed," he answered. "It seems your duty to act in secret as her protector."

"Exactly. That's my object in going down to Whitton. Somehow I feel sure that her life is insecure, for the facts plainly show that Wynd's motive was to get rid of her."

"Without a doubt. Go down to Hounslow to-morrow and discover what you can regarding these friends of hers, the Chetwodes, and their associates. In inquiries of this sort you must carefully work back."

Now, I had for years rather prided myself upon my shrewdness. I had often set myself the task of clearing up those little unimportant mysteries of life which occur to every man; and more than once, while at the hospital, I had rendered service to the police in their inquiries.

That same afternoon, while Bob was out visiting his patients, I chanced to put my hand in the ticket-pocket of my frock-coat, and felt something there. The coat was the one I had worn when called out to become the husband of Feo Ashwicke, and from the pocket I drew a half-smoked cigarette.

I am not in the habit of placing cigarette ends in my pockets, and could not, at first, account for its presence there; but, on examination, I saw that it was the remains of one of an unusual brand, for upon the paper were tiny letters in Greek printed in blue ink. A second's reflection, however, decided me: it was the cigarette which the Major had given me. It had gone out while I had been speaking, and with it in my hand I had rushed upstairs to my wife's room, and instead of casting it away had, I suppose, thrust it into my pocket, where it had remained unheeded until that moment.

I examined it with the utmost care and great interest. Then I descended to Bob's little dispensary, at the back of the house, and, finding a microscope, took out some of the tobacco and placed it beneath the lens. Tiny but distinct crystals were revealed clinging to the finely-cut tobacco, crystals of some subtle poison which, dissolved by the saliva while in the act of smoking, entered the system.

The cigarette had narrowly proved fatal to me.

At once I lit the spirit-lamp, cleaned and dried some test-tubes, and set busily to work to make solutions with the object of discovering the drug. But although I worked diligently the whole afternoon, and Bob, on returning, assisted me, we were unable to determine exactly what it was.

The remainder of the cigarette, including the paper bearing the mark of manufacture, I carefully preserved, and on the following morning went down to Hounslow to ascertain what I could regarding my unconscious wife. Bob remained at Rowan Road to look after his patients, but declared his intention of relieving me if any watching were required. Therefore, I went forth eager to ascertain some fact that would lead me to a knowledge of the truth.

Hounslow, although but a dozen miles from Charing Cross, was, I found, a dull, struggling place, the dismal quiet of which was only relieved by a few boisterous militiamen in its long street.

I took up my quarters at the historic Red Lion, and over a whisky-and-soda made inquiries of the plethoric landlord as to the whereabouts of Whitton. It lay beyond the town, half-way towards Twickenham, he told me.

"There's a Whitton Park, isn't there?" I inquired.

"Yes; Colonel Chetwode's place. That's just before you get to Whitton Church."

"It's a large house, I suppose?"

"Oh, yes; he's the squire there, and magistrate, and all that."

"I've heard his name," I said, "but I've never seen him. What sort of a man is he?"

"Oh, a bit stand-offish, tall, thin, and grey-haired. We hotel-keepers don't like 'im, because he's always down on us on the licensing-days over at Brentford," the man replied, chewing his cheap cigar.

"He's married, isn't he?"

"Yes; he married 'is second wife about three years ago. She's a good-looking woman with reddish hair. They say she don't get on very well with the Colonel's grown-up son."

"Oh," I remarked, at once interested. "How old is the son?"

"About twenty-five. He's a jolly fellow 'e is. He's a lieutenant in the 7th Hussars, and they're stationed here just now. He often comes in and gets a drink when e' passes."

"And he doesn't hit it off well with his stepmother?"

"No; I've heard some queer stories about their quarrels from the servants," he answered. He was a gossip, like all landlords of inns, and seemed extremely communicative because I had asked him to drink with me. The effect of a shilling spent upon drink is ofttimes amazing.

"Stepmothers are generally intruders," I laughed. "Well, things came to such a pass down at the Park, a month or two ago, that Mrs Chetwode demanded that the Colonel should turn young Mr Cyril out of the house, and threatened that if he did not she would leave. The Colonel, so it's said, grew furious, stormed down the place, and in the end Mrs Chetwode packed her trunks and went with Sherman, her maid, to Switzerland. About three weeks ago the Colonel followed her and brought her back, so I suppose they've made it up again."

"Do they entertain many friends?"

"Oh yes, there's always visitors there; it's so near to London, you see."

"Do you know the names of any of the visitors?" I inquired. Adding, "I think a friend of mine comes down to see them sometimes—a Sir Pierrepoint-Lane."

"Oh yes," he said; "I've seen both Sir Henry and his wife driving. They've got a place somewhere in Wiltshire, I've heard. They're great friends of Mrs Chetwode's."

"And there's a Miss Ashwicke who comes with them," I said eagerly. "Do you know her?"

"I may know her by sight," the man replied, "but I don't know her by name."

"She's tall, blue-eyed, with golden-brown hair. Very pretty, and always very smartly dressed."

"Yes; she wears a big black hat, and very often a drab-coloured dress. When she smiles she shows her teeth very prettily," he said.

"That's her, no doubt."

"Well," he said, "her description is exact. She's Mr Cyril's young lady."

"What?" I cried, starting up in surprise.

"When she's down here she's always about with the Colonel's son, and everybody says they're engaged," he went on. "The servants have told me that they're a most devoted couple."

"But is that lady the same one that I mean?" I inquired dubiously.

"I don't know her surname, but her Christian name is Miss Beryl."

"Beryl?" I gasped. Could this be the actual truth, that she was engaged to young Chetwode?

Beryl! Then she was evidently known here by the name in which she had married me—Beryl Wynd.

"Is she often here?" I asked at last, when I found voice again. I was so upset by this statement, that with difficulty I remained calm.

"Oh yes, very often; especially now that Mr Cyril is at the barracks. They ride out together every morning, and are very often about in the town in the afternoon. You'll no doubt see them."

"Ah," I said, with the object of misleading my garrulous informant, "it can't be the lady I mean, as her name is not Beryl."

"The description is very much like her," he observed, knocking the ash from his cigar.

"Is there any talk of young Chetwode marrying?" I inquired.

"Well, yes, there are rumours of course," he answered. "Some say that the Colonel is against it, while others say that Mrs Chetwode is jealous of her stepson, so one doesn't know exactly what to believe."

"I suppose you hear a lot of gossip about them, eh?"

"Oh, a lot. Much, too, that ain't true," he laughed. "Why, somebody said once that Miss Beryl was the daughter of an officer who got sent to penal servitude."

"Who said that?" I said, at once pricking up my ears. Was it not Major Tattersett who had accompanied her to the registry at Doctors' Commons, and who had given me that cigarette?

"Oh, it was a story that got about."

"Did they say who the officer was? or what was his offence?"

"He was a major in the Guards, they said."

"You didn't hear his name?"

"No, I've never heard her name. Everybody here knows her as Miss Beryl. But it would be easy enough to find out." And, rising, he leant forward into the tap-room, where a rural postman was sitting, hot and dusty, drinking ale from a pewter, and shouted, "I say, Allen, what's the name of Mr Chetwode's young lady?"

"The young lady that's so often at the Park? Why, Miss Beryl Wynd."

I sat motionless for some moments. The truth seemed plain—that she had allowed herself to be introduced to me at Gloucester Square under an alias. For what reason, I wondered?

She was undoubtedly in love with this young lieutenant of Hussars. If so, then she would seek to preserve the secret of her marriage, and even repudiate it if necessary. The rumours of her being the daughter of a disgraced officer was another curious feature. It almost appeared as if there were some truth underlying it.

"You hear what the postman says, sir," observed the landlord, turning again to me. "He knows, because he delivers the letters at the Park. Her name is Wynd—funny name, isn't it?"

"Yes," I answered mechanically, for the discovery that this young Chetwode was the accepted suitor of my love was a staggering blow. What could I do? How should I act?

She was my wife by law—mine.

I rose, announcing that I was going for a stroll, and, walked unsteadily out into the long, deserted street. I wandered down the Hanworth Road, past rows of cottages with gardens filled with flowers, to the station, and, crossing the bridge, soon found myself before the old-fashioned lodge at the entrance to Whitton Park.

I was curious to investigate the place, and, noticing that the lodge-keeper's house was shut, while one of the smaller of the great ornamental iron gates stood open, I strolled in, continuing up the avenue for a quarter of a mile or so, when suddenly the drive swept round past a pretty lake, and I came in full view of the house.

It was a splendid old Elizabethan mansion. Before it was a pretty, old-world garden with an ancient sundial in the centre, while to the right was a well-kept modern tennis-court where people were playing, while afternoon tea was being served to the remainder of the house-party.

There were fully a dozen people there, the men in flannels and the women in cool muslins with bright sunshades. Risks of detection, however, prevented me from approaching close enough to clearly distinguish the faces of the hostess and her guests; therefore I stood hidden by the bushes, watching the game, and trying in vain to catch a glimpse of the countenances of the chattering circle of tea-drinkers.

Suddenly a figure in pale yellow rose and crossed to the side of a foppishly-dressed young man who, sitting somewhat apart, was smoking and intently watching the game. The smartness of the figure, the narrow waist, wide hips, and swinging gait were familiar.

Although I could not distinguish her features, I knew that it was my wife—the woman who was ignorant of her marriage, and whom I loved with such a fond, mad passion.

The man rose, pulled a chair forward for her, and then both sat down together to chat. He fetched her some tea, and then sat hugging his knees, apparently engrossed in conversation. She seemed to hold him beneath the spell of her marvellous beauty, just as she held me.

Could it be that that man, whose face I could not see clearly, was Cyril Chetwode, her lover?

I was standing there, my eyes riveted upon the pair, when the sound of a footstep on the gravel caused me to turn quickly. Some one was approaching. I at once drew back behind the trunk of a great elm near which I was standing, for my discovery there as an intruder might upset all my plans.

The figure came forward slowly, for I could hear that they were deliberate footsteps, as though of a person waiting and pacing up and down. I peeped out to ascertain who it was, and as I did so the figure of a man in a soft felt hat and a suit of grey tweed came cautiously into view.

My heart leapt up in quick surprise.

It was the man who, by giving me that cigarette, had made the dastardly attempt upon my life that had been so nearly successful—the man of whom I had been in active search—Major Tattersett.

His single eyeglass was still in his eye, and his hat was set upon his head as jauntily as on the day when we had first met, but, for the eagerness of his countenance as he gazed forward to where my wife sat, I saw that he was not one of the house-party, and felt confident that his presence there was with secret and evil intent.

Chapter Eleven.

Voices of the Night.

From my place of concealment I was able to watch the Major closely without risk of detection.

His presence there boded no good. He had crept slowly up the avenue until within sight of the house, and was intently scanning the gay party assembled on the lawn. Was it possible that he had walked behind me and watched me enter there?

He was scarcely as smart in appearance as on the day when he led my bride up the aisle of the church, and had afterwards handed me the cigarette; but, nevertheless, he retained the distinctly foppish air of the man-about-town. For a few moments only he remained there eagerly scanning the distant group, and then, as though reassured, he turned on his heel and retraced his steps towards the lodge.

Determined to watch his movements, I followed him until he gained Hounslow Station, and there I saw him turn into a low-built, old-fashioned inn, where I afterwards discovered he had been staying for a couple of days.

That some conspiracy was being formed, I could not doubt, therefore I set myself to keep strict watch upon him—no easy matter, for from hour to hour I feared that he might recognise me. It was he who had petitioned the Archbishop for the special licence for our marriage; he who had, with some mysterious motive, posed as the father of the woman I now loved. Surely she must have known that he was not her father, and, if so, she herself had taken a part in a plot which had so nearly cost her her life.

But was she not dead when I found her lying there? The puzzle was bewildering.

The Major's movements might possibly give me some clue. It was fortunate that we had met.

At a cheap clothier's I had purchased a rough secondhand suit and a bowler hat, much the worse for wear, and these I had assumed in order to alter my appearance as much as possible. About nine o'clock that same night, while I stood idling about the station with my eye ever upon the inn opposite, my vigilance was suddenly rewarded, for the Major emerged leisurely, carefully lit a cigar, and then strolled across the railway bridge and down the road towards Whitton. Darkness had not quite set in, therefore I hesitated to follow him; but, fortunately, I had explored the neighbourhood thoroughly during the past few hours, and knew that by crossing to the opposite platform of the station, I could gain a footpath which led through fields and market-gardens, emerging into the high-road almost opposite the gates of the park.

This byway I took, and, hurrying down it, arrived at the point near the lodge fully five minutes before he appeared along the road. The gates were, however, closed.

Would he ring and demand admittance? I wondered.

When about two hundred yards from the gates he suddenly halted, glanced up and down the road as though to make certain that no one was watching, and then, bending down, squeezed himself through a hole in the wooden fencing and disappeared. He evidently knew that the gates were locked, and had already discovered that mode of entry, if indeed he had not broken away the palings himself earlier in the day.

Without hesitation I hurried forward over the grass by the roadside, so that he might not hear my footsteps, and, discovering the hole in the paling, entered after him. I found myself in the midst of hawthorn bushes and thick undergrowth, but, pausing and listening intently, I soon detected which direction he had taken by the noise of breaking twigs. For some ten minutes I remained there, fearing to move lest the noise might alarm him; but when at last he was out of hearing I crept forward, breaking my way through in the direction of the avenue. The night was hot and so still that each sound seemed to awaken the echoes.

With the greatest caution I crept on, walking noiselessly over the grass in the direction of the house.

As soon as the old mansion came into view I saw that lights burned in many of the windows, and from the drawing-rooms, where the open doors led on to the lawn, came the living strains of dance music.

From where I stood I could see the high lamps with their shades of yellow silk, and now and then bright dresses flashed past the long windows. A couple of figures were strolling up and down before the house. I could see their white shirt-fronts in the darkness, and knew that they were men smoking and enjoying the night air.

The two men at last tossed away their cigar ends and entered the house: thus I became encouraged to approach closer, cross the lawn, and peep through one of the side windows of the drawing-room. Fully a dozen people were there, but as I gazed around I was disappointed not to see my love. I had risked discovery and detection to obtain sight of her, but she was not present, neither was her cousin Nora. Most of the guests seemed smart people, judging from the women's toilettes, and all were lolling about with the air of laziness which overcomes one after a good dinner. Dancing had ended, and, as I watched, a young dark-haired girl approached the piano and commenced to sing a song by which I knew that she was French.

I peered in through those windows eager for a glimpse of Beryl. Surely she was not like those others? No, I recollected her calm dignity and sweet grace when I had spoken to her. She, at least, was high-minded and womanly. I was glad she was not there to hear that song.

The singer sat down, having finished, amid roars of applause, and then the conversation was resumed; but at that instant I became conscious of some one passing near me, and had only just time to draw back into the shadow and thus escape observation. It was one of the guests, a man who lounged slowly along, the glowing end of his cigar shining in the darkness, alone; he was apparently full of recollections, for he passed slowly and mechanically onward without noticing me. Unable to see his face, I could only detect that he was rather above the average height, and, by his silhouette, I saw that he stooped slightly.

The encounter, however, caused me to recede from the house, for I had no desire to be detected there and compelled to give an account of myself. I was in shabby clothes, and if found in the vicinity might be suspected of an intention to commit a theft.

Where was the Major? He had certainly entered there, but had escaped my vigilance by passing through the thicket. I had been there nearly half an hour, yet had not been able to re-discover him. The lawn on one side was bounded by a light iron fencing, beyond which was a thick wood, and upon this fencing I mounted, and sat to rest in full view of the house and the long window of the drawing-room. In the deep shadow of the trees I waited there, safe from detection, listening to the music, which had recommenced, and wondering what had become of the man whom I had tried to follow. He seemed to have avoided the house and gone to the opposite side of the park.

Although I could actually see into the circle of assembled guests, yet I was so far off that I could only distinguish the women by the colour of their gowns. Had Beryl returned to join them? I wondered. I was longing for a single glance at her dear face—that face sweeter than any other in the world.

A woman in a cream dress, cut low at the neck, came suddenly to the doorway and peered forth into the night as though in search of some one, but a moment later had disappeared; and again the piano broke forth with the pretty minuet from Manon.

I had, I felt certain, been there almost, if not quite, an hour; therefore I was resolved to make a tour of the park in an endeavour to find the man whose suspicious movements had so interested me earlier in the evening. With that object in view I leaped down upon the lawn, crossed it until I reached the edge of the lake, which I skirted until I gained a rustic bridge which crossed the tiny brook that rippled over the stones and fell into the pool.

Of a sudden I heard a sound. It was quite distinct, like a half-suppressed cough. I halted in surprise, but no other sound reached my ear. Could I have been mistaken? The noise seemed very human, yet I knew that in the darkness of night the most usual sound becomes exaggerated and distorted. Therefore reassured I continued my way by the narrow, unfrequented path, which, leaving the lakeside, struck across the park and led me across a stile into a dark belt of wood.

Scarcely had I entered it, however, when I heard human voices distinctly. I halted and listened. An owl hooted weirdly, and there was a dead silence.

I wondered whether the persons I had surprised had detected my presence. I stood upon the narrow path holding my breath so that I could catch every sound.

A couple of minutes passed. To me they seemed as hours. Then, again, the voices sounded away to the left, apparently on the edge of the wood. Noiselessly I retraced my steps to the stile, and then found that from it there ran a path beside the iron railing, whither I knew not. But somewhere down that path two persons were in consultation.

Treading carefully, so that my footsteps should not be overheard, I crept down the path until, of a sudden, I caught sight of a woman's white dress in the gloom. Then, sufficiently close to overhear, I halted with strained ears.

I was hidden behind a high hazel bush, but could just distinguish against that reddish glare which shines in the sky of the outskirts of London on a summer's night, two silhouettes, those of a man and a woman. The former had halted, and was leaning against the railing, while the latter, with a shawl twisted about her shoulders, stood facing him.

"If you had wished you could certainly have met me before this," the man was grumbling. "I've waited at the stile there a solid hour. Besides, it was a risky business with so many people about."

"I told you not to come here," she answered; and in an instant I recognised the voice. They were the sweet, musical tones of the woman who was my wife.

"Of course," laughed her companion sardonically. "But, you see, I prefer the risk." And I knew by the deep note that the man who stood by her was the Major.

"Why?" she inquired. "The risk is surely mine in coming out to meet you?"

"Bah! women can always make excuses," he laughed. "I should not have made this appointment if it were not imperative that we should meet."

"Well?" she sighed. "What do you want of me now?"

"I want to talk to you seriously."

"With the usual request to follow," she observed wearily. "You want money—eh?"

"Money? Oh no," he said, with bitter sarcasm. "I can do without it. I can live on air, you know."

"That's better than prison fare, I should have thought," she answered grimly.

"Ah, now, my dear, you're sarcastic," he said, with a touch of irony. "That doesn't become you."

"Well, tell me quickly what you want, and let me get back, or they will miss me."

"You mean that your young lover will want to know with whom you've been flirting, eh? Well, you can mislead him again, as you've done many times before. What a fine thing it is to be an accomplished liar. I always envy people who can lie well, for they get through life so easily." He spoke in a familiar tone, as though he held her beneath an influence that was irresistible.

"I am no liar," she protested quickly. "The lies I have been compelled to tell have been at your own instigation."

"And to save yourself," he added, with a dry, harsh laugh. "But I didn't bring you here for an exchange of compliments."

Chapter Twelve.

The Morning After.

"Then why have you compelled me to meet you again?" she demanded fiercely, in a tone which showed her abhorrence of him. "The last time we met you told me that you were going abroad. Why haven't you gone?"

"I've been and come back again."

"Where?"

"That's my business," he answered very calmly. "Your welcome home is not a very warm one, to say the least."

"I have no welcome for my enemies."

"Oh! I'm an enemy—eh? Well," he added, "I have always considered myself your friend."

"Friend!" she echoed. "You show your friendliness in a rather curious manner. You conceive these dastardly plots, and then compel me to do your bidding—to act as your decoy!"

"Come, come," he laughed, his temper quite unruffled by her accusation, "you know that in all my actions I am guided by your interests as well as my own."

"I was certainly not aware of it," she responded. "It cannot be to my interest that you compel me to meet you here like this, at the risk of discovery. Would it not have been better if our meeting had taken place in London, as before?"

"Necessity has driven me to make this appointment," he responded. "To write to you is dangerous, and I wanted to give you warning so that you can place yourself in a position of security."

"A warning!—of what?" she asked breathlessly.

"La Gioia is here."

"La Gioia!" she gasped. "Here? Impossible!" La Gioia! It was the name I had found written upon the piece of paper beneath her pillow.

"Unfortunately, it is the truth," he responded in an earnest voice. "The contretemps is serious."

"Serious!" she cried in alarm. "Yes, it is serious; and through you I am thus placed in peril!"

"How do you intend to act?"

"I have no idea," she responded, in a hoarse tone. "I am tired of it all, and driven to despair—I am sick to death of this eternal scheming, this perpetual fear lest the terrible truth should become known. God knows how I have suffered during this past year. Ah, how a woman can suffer and still live! I tell you," she cried, with sudden desperation, "this dread that haunts me continually will drive me to take my life!"

"Rubbish!" he laughed. "Keep up your pluck. With a little ingenuity a woman can deceive the very devil himself."

"I tell you," she said. "I am tired of life—of you—of everything. I have nothing to live for—nothing to gain by living!"

Her voice was the voice of a woman driven to desperation by the fear that her secret should become known.

"Well," he laughed brutally, "you've certainly nothing to gain by dying, my dear."

"You taunt me!" she cried in anger. "You who hold me irrevocably in this bond of guilt—you who compel me to act as your accomplice in these vile schemes! I hate you!"

"Without a doubt," he responded, with a short laugh. "And yet I have done nothing to arouse this feeling of antagonism."

"Nothing! Do you then think so lightly of all the past?"

"My dear girl," he said, "one should never think of what has gone by. It's a bad habit. Look to your own safety, and to the future."

"La Gioia is here!" she repeated in a low voice, as though unable to fully realise all that the terrible announcement meant. "Well, how do you intend to act?"

"My actions will be guided by circumstances," he replied. "And you?"

She was silent. The stillness of the night was broken only by the dismal cry of a night-bird down near the lake.

"I think it is best that I should die and end it all," she replied, in a hard, strained voice.

"Don't talk such nonsense!" he said impatiently. "You are young, graceful, smart, with one of the prettiest faces in London. And you would commit suicide. The thing is utterly absurd!"

"What have I to gain by living?" she inquired again, that question being apparently uppermost in her mind.

"You love young Chetwode. You may yet marry him."

"No," she answered with a sigh; "I fear that can never be. Happiness can never be mine—never."

"Does he love you?" inquired the Major, with a note of sympathy in his voice.

"Love me? Why, of course he does."

"You have never doubted him?"

"Never."

"And he has asked you to marry him?"

"Yes, a dozen times."

"When was the last occasion?"

"To-night—an hour ago."

"And you, of course, refused?"

"Of course."

"Why?"

"Because of the barrier which prevents my marriage with him."

"And you will allow that to stand in the way of your safety?"

"My safety!" she echoed. "I don't understand."

"Cannot you see that if you married Cyril Chetwode at once, La

Gioia would be powerless?"

"Ah!" she exclaimed suddenly, impressed by the suggestion. "I had never thought of that?"

"Well," he went on, "if you take my advice, you'll lose no time in becoming Chetwode's wife. Then you can defy your enemies, and snap your fingers at La Gioia."

A deep silence fell. The woman who was my wife was reflecting.

"You say that by marriage I could defy my enemies; but that is incorrect. I could not cut myself free of all of them."

"Why? Whom would you fear?"

"You yourself," she answered bluntly.

"You have no confidence in me," he protested with a dissatisfied air.

"I can have no confidence in one who holds me enslaved as you do."

"And yet I have come here at considerable risk and personal inconvenience to give you warning."

"Because you fear discovery yourself."

"No," he laughed; "I'm quite safe. I merely came here to make two suggestions to you. One I have already made, namely, that you should marry Chetwode without delay. And the other—"

He paused, as though to accurately gauge the extent of his power over her.

"Well? Go on. I am all attention."

"The other is that you should, as before, render me a trifling assistance in a little matter I have in hand which, if successfully carried out, will place both of us for ever beyond the reach of La Gioia's vengeance."

"Another scheme?" she cried wearily. "Well, what is it? Some further dastardly plot or other, no doubt. Explain it."

"No; you are under a misapprehension," he responded quickly. "The affair is no dastardly plot, but merely a little piece of ingenuity by which we may outwit La Gioia."

"Outwit her!" she cried. "The very devil himself could not outwit La Gioia."

"Ah!" he laughed; "you women are always so ready to jump to ill-formed conclusions. She has one weak point."

"And you have discovered it?"

"Yes; I have discovered it."

"How?"

"That is my affair. It is sufficient to be aware that she, the invincible, is nevertheless vulnerable."

There was another pause; but at last the woman I loved responded in a firm, determined tone—

"Then, if that is true, I leave it to you. You declare you are my friend, therefore I can, at least, rely on you for protection, especially as we have so many interests in common."

"But you must assist me," he observed.

"No," she answered, "I refuse to do that. You are quite capable of carrying out any villainy without my assistance."

"Need we use the term villainy where La Gioia is concerned?" he asked. "You know her well enough to be aware that if she finds you she will be merciless, and will gloat over your downfall."

"I would kill myself before she discovers me," my wife declared.

"But you might not have time," he suggested. "To die willingly demands considerable resolution. Women's nerve usually fails them at the extreme moment."

"Mine will not, you may rest assured of that," she answered.

"You don't seem capable of listening to reason to-night," he protested.

"I am capable of listening to reason, but not to conspiracy," she replied with some hauteur. "I know well what is passing in your mind. You would plot to take her life—to murder La Gioia!"

He laughed outright, as though there was something humorous in her words.

"No, no, my dear," he answered quickly. "You quite misunderstood my intention."

"I misunderstood your intention on a previous occasion," she said meaningly.

"But in this affair our interests are entirely mutual," he pointed out. "You must assist me."

"I shall not."

"But you must. We have everything to gain by securing her silence."

"And everything to lose by meeting her."

"But when we meet her it will be in defiance. I have thought out a plan."

"Then carry it out," she said. "I will have nothing whatever to do with it."

"I may compel you," he said, with slow distinctness. "You have already compelled me to act as your accomplice, but you have strained my bonds until they can resist no longer. I intend to break them."

"That is indeed very interesting!" He laughed, treating her as though she were a spoilt child.

"Yes," she cried furiously, "I will kill myself!"

"And leave me to make a scandalous explanation."

"Then you would besmirch my good name after my death?" she said, turning upon him quickly. "Ah, yes! You show yourself in your true colours. You would even weave about me a web of infamy, so as to prevent me taking my life. I hate and detest you!"

"That's not the first time you have informed me of that fact, my dear," he responded, perfectly coolly.

"If it were not for you I should now be a happy girl. Thanks to you I am, however, one of the most wretched of all God's creatures."

"You need not be. You are petted in your own circle of friends, and your reputation remains unsullied."

"I occupy a false position," she declared. "What would Cyril say if he knew the truth?"

"A woman should never study the man who is to be her husband. It makes him far too conceited; and, moreover, she is sure to regret it in after-life."

He was at times shrewdly philosophical, this scoundrel who held my wife beneath his thrall.

"I have you—only you—to thank for my present position. Believed by the world to be an honest, innocent girl, and accepted as such, I nevertheless fear from hour to hour that the truth may be revealed, and that I may find myself in the hands of the police. Death is preferable to this constant, all-consuming dread."

"The unreasonableness and pertinacity of woman is extraordinary!" he exclaimed in a tone of impatience.

"What good can possibly result from this duel between us? Why not let us unite in defeating La Gioia?"

"That I refuse to do."

"But our position is serious—most serious," he pointed out. "Suppose that she discovers you!"

"Well, what then?"

"You must be entirely at her mercy," he said in a deep voice. "And you know the fiendishness of her vengeance."

"I know," she responded in a voice scarcely above at whisper, the voice of a woman driven to desperation.

"But you must arm yourself against her," he urged.

"Together we are strong enough to defeat any attack that she may make."

"Tell me plainly," she asked, dropping her voice until it was scarcely above a whisper, "do you, yourself, fear her?"

"Yes. She is the only person who, besides ourselves, knows the truth," he responded in a low tone.

"And you would set a trap into which she will fall?" she went on, still in a whisper. "Come, do not let us prevaricate longer. You intend to kill her?"

There was dead silence. At last her companion spoke.

"Well," he answered, "and if your surmise is correct?"

"Then, once and for all," she said, raising her voice, "I tell you I'll have no hand whatsoever in it?"

He was apparently taken aback by the suddenness of her decision.

"And you prefer to be left unprotected against the vengeance of La Gioia!" he said harshly.

"Yes, I do," she said determinedly. "And recollect that from to-night I refuse to be further associated with these vile schemes of yours. You deceived me once; you shall never do so again!"

He laughed aloud.

"And you think you can break from me as easily as this. Your action to-night is foolish—suicidal. You will repent it."

"I shall never repent. My hatred of you is too strong!"

"We shall see," he laughed.

"Let me pass!" she cried, and leaving him, walked quickly down the path, and in a few moments the flutter of her light dress was lost in the darkness.

Her companion hurried after her.

I emerged quickly from my hiding-place, and followed them as far as the stile. He had overtaken her, and was striding by her side, bending and talking earnestly as they crossed the open grassland.

To follow sufficiently close to overhear what he said was impossible without detection, therefore I was compelled to remain and watch the receding figures until they became swallowed up in the darkness. Then, turning, I passed through the belt of wood again, and, scaling a wall, gained the high-road, which, after a walk of half an hour, took me back to Hounslow.

That night I slept but little. The discovery I had made was extraordinary! Who was this woman with the strange name? "La

Gioia" meant in Italian "The Jewel," or "The Joy." Why did they fear her vengeance?

In the morning, as I descended to breakfast, the landlord of the inn, standing in his shirt-sleeves, met me at the foot of the stairs.

"Have you heard the terrible news, sir?" he inquired.

"No," I said in surprise. "What news?"

"There was murder committed last night over in Whitton Park!"

"Murder?" I gasped. "Who has been murdered?"

Chapter Thirteen.

I Practise a New Profession.

"Why, the Colonel—Colonel Chetwode!" the man answered excitedly.

"Colonel Chetwode!" I gasped. "Impossible!"

"It's a fact," he declared. "The whole thing's a deep mystery. They found him at five o'clock this morning."

"Tell me all about it," I urged.

"Mr Plummer, sergeant of police, was in here half an hour ago, and he told me all about it. According to what he says, it seems that a workman going across the park to Twickenham early this morning, saw the body of a man on the edge of the lake, half in the water. He rushed forward, and to his horror found it was the Colonel, quite dead."

"Drowned?"

"No; he wasn't drowned. That's the curious part of it. He was murdered."

"How?"

"By a blow on the head, the police believe. Plummer says that there are lots of marks near the edge of the lake as though a struggle took place."

"Extraordinary!" I ejaculated. "You say he was quite dead when discovered. Was a doctor called?"

"Yes; the police surgeon, Doctor Douglas. He declared that the poor Colonel had been murdered, and had been dead several hours."

"Is there no suspicion of the assassin?" I inquired, as the thought of the man whom I had watched in the Park dashed through my brain.

"None whatever," he answered. "The Colonel was very popular everywhere, and was always good to the poor. It's his wife who isn't liked; she's a rum un', they say."

"Where was the body found?" I inquired, when I had seated myself at the table while he had taken up a position before the empty fireplace to continue gossiping.

"Ah!" he said, "you wouldn't, of course, know the spot, for you've never been in the park. There's a path which leads across the grass at the back of the house through some thickets, and, skirting the lake, crosses the brook by a little bridge. It was just by that bridge that the poor fellow was found. They think that just as he had crossed the bridge he was struck down, and then fell backwards into the lake."

"Ah! I understand," I said. "Let's hope that the detectives will discover something when they arrive. It was evidently a most dastardly bit of work."

The man's remark that I had no knowledge of the spot where the body was found aroused me to a sense of my own position. If it were known that I had entered the park that night, might not a serious suspicion fall upon me?

I recollected how, as I had crossed the bridge, I had heard distinctly a short cough. The murderer was, without doubt, lurking there when I had passed.

"Every one is talking of it. Lots of people are going down to see the spot. I shall go down presently. Do you care to come?" the landlord asked.

I acceded willingly, for I wished to see the place in daylight, and, as one of a crowd of sightseers, I should escape observation.

While I ate my breakfast, the man, full of the mystery, continued discussing it in all its phases. I allowed him to run on, for every word he spoke was, to me, of intense interest.

"The poor Colonel was the very last man to have an enemy who would take his life," he said.

"But his second wife?"

"Ah!" he said with a knowing air, "he was never quite the same after he married again. They say that she flirted indiscriminately with every man she came across, no matter who he was."

"As bad as that—eh?"

"Of course I don't know for certain. I only tell you what I've 'eard."

"Of course, of course," I said. "People will always talk. But do you really think it's true that she is as giddy as reported?"

"I really don't know," he responded, raising his eyebrows. "These women of the upper ten are a queer lot sometimes."

"Well, the Colonel's death is a very mysterious affair, at any rate," I observed.

"Very," he said. "And one or two evil-tongued people are already suggesting that she might have had a hand in it."

"That is cruel," I answered. "She may be unpopular, but that's no reason why she should be a murderess. I suppose they base their suspicions upon the quarrel of which you told me yesterday."

"I suppose so. The first Mrs Chetwode was a born lady, but of this woman nobody ever knew anything of who or what she was before he was so misguided as to marry her."

"Perhaps the police inquiries will throw some light upon that," I remarked.

"Let's hope so," he responded. And then, having finished my breakfast, we went together to the park.

Fortunately, on the previous night, I had been able to slip out and in unobserved, for the landlord had been absent with his wife at a neighbour's, and was therefore not aware of a fact which might prove damning against me—namely, that I had disguised myself in a suit of secondhand clothes.

The tragedy had been enacted at the bridge I had crossed. I had passed over that very spot, and had actually heard the sound of the assassin's cough.

Was that a signal to an accomplice? It seemed very much as though there had been two persons lying in wait for the Colonel, and I, having passed at the moment when they expected him, had narrowly escaped being struck down. That cough was possibly the signal that had saved me.

"Pass along, please! Pass along!" said a constable, as I stood staring in wonder at the spot where the body had been found half in the water among the waving reeds.

We receded for some distance, while the publican pointed out the geographical position of the spot with its relation to the house and the high-road.

"It's a lonely place 'ere of a night," he said. "Just the place where a man might commit a murder. Funny, however, that the Colonel was wandering about in the park alone!"

"Curious, too, that his presence was not missed by his wife, or any of the household."

"Yes," he said. "Very mysterious, indeed. He must have gone out unknown to any one, and, when the place was locked up for the night, it was believed he was indoors."

"He was wearing evening dress," I said.

"Oh, I believe so. But I'm not certain. I've not heard how he was dressed—I say, Harding," he cried, turning to a bent old man who chanced to be passing, "how was the Colonel dressed when he was found?"

"In his cut-away coat and shirt," was the reply. "They said that his shirt-stud was stolen."

"Ah!" exclaimed my garrulous friend, the publican, "that looks as though it was done with a motive of robbery—don't it?"

"Yes," I said, my thoughts reverting again, as they constantly did, to that strange conversation which I had overheard in the darkness, the words of a man who had practically acknowledged himself to be an assassin.

When we again emerged upon the high-road I parted from my companion, he returning to Hounslow and I continuing my walk along the highway leading to Twickenham.

I wandered aimlessly, trying to form some resolution. Had any person seen me enter or leave the park on the previous night? If they had then my position was certainly one of peril, for, if arrested on suspicion, I should experience the utmost difficulty in clearing myself.

Where was Beryl? I called her Beryl, for that was the name by which I had first known her, and it appeared to me that her cousin had falsely introduced her to me as Feo. Had they both returned to London, or were they still at the Park?

At a point beyond Kneller Hall, just then within sight of Twickenham Town, I turned back, and, passing along the boundary of the park to Hounslow railway station, made inquiries of a friendly ticket collector, from whom I learnt that the two ladies had left, with several of the other guests for Waterloo half an hour before.

This information decided me. I went on into the town, and, entering the police-station, sought an interview with the inspector. It fortunately happened that Mr Rowling, the sub-divisional inspector from Brentford, a tall, rosy-faced, smart-looking man, was there, and he being the chief of that sub-district of the T Division, I gave him my card and placed myself at his disposal.

He had ridden over from Brentford in response to a telegram, and looked a veritable giant in his long police riding-boots and spurs. When I told him that I was a medical man who took a great interest in the detection of crime, and therefore wished to assist in the inquiries regarding the Colonel's death, he looked at me curiously with his merry blue eyes, and again glanced at my card.

"Well, Doctor," he said, "I've sent to Scotland Yard as well as to my superintendent at Hammersmith, and we are expecting three or four men from the Criminal Investigation Department to take up the case. They left by the 09:05 from Waterloo, and will arrive here in a few minutes, I hope."

"But cannot you give me permission to assist them?"

"That, I fear, is beyond my power. The inquiries are, you see, left entirely to them."

"But you are chief of this division of police. Surely you can give me permission?"

Before replying he made further inquiries as to who I was and where I lived.

While we were talking three men in plain clothes entered the office and saluted. Then, after briefly explaining the discovery to them, Rowling introduced me as an assistant.

The elder of the three, a thin-faced, dark-haired man, who was an inspector—Bullen by name—while his companions were sergeants, seemed greatly surprised at my application.

"It's quite irregular, you know," he said briefly.

"But I think, under the circumstances," said Rowling, "that the Doctor might be of some service. He has had previous experience in murder cases, and has just applied to me. Of course I referred him to you, as you are to direct the inquiry."

"The difficulty is that any little indiscretion on his part might upset our plans," responded the detective.

"I will give you my word of honour to preserve secrecy in everything, and likewise to obey your orders as though I were a subordinate," I said eagerly.

"Very well," he replied at last, but not without some reluctance. "Of course, you are not attached to the inquiry officially, but I will give you permission to act with us."

I thanked him, declaring my intention to use every discretion; and then Rowling gave them a brief description of the character of the man who had discovered the body, and handed them a written report made by the police surgeon, Doctor Douglas, who had been called to examine the body.

"There are no suspicions against any one?" inquired Bullen, after he had read the medical statement aloud to his two companions.

"None," answered Rowling. "The boundary of the Park is patrolled, but the man on duty last night declares that he saw nobody of whom he could entertain, any suspicion."

Then, going to the wall, he pointed out on the ordnance map the position of the park and mansion. This having been examined carefully by all three, Rowling gave them a brief description of the murdered man, his wife and his son, very similar to that given by my gossiping friend of the Red Lion.

"There were a lot of visitors at the Park, you say," Bullen observed. "Are they still there?"

"No. Most of them have returned to London, I believe," I responded.

"Ah!" said the detective, in a tone of disappointment; "it would have assisted us greatly if we could have seen what kind of persons they were. But we'd better go down to the house and have a look round."

Chapter Fourteen.

A Theory.

Half an hour later I stood beside the body of Colonel Chetwode, making a thorough and complete examination.

It was still clothed, just as it had been found, for the local police had given orders that it should not be touched before the arrival of the detectives from headquarters.

The body was that of a tall, thin man, with aquiline, refined features, about sixty or so, with iron-grey hair and moustache, and a brow lined by care and anxiety. His evening clothes, wet and muddy, in the broad light of day gave the corpse a disreputable, neglected appearance, which was rendered even more striking by his dishevelled hair and moustache matted with dried mud.

Bullen was alone with me, his companions being at the spot where the body was found, and as I proceeded to draw up the blind and examine the wound in the dead man's scalp, the detective stood by in silence watching my examination.

The wound near the base of the skull was, I found to my surprise, quite a superficial one. By its appearance I saw that the police doctor had probed it and quickly found that the injury was not of such a nature as to have caused death.

"Well?" Bullen asked anxiously. "What do you make out of it.

Doctor?"

"At present, I can only say that death was not caused by that wound," I responded.

"Then how, in your opinion, was the crime committed? What, in your opinion, was the weapon used?" he asked.

"At present I am unable to say," I responded. "The natural conclusion is that it was caused by a blow from a life-preserver, yet a round knob could never have inflicted such a wound. I incline to the opinion that the wound might have been caused by a fall from the bridge upon the rough stones below."

By the aid of my probe I satisfied myself that the bone was not fractured, as it would have been by a deliberate blow dealt from behind. The nature of the wound, indeed, was very much as if it had been caused by the unfortunate man's head coming into contact with some sharp stone.

Then, after very careful investigation, lasting over half an hour, during which I took a number of accurate measurements which might be used later in the identification of the weapon, I came to the rather vague conclusion that the crime had been committed not by a blow, but by hurling the victim from the little bridge below which he had been found.

"Do you believe that death was instantaneous?"

"I am not certain," I responded. "There is no injury to the spinal column which could have caused death. He was, without doubt, pinioned from behind, at the moment he had crossed the foot-bridge, and thrown backward, rolling down the bank into the lake."

"His shirt-stud has gone," remarked the detective. "That looks like robbery."

"I don't think so," I answered.

"Why not?"

"Well, do you notice a long green mark there?" I said, pointing to the limp shirt-front. "You see that it runs straight across the stud-hole. By that mark I feel assured there was no robbery."

"I see the mark," Bullen answered, "but at the same time, I don't quite see your argument."

"That mark was made by a damp branch or bramble. When he fell he tumbled backward into the bushes, and, crashing through them, rolled into the water. One of the branches caught his shirt-stud and broke it out. If you have a strict search made you will find it somewhere near where he fell. His watch and chain and ring are still upon him, you will notice."

"I quite understand your theory," he responded. "I will order active search to be made, for it is an important point whether the murder was done by thieves whom he discovered upon his property. It might have been that burglars were lurking there, and, being disturbed by him, they killed him in order to prevent an alarm being raised."

"I scarcely think that," I argued. "If they were burglars they would not have attacked him from behind without any ulterior motive. They would have remained in hiding."

"But how do you account for him wandering about the park at that hour?" asked the detective.

"That point can only be cleared up by his widow," I exclaimed. "I think we should see Mrs Chetwode without delay."

With this suggestion he agreed, and having rearranged the body, I left it to the police surgeon to make his post-mortem.

Out in the corridor we met the butler, by whom Bullen sent his card to the widow with the request that she would grant us an interview.

Ten minutes later we were received in the morning-room by a pale, fair-haired, rather fragile woman, the redness of whose eyes told plainly that she had been crying, but whose improvised mourning became her well. She was perhaps thirty, certainly not more, rather handsome, with an air of self-conceit, and a slightly cockney accent in her voice, which told me that she was not quite so well bred as one might have expected the mistress of Whitton to have been.

Bullen apologised for being compelled to intrude upon her privacy, but explained that it was necessary to make searching inquiries into the painful affair, and he would therefore esteem it a favour if she would answer one or two questions.

To this she assented willingly, and, asking us to be seated, sank into an armchair.

The detective had not introduced me, therefore she no doubt believed me to be an emissary of Scotland Yard.

"Have you any idea of the hour at which the Colonel left the house?" asked Bullen.

"No. I think, however, it must have been about half-past ten," she responded in a hard voice.

I was watching her carefully, and saw by the nervous twitching of her hands that she was striving to calm the conflicting emotions within her. She kept her eyes—beautiful eyes of almost a violet tint—fixed upon her examiner.

"But if he went out as early as that, you would surely wonder why he did not return?" observed the detective.

"Ah, no," she said quickly. "I was in ignorance of his absence until—until my maid awoke me at a quarter-past five this morning, and told me of the awful discovery."

She pursed her lips very slightly. That almost imperceptible movement aroused my suspicions. I had been told that she was on bad terms with the dead man, and probably that had prejudiced me against her.

"Then he went out without your knowledge? Will you kindly tell me how you spent the evening?!"

"How I spent the evening?" she asked with a slight start.

"I mean how you all spent the evening," he said, correcting himself. "You had guests here, I understand."

"Yes; we had quite a number of people. And after dinner, as usual, the men played billiards and smoked, while we women remained in the drawing-room. About half-past nine the men joined us, a couple of dances were played, some songs were sung, and the evening passed without further event, as far as I am aware."

"But your husband?"

"Well, about half-past ten he came to me and said that he was not feeling very well, therefore he should go to his room."

"And you never again saw him alive?"

"No," she faltered. "When I saw him again he was down in the hall. Some men were carrying him in—dead! Oh, it's awful! I—I can't realise it!" And she burst into a torrent of tears.

"It certainly is a most painful affair," said Bullen, sympathetically; "but we are striving our utmost to solve the mystery. Therefore, I trust you will forgive me for seeking this interview. Whatever information you can give us will assist us very materially in our inquiries."

"I don't think I can tell you anything more," declared the distressed woman.

"But what is your theory? Do you believe that the announcement that he was not feeling well was a mere excuse for absence?"

"Ah, that I cannot tell," she responded. "The house was locked up at midnight, and it was evident that he was out then, for this morning all the doors were bolted, and the windows were found fastened, just as the servants had left them."

"Well," he said, "that shows that he went out before the house was locked up. Were any of the other guests out in the park?"

"Not to my knowledge," she replied, after a second's hesitation. "Of course the men went out upon the drive in front of the house, and walked up and down to smoke after dinner."

"From your statement it would almost appear as though your husband went out to keep some secret appointment. Have you any suspicion that he had arranged to meet any one?"

"None whatever."

"And he had never mentioned to you any single person with whom he was at enmity?"

"Never."

"I presume that most of the guests who were here last night have since left?"

"All have left. I am practically alone."

"I shall be glad if, as soon as you can do so, you will kindly make me out a list of your guests, together with their addresses. We may not require it, but in this matter we must not overlook a single point."

"But surely you don't suspect any of them?" she exclaimed quickly.

"We suspect no one, at present," he responded. "But in order to prosecute our inquiries satisfactorily, it is necessary to know exactly who was in the house at the time of the tragedy."

"Oh, of course—of course," she said. "I will make out the list and let you have it in the course of an hour—if that will do?"

"Excellent," the detective said.

Bullen glanced across to a half-open door, which appeared to give entrance to the library, saying—

"If you will permit us, we will examine the Colonel's papers; they may give us some clue. It is just possible that he received a letter making the appointment in the park."

"You are quite at liberty to act just as you think best," she answered with perfect frankness.

He thanked her, and then tactfully turned the conversation back to the events of the previous night. It might have been owing to the prejudice which I entertained towards her, but somehow she seemed anxious to avoid any remark regarding the period immediately preceding the tragedy. Naturally a wife whose husband has been foully assassinated in a manner so mysterious, would look back in horror upon past events; but in some strange, indefinite way she seemed to hold our presence in dread.

Bullen, not slow to notice this, continued to ply her with questions in order to obtain further details of how the hours after dinner had been spent.

"Who saw your husband last?" he inquired.

"I don't know for certain. I believe it was one of the guests—a Mr Durrant, with whom he had played billiards."

"After he had complained to you of not feeling well?"

"No; he played billiards before," she answered. Then readily added, "On leaving me he returned to the billiard-room to fetch his cigar-case. It was then he wished Mr Durrant good-night."

"Did he tell him, also, that he was unwell?"

"Yes, I believe so. But Mr Durrant sent a card of sympathy to my room and left without seeing me. I therefore only know this by hearsay from the servants."

"You have a stepson—Lieutenant Chetwode. Where was he?"

"With me in the drawing-room. Ah! here he comes." And at that moment a thin, dark-haired, well-set-up young man entered, eyeing us with an inquiring glance.

This, then, was my wife's lover.

Briefly the widow explained who we were, and, in reply to Bullen's questions, the dead man's son described how his father had managed to slip out unobserved, and how his absence had passed unnoticed until the awful discovery had been made in the morning.

"You have no suspicion that he had any enemy, I suppose?" the detective asked.

"None whatever. The terrible affair is a most profound mystery."

"Yes," said Bullen reflectively, his grey eyes fixed upon those of the widow; "it's a mystery we must try to solve."

"I hope you will," the young man exclaimed. "My father has fallen beneath the hands of some cowardly assassin concealed in those bushes down by the lake—he was the victim of the revenge of some person unknown."

"What makes you think the motive was revenge?" inquired the detective, quick to scent any clue.

The widow and her stepson exchanged rapid glances. I was watching, and it occurred to me that some secret understanding existed between them. My friend of the Red Lion had declared that they were enemies, but to me it certainly appeared as though they were acting in complete accord.

"Oh," responded Cyril Chetwode, rather lamely, "I merely suppose that."

"Revenge for what?"

"Ah! if we only knew the reason it would not be difficult to find the murderer," answered the man who loved my wife. "It may be that some person sought revenge for an imaginary grievance."

"But why was the Colonel walking at that lonely spot at that hour? He must have had an object. It looks suspiciously as though he went to keep a secret appointment. The excuse that he was ill seems to have been made with a view to securing his room from intruders who might disturb him."

"He may have kept an appointment," his son replied. "But only he himself could tell us the truth."

The detective acquiesced, and after some further conversation, in which I joined, he rose, and passing through into the library, commenced an examination of the papers lying on the writing-table. With my rival in the affections of the woman who was my wife, I assisted him, while the widow stood behind us watching, her face pale and anxious and her nervous hands trembling.

She was in fear. Of that I felt absolutely convinced. But what discovery did she dread?

While we were bending, examining the contents of one of the drawers, which was full of papers relating to the Colonel's duty as a justice of the peace—for it was here that he performed his judicial work—his widow stood behind me, and, with a quick movement, sidled up to her stepson. The next instant it occurred to me that she had passed something to him; but, pretending to be engrossed in the papers, I made no sign that I had observed their rapid exchange.

"Have you found anything?" she inquired calmly, after a few moments.

"No; nothing, unfortunately," Bullen responded. And then, having searched the room from top to bottom, suggested a move to the Colonel's bedroom.

Here the search, both of the clothes in his wardrobe and of the room wherein he usually slept, likewise proved fruitless. After twenty minutes or so, however, I contrived, while the others were busy turning over the dead man's effects, to slip back to the library. Young Chetwode had, at the moment when the suspicious movement had been made behind me, stood with his back to the black marble mantelshelf, and it was to examine this that I returned. While doing so I suddenly found a crack between the wall and the upright marble support, where the plaster had dried out by the heat of the winter fires, and, peering within, I saw something concealed there.

With the aid of my scarf-pin I managed to pick it out, and found that it was an unmounted photograph that had been crumpled in the hand and was dirty. Mrs Chetwode had managed to seize it before we could discover it, and the stepson had concealed it in that ingenious hiding-place.

I spread it out; the picture I gazed upon was both startling and ghastly. It was a portrait of Beryl, my love, supported by pillows, her face expressionless, her eyes closed.

The hideous truth was plain. The photograph had been taken after death!

Chapter Fifteen.

The Grey House.

I placed the mysterious picture in my pocket and remained silent. That my wife had been photographed after death there could be no doubt, for I, as a medical man, was, alas! too well acquainted with the appearance of a face from which life had faded, as distinguished from that of one asleep or under the influence of an anaesthetic.

Yet she was now living, bright, vivacious, and defiant! Had I not stood near her, seen her silhouette in the darkness, and heard the sweet music of her voice only twelve hours ago? It was incomprehensible—an absolute and complete enigma.

Fearing lest suspicion might be aroused by the missing photograph, I took a small scrap of paper from the waste-paper basket and thrust it into the crack. No doubt they would return for it, but, finding another piece of paper there, would probably believe that the photograph had gone so deeply into the crack as to be hidden successfully in the heart of the wall.

Bullen was still with the widow and her stepson when I rejoined him in the drawing-room, accounting for my absence by saying that I had been around the exterior of the house. He was again questioning Mrs Chetwode, and I could discern by her manner that she was acting in accord with her stepson. To the latter I had taken an instinctive dislike. Although an officer of hussars, he was an over-dressed youth with a three-inch collar, a cravat of an effeminative shade of lavender, a fancy vest, and a general get-up which stamped him as an interesting specimen of the "saltator Britannicus," or common or garden "bounder."

Presently we took our leave of the pair, and together went down to the spot where the body had been found. One of the detectives had discovered the missing shirt-stud, as I had predicted, while the various marks in the vicinity had been carefully examined and noted.

I spent the whole morning striving to obtain some clue, sometimes with the others and often wandering by myself.

My lunch I took in the bar of the Station Hotel. I had a purpose in doing this, for during a chat with the proprietor I learned that the Major had remained there three days, and had paid his bill and left on the previous evening. That in itself certainly appeared a suspicious circumstance. He had left the place ostensibly to return to London, yet he had kept that appointment in the park and had afterwards gone—whither? The last train left Hounslow for Waterloo at 11:05. He had, however, not taken that, for eleven o'clock struck from Whitton church tower just after I had watched them disappear into the night.

During the greater part of the afternoon I was with Bullen, and at the latter's request assisted the police surgeon to make his post-mortem. But we discovered nothing further to account for death, absolutely nothing.

"What is your opinion?" I asked of my friend, the detective-inspector, when alone with him.

"I have no opinion," he responded, "except that that woman knows something more than she will tell us."

"Exactly?" I exclaimed. "I wonder what her object is in concealing any facts she knows?"

"Ah, Doctor," he replied, "women are funny creatures; one never knows what motive they may have. In this case we shall be compelled to act very warily, and, if possible, mislead her and place her off the scent. She has given me a list of the guests, which may be useful."

He took from his pocket a sheet of writing-paper with stamped heading, and I quickly glanced down the list of names. In an instant I saw that it was incomplete. The two persons whom I knew had been there she had omitted; their names were Lady Pierrepoint-Lane and Beryl Wynd.

Without comment I handed it back to him. It occurred to me that it might be best to keep my knowledge to myself, for by so doing I might perchance discover a clue.

That evening, having resolved to remain and watch the inquest on the morrow, I scribbled a hasty line to Bob, and then spent the hour after dinner in company with Bullen and Rowling in the bar parlour of a neighbouring public-house.

At the inquest held in the billiard-room at Whitton next morning, reporters were present in dozens, and the "note" taken by all was verbatim, for being the dead season, such a mystery came as a welcome "scoop" to those journals whose only claims to notoriety are the sensationalism of their contents bills and their remarkable "cross-heads."

The same evening I returned to Rowan Road, where I found Bob in his den, stretched out lazily in his cane deck-chair, smoking his big pipe with a whisky-and-soda at his elbow.

"Hullo, old chap!" he cried, jumping up as I entered. "Back again, eh? And with a murder case on hand, too?"

"Yes," I responded, sinking into a chair, wearied and tired out. "Most extraordinary, isn't it?"

Then at his request, I gave him a minute and detailed account of all that had occurred, and placed in his hands the hideous post-mortem photograph.

"Well?" I asked. "What do you think of it?"

"Think of it?" he said. "Why, the mystery becomes more involved than ever. You are certain that this photograph is of her?"

"Absolutely certain."

"Then it seems to me very much as though she is hand-in-glove with the Major, her lover, and Mrs Chetwode, and that they all of them know the truth regarding the tragedy."

"That's exactly my theory," I responded, taking down my pipe from the rack, and filling it while Bob poured me out a drink.

"But the injuries?"

I described them in terms which, being technical, are of no interest to you, my reader, and he sat listening with a dark, thoughtful expression upon his round, usually merry countenance.

"A fact which is very puzzling to me, old fellow," he said at last, blowing a cloud of smoke from his lips, "is the reason her ladyship was so extremely eager to make your acquaintance."

"Yes; I can't understand it in the least. It is fortunate, however, that she is in ignorance of my visit to Whitton."

"Most fortunate," he answered. "My idea is that the truth is only to be obtained here, in London—and not down there."

"Do you think. Bob, that I acted wisely in keeping the secret of that midnight meeting to myself?" I asked earnestly, for I felt that perhaps I had, by so doing foiled the activity of the police.

"Certainly. You are in possession of two distinct facts which may lead us to a clue, not only to the murderer, but to the motive of your marriage to this mysterious wife of yours."

"Does it strike you that the Major may be the actual assassin?"

He was silent, puffing thoughtfully at his pipe.

"No," he responded. "To tell you the truth, that isn't my theory."

"Then what is?" I asked.

"If Mrs Chetwode and this mysterious wife of yours are acting together, Tattersett cannot be the culprit. It would rather be to their interest to denounce him."

I saw the trend of his argument, but nevertheless clung to my theory that the man who had in my hearing proposed murder had committed the crime.

The mystery at Whitton, startling though it was, was quickly forgotten by the public. Several times, in the days that followed, I went down to Hounslow and held consultations with Bullen and his assistant, but no fresh discovery was made, for not the slightest clue presented itself. A verdict of "Wilful murder against some person or persons unknown" had been returned, and the matter left in the hands of the police.

A week went past, but I could not decide whether it would be policy to call at Gloucester Square and have an interview with Beryl and her cousin. I recollected that the Colonel's widow had not given their names to the police—a fact full of significance, for it appeared as though she desired to conceal their visit to Whitton.

I longed to see my love to speak with her, to hold her hand and bask in the sunshine of her smiles.

She had defied the man who had tempted her to revenge, she had declared her intention of renouncing all the past. Ah, that past! If I could only glean something regarding it! If I could only stand by her as her champion without arousing any suspicion within her.

This impulse to see her proved too strong. I could not resist it, therefore one day I went to Gloucester Square to make an afternoon call, but found the blinds down.

"Her ladyship is out of town, sir," the maid-servant answered in response to my inquiry.

"And Miss—Miss Ashwicke?" I said, quickly remembering that she had been introduced to me by that name.

"Ashwicke," repeated the girl, puzzled. "There is no Miss Ashwicke in the family, sir."

"Oh, of course," I said, rather lamely I fear; "it's my mistake. I meant Miss Wynd."

"She's with her ladyship in Wiltshire, sir."

"At Atworth?"

"Yes, sir."

"When did they leave?"

"Three days ago, sir. Sir Henry went with them."

"Did a young gentleman named Chetwode accompany them?"

"I don't know, sir."

"But you know Mr Chetwode, of course?" I said.

"Oh yes, sir. They say he is to marry Miss Beryl," answered the girl, smiling.

"And his mother is a frequent visitor also, isn't she."

"Yes; she's here very often indeed."

"And Major Tattersett?"

"He's only been here once, I think—a long time ago. He's a round-faced gentleman who wears a single eyeglass, isn't he?"

"Yes. Did he call to see Sir Henry?"

"No, sir. He came to see Miss Beryl."

"And he has only been here once, you say?"

"Yes—only once, as far as I know."

"I suppose you don't expect the family back till the end of September—eh?"

"Oh, not before the middle of October. They'll stay there through the shooting."

Other questions I put to her she answered frankly, and I left a coin in her hand as I turned and went down the steps. Why, I wondered, had her ladyship thought fit to introduce Beryl to me as Feo Ashwicke?

In deep disappointment I returned to Rowan Road. Every effort I made seemed unavailing.

As the weeks passed in inactivity, and I was still Bob's guest, assisting him among the few patients who rang the surgery bell, I began to feel that I must stir myself and find a fresh post as assistant. Rather than borrow off Bob, I had slid into a pawnbroker's one evening and exchanged the watch which my mother had given me in my schoolboy days for two pounds and a ticket upon which was inscribed a false name and address. Of this money only a few shillings remained, and I was existing upon my friend's charity.

While in this unsettled state of mind I was called out one morning to visit a patient over in Brook Green, and on my return entered a saloon-bar opposite Hammersmith Station for a glass of that homely and inexpensive beverage vulgarly known as "bitter." Upon the counter before me the London Post-office Directory lay open, and of a sudden it occurred to me that I had never searched for the name of Ashwicke.

I turned over the pages curiously until I reached that headed "Ash," and suddenly, half-way down, I came across the name I wanted: "Ashwicke, Alan Wynd, 94, Queen's-gate Gardens, S.W."

Without hesitation I went forth and mounted an omnibus, which set me down at the corner of the Cromwell Road, and ten minutes later I stood before the house which the directory indicated.

Instantly I saw that its exterior was identical—a large grey place with a great dark portico supported by four huge columns. It was the house to which I had been called on the day the strange marriage had taken place.

Chapter Sixteen.

The Veiled Lady.

The neighbouring houses were mostly closed, their owners being out of town for the summer; but the one before which I halted was apparently occupied, therefore I boldly ascended the steps and rang the bell.

My summons was answered by a burly, ill-dressed man in carpet slippers, who, when I inquired for Mr Ashwicke, responded—

"He don't live here; this is Mrs Stentiford's."

"But he did live here," I protested. "How long has he been gone?"

"I don't know. I've only been here a fortnight, but I believe the mistress has lived here for three or four years."

"Is your mistress in?"

"No; she's away in Switzerland."

"And you're taking charge of the house?"

"That's so."

"Well," I said, "Mr Ashwicke lived here until a short time ago, that's very certain. I feel sure I haven't mistaken the house; I used to be a visitor here. Would you mind me glancing at some of the rooms?"

He eyed me with distinct suspicion.

"No," I laughed, "I'm not a swell mobsman, nor a burglar on the look-out for a likely house to rob—I'm a doctor." And, to convince him, I took off my silk hat and displayed my stethoscope in the lining, as well as giving him a card.

"Well," he answered, rather ill-manneredly, "I don't see why I should satisfy you. You aren't a friend of Mrs Stentiford's?"

"No," I admitted; "but I only desire a glance at the library and at the bedrooms upstairs, just to satisfy my curiosity."

"Why?"

"Well, to tell you the truth, there occurred here, in this house, an incident which was the crisis of my life. For that reason I am full of curiosity to see the rooms again, and I ask you as a favour to allow me to do so."

"Very well," he said at last, after a moment's hesitation, "come along. You say you want to see the library." And I followed him down the hall, at the end of which he opened a door.

I went in and looked around. Yes; it was the same. Nothing had apparently been moved.

I looked into the dining-room—that same handsome apartment in which champagne had been drunk to my health and happiness. Bah! what a mockery it had been!

We went into several of the other rooms after that, and all of them were, I found, well furnished in a style rather out-of-date but nevertheless comfortable.

"And how long have you been in Mrs Stentiford's service?" I inquired, as we descended the stairs.

"Just a fortnight."

"You're a police-officer, aren't you?" I inquired.

"Yes—a sergeant," he answered. "But how do you know?"

"Oh," I answered, laughing, "when a man's been in the police there's little mistake about it. We doctors have our eyes open, you know."

He smiled, but was apparently surprised that I should have detected his calling.

"There are none of the other servants here, I suppose?"

"No—none. Why?"

"Because I'm anxious to find out whether Mrs Stentiford has ever let her house furnished."

"I don't think so."

"What gives you that impression?"

"Because before she went away she told me that she preferred to close the place and pay me, rather than to let her things be ruined by strangers."

"And I suppose you've heard from neighbours about the house?"

"Yes," he replied; "I've heard that a gentleman lived here about four years ago—I think the name was Ashwicke."

"But he was living here a few weeks ago," I declared; "I visited him here."

The retired police-sergeant looked at me incredibly.

"I think you must be mistaken. Mrs Stentiford was certainly occupying the house then."

"But you were not here?"

"No; I wasn't here, that's true."

"She might have let it for a few weeks, during the London season—eh?"

"She certainly might," he responded; "but, if she did, she kept the matter a secret, for none of the neighbours are aware of it."

"Then you have already inquired?" I asked, somewhat surprised, for he spoke so positively.

"Yes," he replied. "Curiously enough, a few days ago I had some one else call and ask for Mr Ashwicke."

"Who was it?" I demanded quickly.

"A lady—a young, rather good-looking lady."

"What was she like? Describe her to me."

"Well, she wore a thick white veil so that I couldn't see her face quite distinctly," the man answered; "but she, like yourself, declared that she knew Mr Ashwicke, and had been a visitor here. She asked to see the very same rooms as you have seen. Very curious, isn't it?"

"Very," I exclaimed in wonder. "Did she give any further explanation?"

"No; she gave me half a sovereign instead," he laughed.

"And she also declared that Mr Ashwicke had lived here recently?"

"Yes; that's what caused me to inquire."

"Very remarkable," I said. "I wonder who she could have been. Can't you give the slightest description of her?"

"I only noticed that she spoke in a soft, refined voice, and that she had very pretty eyes, blue-grey, I believe they were. But those thick white veils, with embroidery on them, make it very difficult to see a woman's face clearly."

"And her hair? Was she fair or dark?"

"Between colours."

"Fair?"

"No; not fair, and not dark. Almost chestnut colour, I think it was."

"Was she tall?"

"Middling. She came in a hansom, and it waited for her. She was evidently a lady."

"She gave no name?"

"No; she was very discreet. And that's what made me scent a mystery when you called and asked for the same person, and to see the same rooms."

"Well, it is extraordinary," I remarked. "Most extraordinary!"

I was sorry that I had no money to give him a tip, but my last half-crown reposed in the corner of my pocket, and I could not summon courage to leave myself penniless; so I merely thanked him, and, descending the steps, left him with disappointment plainly depicted upon his face.

The man might be useful, I felt, therefore I had decided to return at an early date, when my funds were not so low, and give him a similar tip to the one he had received from the veiled lady.

Who was she? I wondered. Surely it could not have been Beryl herself.

By good fortune, on my return to Rowan Road, I found a letter awaiting me, and on opening it discovered that it was from a doctor practising in Bayswater, who, in reply to my application a week before, appointed me his locum tenens. Therefore, on the following day, I thanked Bob warmly, for all his hospitality towards me, and bade him good-bye.

"Promise me one thing, Dick," he said, as he stood in the hall, holding my hand in a firm, friendly grip of farewell.

"Well," I asked, "what is it?"

"That you'll try and forget all about this mystery of yours," he said earnestly. "You'll be getting brain fever, or something equally disagreeable, if you don't try to control yourself and think no more of it. The experience is unusual, but, depend upon it, the mystery is so well-kept by the set of scoundrels into whose hands you fell, that you'll never get to the bottom of it."

"But I mean to solve it," I said resolutely. "I'm married, my dear fellow, and—well, I love her."

"I know. That's just the devil of it," he answered bluntly. "You're gone on her, and the mystery makes you the more eager to claim her as your wife!"

"Exactly, old fellow," I answered. "I know that you're my best friend. Indeed, you have kept me out of the gutter or the common lodging-house these past weeks, and I am ready to repay you in any way in my power; but as to taking your advice in this matter, I really can't."

"Then, you're a fool, Dick."

"I may be," I responded; "but I mean to clear up the mystery."

"Because you are jealous of this young Chetwode."

"I don't deny that I'm jealous," I replied with perfect frankness. "But I know that Beryl is in danger, and, as her husband, I should be at her side to protect her."

"That's all very well; but, after all your exertions, you've really discovered absolutely nothing."

His words were, alas! only too true. I had made many discoveries, but each of them had only served to render the veil of mystery more impenetrable.

"But why do you urge me to give it up?"

"For your own sake," he responded. "You can't practise properly when your head is full of such a bewildering puzzle. Don't you see that in this affair your reputation is at stake?"

"But her life is of greater moment to me than my own reputation," I declared. "Let me have my own way, there's a good chap." And I wished him good-bye.

An hour later I became installed as temporary assistant to a surgeon in Richmond Road, Bayswater, who, having been "run down" by the unusual number of cases of influenza, had resolved to take a month's vacation.

The Bayswater surgeon proved a genial fellow, but I saw little of him, for he left for North Wales with his family early next morning, after handing me his visiting-book and giving me general instructions. A fortnight went by, and so large was the practice—for I had to attend a number of the large drapery establishments in Westbourne Grove, where my principal was medical officer—that I had but little leisure. To forget the strange enigma which so troubled my brain I had thrown myself heartily into the work.

One hot, oppressive evening, after I had been in Richmond Road about three weeks, I was busy seeing the patients who, crowding the waiting-room between the hours of seven and nine, entered the consulting-room one by one to describe their physical ills, when the servant came in with a card, saying—

"A lady wishes to see you at once, sir."

I took the card she handed me, and started with mingled surprise and satisfaction when I recognised the name—Lady Pierrepoint-Lane. At last she was in London again! But how, I wondered had she discovered my whereabouts. Quickly I went into the hall, and there found her with blanched face and in a state of great agitation.

"Ah, Doctor," she gasped breathlessly, as I greeted her and our hands met, "I am so glad I've found you? I went to Hammersmith, but your friend, Doctor Raymond, told me you were here."

"What is the matter?" I inquired, surprised at her eager manner. "Has anything occurred?"

"Yes, something most mysterious!" she answered hoarsely. "You are the only doctor whom I can trust. Will you come with me at once? I have a cab in waiting."

"Where?" I inquired. "To your house?"

"Yes," she urged. "Do not let us lose time. Apologise to your other patients here, and come at once. It's a matter of life or death."

"Of life or death?" I cried. "Who is ill?"

"It's all a mystery," she answered in the same breathless manner. "But you will keep it a secret—promise me."

"I have many family secrets entrusted to me," I answered. "Rest assured that I shall betray no confidence."

"Then come quickly, and recollect that what you may see or hear to-night you must never divulge. On your word of honour as a gentleman."

"I give you my word of honour," I answered, wondering what fresh mystery was in store for me.

Then, turning, I asked a servant, who stood near, to tell the patients waiting for me that I had been unexpectedly called out to an urgent case, and would return in an hour.

"Good!" her ladyship exclaimed. "Let us not lose an instant."

Instinctively I placed my instrument case in my pocket, and took down my hat.

"Tell me the nature of the illness," I urged. "How did it occur? Who is the patient?"

"How it occurred nobody knows. It is a mystery, as I tell you. My cousin Feo, to whom I think I introduced you, is dying!"

"Dying!" I gasped, staring at her amazed. "Here in London?"

"Yes, at my house. I have called you because you are a doctor, and I can rely upon your secrecy."

Chapter Seventeen.

In Peril.

Without loss of a moment we entered the hansom and drove along Bishop's Road and Westbourne Terrace, and thence across Sussex Gardens to Gloucester Square.

Beside me my companion sat pale, erect, and rigid, responding only in monosyllables to my questions, and refusing to tell me anything beyond what she had already said—that her cousin was dying. Her manner was strange, as though she were in deadly fear.

I had taken her hand to assist her into the cab, and found it was cold as ice. Her face was the face of a woman haunted by some imminent terror, a white countenance with eyes dark and deep sunken. How changed she was from the bright, pleasant woman who had consulted me under such curious circumstances, when I had first taken Bob's place at Rowan Road. Could this change in her be in any way due, I thought, to the tragedy at Whitton? I recollected the singular fact that Mrs Chetwode had omitted the name and that of Beryl from the list furnished to the police. Again I glanced at her ashen face as we rounded the corner into Gloucester Square; it was that of a woman absolutely desperate. She was trembling with fear, yet at the same time striving to preserve an outward calm. My suspicion of her was increased.

The hall door having been thrown open by a servant, my companion led me through into a pretty boudoir on the left, where, lying fully dressed upon a divan of yellow silk, I saw my love. Her wonderful hair had become disengaged from its fastenings and fell dishevelled about her white face, and her corsage was open at the throat as though some one had felt her heart.

In an instant I was at her side, and, while her cousin held the shaded lamp, I examined her. Her great fathomless eyes were closed, her cheeks cold, her heart motionless. Every symptom was that of death.

"Is she still alive?" asked the terror-stricken woman at my elbow.

"I cannot decide," I answered, rising and obtaining a small mirror to test whether respiration had ceased.

Hers was no ordinary faintness, that I at once saw. The limbs were stiff and rigid as in death, the hands icy cold, the lips drawn and hard-set, the whole body so paralysed that the resemblance to death was exact.

All the startling events of my fateful wedding day came back to me. From that white throat that lay there exposed I had taken the tiny gold charm, which now hung round my own neck, reminding me ever of her. That sweet face, with the halo of gold-brown hair, was the same that I had seen lying dead upon the pillow in that house of mystery in Queen's-gate Gardens, the same that I had bent and kissed.

I took her hand again; there were rings upon it, but all were set with gems. The bond of matrimony that I had placed there was absent.

For a moment I stood gazing at her, utterly confounded. But I saw that to save her life no time must be lost, therefore, rousing myself, I obtained her ladyship's assistance to unloose my loved one's corset, and then made a further examination.

"This is a serious matter," I said at last. "I shall be glad if you will send a servant in a cab to Bloomsbury with a message."

"To Bloomsbury? Why?" she asked. "Cannot you treat her yourself?"

"Not without consultation," I responded; and taking a card from my pocket, I wrote upon it an urgent message to accompany the bearer at once.

She gave me an envelope, and, enclosing the card, I wrote the superscription, "Doctor Carl Hoefer, 63, Museum Mansions, Bloomsbury."

Her ladyship at once sent the servant on the message, and then without delay returned to my side.

"Well, Doctor," she asked in a low, strained voice, "what is your opinion? Will she recover?"

"I cannot say," I responded mechanically, my eyes still fixed upon my patient's face, watching for any change that might occur there.

At my request her ladyship brought the brandy decanter from the dining-room, and I managed, after some difficulty, to force a few drops between her cousin's lips.

"Now tell me," I said firmly, turning to the agitated woman at my side, "how did this occur?"

"I don't know."

"But if her life is to be saved we must know the truth," I said, my eyes fixed upon her. "In this manner to prevaricate is useless. Tell me how it is that I find her in this condition of fatal collapse."

"I cannot tell you things of which I myself am ignorant," she answered, with a well-feigned air of innocence.

"You wish to save your cousin's life?" I inquired.

"Certainly. She must not die," she cried anxiously.

"Then answer my questions plainly, and leave the rest entirely in my hands," I replied. "From your manner I know that you have some secret which you are striving to conceal. Knowledge of this secret will, no doubt, place me in a position to combat this extraordinary attack. If because you maintain silence she dies, then an inquest will be held, and the truth must come out—and a scandalous truth it will be."

"Scandalous!" she exclaimed with some hauteur. "I don't understand."

"An attempt has been made upon her life," I said as calmly as I could. "Those who are responsible for this must, if she dies, be discovered."

"An attempt upon her life? How do you know?" she gasped.

I smiled, but made no direct answer to her question.

"I am aware of it by the same means that I know that Feo Ashwicke and Beryl Wynd are one and the same person."

She started quickly.

"Who told you that?" she asked, with a strange flash in her eyes.

I smiled again, answering, "I think it would be best if you confided in me in this matter, instead of leaving me to obtain the truth for myself. Remember, you have called me here to save your cousin, and yet, by her side, while her young life is slowly ebbing, we are engaged in a battle of words. Now tell me," I urged, "how did this occur?"

She shook her head.

"Shall I begin?" I suggested. "Shall I say that you came up with Miss Beryl from Atworth yesterday, quite unexpectedly, in order to keep an appointment? That you—"

"How did you know?" she gasped again. "How did you know our movements?"

"I merely ask whether this is not the truth," I responded calmly. I had noticed that the furniture in the room was undusted, and therefore knew that they had returned to town unexpectedly. "Shall we advance a step further? I think, if I am not mistaken, that there was a strong reason for your return to town, and also for keeping your presence in London a secret. That is the reason that you communicated with your friend."

"With whom?"

"With Mrs Chetwode."

The light died from her face. She swayed slightly, and I saw that she gripped the edge of the little glass-topped table to steady herself.

Then her features relaxed into a sickly smile, and she managed to stammer—

"You are awfully clever, Doctor, to be aware of all these things. Is it clairvoyance—thought-reading, or what?"

"Those who have secrets should be careful not to betray them," I responded ambiguously.

"Then if I have betrayed myself, perhaps you will tell me something more of equal interest."

"No," I answered. "I have no desire to make any experiments. In this matter your cousin's life is at stake. It will be, at least, humane of you if you place me in possession of all the facts you know regarding the dastardly attempt upon her."

"I tell you that I know nothing."

"Nothing beyond what?" I said very gravely.

Again she was silent. I watched the inanimate body of the woman I loved, but saw no change. In what manner that state of coma had been produced I knew not, and I was in deadly fear that the last breath would leave the body before the arrival of Hoefer, the great German doctor whose lectures at Guy's had first aroused within me a desire to become a medico-legist. There was, I knew, but one man in all the world who could diagnose those symptoms, and it was Hoefer. I only prayed that he might not be out of town.

"Well," I went on, "it seems that you hesitate to tell me the truth, because you fear that I might divulge your secret. Is that so?"

"I believed that I might trust you to attend my cousin, and preserve silence regarding her illness and her presence in London," was the haughty reply. "But it seems that you are endeavouring to ascertain facts which are purely family affairs."

"The doctor is always the confidant of the family," I answered.

"But the other—the doctor who is coming?"

"He is an old friend and will promise to keep your secret," I said. "Come, tell me."

She stood hesitating, erect, statuesque, her eyes fixed immovably upon me.

"I know you are in trouble," I added in a tone of sympathy. "I am ready to assist you, if you are open and straight forward with me. I have already given you my pledge of secrecy. Now tell me what has occurred."

She wavered in her resolution to tell me nothing. My sympathetic tones decided her, and she said in a low, hoarse voice—

"It is a mystery."

"In what way?"

"As you have already said, we left Atworth in order to keep an appointment here. I was entertaining a house-party, but made an excuse that one of my aunts in Cheltenham was dangerously ill. I left, and, unknown to my husband or any other person, travelled with Beryl to London."

I noted that she inadvertently used my love's proper name instead of Feo, the name by which she had introduced us.

"The appointment was with Mrs Chetwode?" I suggested.

"Yes," she answered. "I had arranged to meet her to-day at two o'clock."

"I have read in the newspapers, reports of the terrible tragedy at Whitton. It was her husband who was murdered, was it not?"

"Yes," she answered in a tone rather unusual. Then she pursed her lips and held her breath for a single instant. "She has been staying with her sister in Taunton since the awful affair occurred, and came to town purposely to meet me."

"I think, if I mistake not, both you and your cousin were at Whitton at the time of the tragedy," I observed with affected carelessness.

"Oh no; fortunately we were not," she answered quickly. "We left the day previously."

That certainly was not the truth—at least, Beryl had been there at four o'clock in the afternoon. But I made no remark. It would not be policy to tell this woman of my visit to Whitton and of all I had overheard and seen.

"Well, and to-day? Did your friend Mrs Chetwode call?"

Again she hesitated, and that aroused within me a further suspicion.

"Yes," she replied. "She remained an hour, then left."

"Alone?"

"No; we went with her?"

"Where?"

"To visit a friend in Cadogan Place."

"And how long did you remain?"

"About half an hour."

"Cannot you tell me the name of this friend?"

"No," she answered; "it is of no account."

"Did you or your cousin eat or drink anything to-day, except here in your own house?"

"Nothing. The person whom we visited offered us port wine, but neither of us accepted."

"No tea?"

"None," she answered. "We afterwards returned home, arriving about five o'clock, took tea here, and dined at half-past six. An hour later, just as we had finished dinner, the servant handed Beryl a card; and she rose, excusing herself on the plea that her dressmaker had called, and, saying that she would return in a moment, left me alone to finish my dessert. I waited for her return for fully twenty minutes, then went across to the morning-room. The light had been switched off, and, when I turned it on, I saw to my horror that she was lying full length on the floor, apparently dead. We carried her here, and then I at once went in search of you."

"And is that all you know?" I inquired rather incredulously.

"Everything," she assured me. "I found Beryl lying helpless and insensible, just as she is now."

"And that was an hour and a half ago?" I remarked.

"Yes."

"But who was this caller? Surely you are able to ascertain that? The servant asked the person in."

"It was a woman, and she asked for my cousin."

"Then you don't actually know that it was the dressmaker?"

"The servant can give no accurate description, except that she was middle-aged, dressed in deep mourning, and wore a veil. She said she was the dressmaker."

"Then the woman escaped from the house without being seen?"

"Yes," her ladyship replied. "No one heard a sound after poor Beryl entered the room. What occurred there no one knows."

"We only know what occurred by the effects," I said. "A desperate attempt was made upon her life. This is no mere fainting-fit."

"But who could this mysterious woman have been?" her ladyship exclaimed. "It is absolutely astounding!" A thought flashed across my mind at that moment. Could the visitor in black actually have been that dreaded person of whom even Tattersett had spoken with bated breath—La Gioia?

Chapter Eighteen.

The Mystery of the Morning-Room.

My eyes wandered from the face of the trembling woman before me to the blanched countenance of my love. In an instant I detected a change there. While I had been speaking the muscles had relaxed until that face I adored had become blank and quite expressionless. No deep medical knowledge was necessary to detect the awful truth. It was the exact counterpart of the photograph which had been in the Colonel's possession.

With a cry of despair I sank upon my knees, touching her cheeks and chafing her hands. I held the mirror against her mouth. But the jaw had dropped, and when I looked eagerly for signs of respiration, there were none. Beryl, my mysterious, unknown wife, was dead.

I pressed her hand, I called her by name, and, aided by her cousin Nora, frantically tried the various modes of artificial respiration. But all in vain. Her frail life had flickered out even while we had been fencing with each other. All was useless. She had, as the Major had predicted during that memorable interview at Whitton, been struck down swiftly and secretly in some manner that was impossible to determine.

"She's dead!" I cried, still holding her thin, cold hand, and turning to the woman who had brought me to her side. "Dead—dead!"

"Impossible!" she gasped. "No, don't tell me that. Do your best to save her, Doctor. You must save her—you must!"

"But she is beyond human aid!" I declared. "Respiration has ceased. She has been murdered!"

"By that woman in black!" she shrieked. "But how?"

"That I do not know," I responded very gravely. "There is no wound; nothing whatever to account for death."

"Oh!" she cried in desperation, "I ought to have told you everything at once, but I feared you would not believe it if I told you. A strange thing has occurred in this house, something very uncanny. It is as though the place is overshadowed by some evil influence."

"I don't understand you," I answered quickly interested; but ere the words had left my mouth there was a tap at the door, and the servant, ushered in my old friend and lecturer, Carl Hoefer.

"Ah, my dear Doctor!" I cried eagerly, rushing forward to welcome him—"You will excuse me calling you so unexpectedly, and at this hour, but something very unusual has transpired—a matter in which I require your assistance."

"Ach!" he answered, shaking my hand, "I was surprised to get your kart, my frient. But, you see, I haf come to you at once."

He was a stout, ill-dressed man, broad-shouldered, short-legged, big-headed, heavy-jowled, about fifty-five, with scraggy yellowish hair upon his furrowed face, a pair of big eyes which blinked through large gold-rimmed spectacles, and a limp shirt-front secured by a couple of common pearl studs. Typically German in figure and manner, he spoke with a strong accent, his English grammar being often very faulty, but he was nevertheless a burly, good-natured man, possessing a keen sense of humour.

I introduced him briefly to the baronet's wife, and then, indicating the inanimate body of my love, gave him a short, technical account of her symptoms. He bent over her, examined her face, and grunted dubiously.

"It looks as though the young lady were dead," he said with his strong accent, his great sleepy-looking eyes blinking at us through his spectacles.

"I see no sign of life," I responded. "What is your opinion?"

He went down on his knees, grunting over the effort, and while I held the lamp for him, examined her throat and neck carefully, as though looking for some mark or other.

"And how did it all happen?" he inquired presently, after a long, thoughtful silence.

I exchanged glances with her ladyship, and then related him the story just as she had told it to me.

"Her ladyship wishes that it should be kept a profound secret," I added.

"Secret!" he snorted. "How are you going to hoodwink the coroner?"

"Then you think poor Beryl is really dead?" her cousin gasped.

"She is dead," the old fellow answered gruffly.

"But can you do nothing?" I urged in desperation.

"If she's dead, that's impossible," he declared.

"No," I said. "I refuse to believe that she is actually beyond your aid. To us she may appear dead, but her state may be only a cataleptic one."

He shook his great shaggy head dubiously, but made no response. This man, one of the greatest chemists of the age, who had been recognised as private docent of pathological anatomy and bacteriology at the University of Naples, and was renowned throughout the world for his excursions into the queer byways of medicine, was a man of few words.

His grunts were full of expression, and his fleshy face with the dull eyes was absolutely sphinx-like. The story he had heard regarding Beryl's sudden seizure did not convince him. His expressive grunt told me so. He had ripped up the tight sleeves of her dress, and was examining the inside of the arms at the elbows, but what he saw did not satisfy him.

I told him of the mirror-test, of the artificial respiration which I had tried, and he listened to me in silence. With his finger he opened the left eye and looked long and earnestly into the pupil. Then after a long suspense he suddenly spoke.

"Ach! we have been meestake; she is not dead."

"Not dead?" I cried joyfully. "Thank God for that! Do your best to restore her to us. Doctor—for my sake! How can I assist you?"

"By remaining quiet," he growled reprovingly.

And again he recommenced the examination of the inside of the elbows after having ordered other lights to be brought. Then, without saying where he was going, he left us, promising to return in a few minutes. He was a queer old fellow, very eccentric, and with a method that was as curious as the particular branch of the profession in which he was a specialist.

Not more than ten minutes passed before he returned grunting, puffing, and carrying a small packet in his hand. He had evidently been to the nearest chemist's.

"Some water!" he commanded—"warm water."

This was at once brought, and, arranging several little packets on the glass-topped table, he seated himself leisurely, and commenced to open and examine the contents of each very slowly.

"You have a hypodermic syringe?" he inquired. I took it from my pocket-case and handed it to him. He grunted and made a disparaging remark about the make—German needles were so much better, he declared. Then, having cleaned the syringe, he mixed a solution with the utmost care, and then administered a subcutaneous injection in Beryl's arm.

He took a chair and sat beside the cold, inanimate form, eagerly watching the effects of the drug he had administered.

Her ladyship stood near, her dark eyes, framed by the white agitated countenance, fixed immovably upon us.

Hoefer glanced at his cheap metal watch, and, grunting, crossed to the table and mixed a second injection, grumbling all the time at the inferior quality of my hypodermic syringe. So rough, unpolished in manner, and unsparing in criticism was he, that her ladyship drew back from him in fear.

The second injection proved of as little avail as the first, and from the great man's grave expression I began to fear the worst. No sign of life asserted itself. To all appearance my adored had passed away.

Suddenly he rose, and, turning to her ladyship, said in broken English—

"Now, madam, you will tell me, please, how this occurred."

"I do not know. Doctor Colkirk has told you all I know about it."

"But, just as Doctor Hoefer entered, you were telling me about something mysterious that had happened here. What was that?"

She pursed her lips for a moment, and glanced quickly at the old German.

"It is a most serious thing. I cannot make it out. There is some mystery in the morning-room."

"Ach!" exclaimed Hoefer, with a grunt—"a mystery! The symptoms of the lady are in themselves mysterious. Please explain the mystery of the room."

"Well," she answered, "when I entered, after the departure of the visitor, and discovered my cousin lying on the floor unconscious, I was quite well; but when I left I experienced a most curious sensation, just as though all my limbs were benumbed. I, too, almost lost consciousness while in the cab in search of Doctor Colkirk. But the most curious part of the affair is that my maid and the housemaid, who rushed in when I raised the alarm, experienced the very same sensation. It was as though we were struck by an icy hand—the Hand of Death."

"There is something very uncanny about that," I observed, puzzled.

"To me it seems as though poor Beryl were struck down in the same way as myself."

"But you say that you felt nothing on entering—only on leaving?" inquired Hoefer, his eyes seeming to grow larger behind his great glasses.

"Only on leaving," she assured him.

"Strange!" he ejaculated. "Let us see the room. We may, perhaps, obtain a clue to this mysterious ailment from which your cousin is suffering."

"But she is not dead?" I asked in doubt.

"No," he responded. "The last injection must be given time to take effect. We can only hope for the best."

"But the electric battery?" I suggested. "Could we not try that?"

"Useless, my dear friend," he responded; "it would kill her. Let us see the room of mystery."

The baronet's wife conducted us along the hall to the further end, where she opened the door, herself drawing back.

"What!" I inquired. "You fear to enter?"

"Yes," she faltered. "I will remain here."

"Very well. We will go in," I laughed, for the idea seemed so absurd that both Hoefer and myself put it down to her excited imagination.

What ill effect could the mere entry into a room have upon the human system, providing there were no foul gases? Therefore we both went forward, sniffing suspiciously, and walking to the window, opened it widely.

The half-dozen lights in the electrolier illuminated the place brightly, revealing a fine, handsome room furnished with taste and comfort. On looking round we certainly saw nothing to account for the extraordinary phenomena as described by the trembling woman who stood upon the mat outside.

While we made a careful examination of the place in which my love had met her strange visitor, the door, creaking horribly, swung slowly to, as doors often will when badly hung. Hoefer examined the floor carefully, seeking to discover whether the unknown woman in black had dropped anything that might give a clue to her identity, while I searched the chairs for the same purpose. We, however, found nothing.

What, I wondered, was the nature of the interview that had taken place there a couple of hours before? Who was the woman who had called and represented herself as Beryl's dressmaker? Could it have been the woman whose vengeance was so feared, the woman whose very name had been uttered by that miscreant with bated breath—La Gioia?

With her ladyship standing in the hall watching us we searched high and low. Neither of us felt any curious sensation, and I began to think that the story was merely concocted in order to add mystery to Beryl's unique seizure. Yet, from that woman's face, it was nevertheless evident that she stood there in fear lest any evil should befall us.

"Do you experience any queer feeling?" she inquired of us at last.

"None whatever," I responded.

"It is only on leaving," she replied.

"Very well," I answered with a laugh, scouting the idea, and then boldly passing out into the hall.

"Good Heavens?" I gasped a few moments later, almost as soon as I had reached her side. "Hoefer! come here quickly. There's something devilish, uncanny in this. I've never felt like this before."

The old German dashed out of the room and was in an instant beside me.

"How do you feel?" he inquired.

I heard his voice, but it sounded like that of some one speaking in the far distance. The shock was just as though an icy hand had struck me as I had emerged from the hall. I was cold from head to foot, shivering violently, while my lower limbs became so benumbed that I could not feel my feet.

I must have reeled, for Hoefer in alarm caught me in his arms and steadied me...

"Tell me—what are your symptoms?"

"I'm cold," I answered, my voice trembling and my teeth chattering violently.

He seized my wrist, and his great fingers closed upon it.

"Ach!" he cried in genuine alarm, "your pulse is failing. And your eyes!" he added, looking into them. "You are cold—your legs are rigid—you have the same symptoms, exactly the same, as the young lady?"

"And you?" I gasped. "Do you feel nothing?"

"Nothing yet," he responded—"nothing."

"But what is it?" I cried in desperation. "The feeling is truly as though the Angel of Death had passed and struck me down. Cannot you give me something, Hoefer? Give me something—before I lose all consciousness!"

The woman near me stood rooted to the spot in absolute terror, while the old German placed me upon an oaken settle in the hall, and ran along to the boudoir, returning with the syringe filled with the same injection which he had administered to my love. This he gave me in the arm, then stood by breathlessly anxious as to the result.

The feelings I experienced during the ten minutes that followed are indescribable. I can only compare them to the excruciating agony of being slowly frozen to death.

Through it all I saw Hoefer's great fleshy face with the big spectacles peering into mine. I tried to speak, but could not. I tried to raise my hand to make signs, but my muscles had suddenly become paralysed. Truly the mystery of that room was an uncanny one.

It ran through my mind that, the house being lit by electric light, the wires were perhaps not properly isolated, and any person leaving the place received a paralysing shock. This theory was, however, completely negatived by my symptoms, which were not in any way similar to those consequent on electric shock.

Hoefer looked anxiously at his watch, then, after a lapse of a few minutes, gave me a second injection, which rendered me a trifle easier. I could detect, by his manner and his grunts, that he was utterly confounded. He, who had sneered at the weird story, like myself was now convinced that some strange, unaccountable mystery was connected with that room.

To enter, apparently produced no ill effect; but to leave brought swiftly and surely upon the fated intruder the icy touch of death. I had laughed the thing to scorn, yet within a few seconds had myself fallen a victim. Some deep, inscrutable mystery was there, but what it was neither of us could tell.

Chapter Nineteen.

Hoefer's Strange Methods.

Twenty or thirty minutes elapsed before I regained my power of speech. The drugs administered by Hoefer fortunately had the effect desired. His sleepy eyes beamed through his great spectacles as he watched with satisfaction the stimulating consequence of the injection. He dissolved in water a tiny red tabloid, which he took from a small glass tube in a case he carried, and ordered me to drink it. This I did, finding it exceedingly bitter, and wondering what it was.

I asked no questions, however. He was a man who had made many extraordinary discoveries, all of which he had kept a secret. In the medical profession he was acknowledged to be one of the greatest living toxicologists, and his opinions were often sought by the various medical centres. Indeed, as every medical man knows, the name of Hoefer is synonymous with all that is occult in the science of toxicology, and the antidotes he has given to the world, from time to time, are as curious as they are drastic in effect.

"Have you experienced any strange sensation?" was my first question of him.

"No, none," he answered. "Ach! it is all very curious—very curious indeed! I have never before seen similar cases. There is actual rigor mortis. The symptoms so closely resemble death that one might so easily mistake. We must investigate further. It cannot be that there is any lethal gas in the room, for the window is wide open; and, again, while actually in the room no ill effect is felt. It is only on emerging."

"Yes," I answered. "I was struck almost at the instant I came out. It was as sudden as an electric shock. I cannot account for it in the least; can you?"

"No," he answered; "it is a mystery. But I like mysteries; they always interest me. There is so much to learn that one is constantly making fresh discoveries."

"Then you will try and solve this?" urged her ladyship, after expressing satisfaction at my recovery.

"Of course, madam, with your permission," he answered. "It is a complex case. When we have solved it we shall then know how to treat the young lady."

"And how do you intend to begin?" I inquired, raising myself, not without considerable difficulty.

"By going into the room alone," he answered briefly.

"You, too, will risk your life?" I exclaimed. "Is it wise?"

"Research is always wisdom," he responded. Then, finding that I was recovering rapidly from the seizure, he gave me some technical direction how to treat him in case he lost consciousness.

He arranged the tiny syringe, and the various drugs and tabloids, upon the hall table, and then, with a final examination of them, he opened the door of the fatal room and entered, leaving us standing together on the threshold.

Walking to the window he looked out, afterwards making several tours of the room in search of its secret. He, however, found nothing. The air was pure as London air can be on a summer's night, and, as far as either of us could discern, there was nothing unusual in the department. The door swung to halfway, and we heard him growling and grunting within. He remained in the room for perhaps five minutes, then emerged.

Scarcely, however, had he crossed the threshold when he lifted his left arm suddenly, crying—

"Ach, Gott! I am seized. The injection—quick!"

His fleshy face went pale, and I saw by its contortions that the left side had become paralysed. But with a quick movement I pushed up his coat-sleeve, and ran the needle beneath the skin.

His teeth were closed tightly as he watched me.

"It is almost unaccountable," he gasped in an awed voice, when I had withdrawn the needle after the injection. "I was cold as ice—just as though my legs were in a refrigerator!"

"Your feet are benumbed?" I said.

"Yes," he responded. "The sensation is just exactly as you have described it. Like the touch of an icy hand."

I felt his pulse; it was intermittent and feeble. I told him so.

"Look at your watch, and in three minutes give me the second injection. There's ether there in the larger bottle."

I glanced at the time, and, holding my watch in my hand, waited until the three minutes had passed. We were silent, all three of us, until I took up a piece of cotton wool, and, saturating it with ether, nibbed it carefully on the flesh. Then I gave him the second injection.

"Good!" he said approvingly. "It acts marvellously. I shall be better in a few moments. Did you feel your head reeling and your strength failing?"

I responded in the affirmative.

"And so did I," he answered. "The seizure is sharp and sudden, the brain becoming paralysed. That is the condition of the young lady: paralysis of the brain and heart, coma and collapse."

"But the cause?" I asked.

He was pale as death, yet he took no notice of his own condition.

"The cause?" he echoed, in his deep guttural German. "It is for us to discover that. I have never met a more interesting case than this."

"Yes, it's interesting enough," I admitted; "but recollect the lady. We must not neglect her."

"We are not neglecting her," he responded reprovingly. "Now that we know something of the symptoms, we may be able to save her. Before, we were working entirely in the dark."

"But you are still ill," I said.

"No, no," he laughed; "it is nothing." And he passed across the threshold and stood just within the room again.

Apparently he thought that the seat of the mystery lay in the doorway. Then he rejoined us, but felt no further symptoms.

There was evidently some uncanny but unseen influence contained within that apartment, but what it was we could not discover. All that was plain to us was the fact that any person emerging from it must be struck down as by an ice-cold hand.

Together we returned to the boudoir, and, to our satisfaction, saw an unmistakable sign that life was not entirely extinct. My love had moved!

"Good!" exclaimed the old German. "I go again to get something else." And, without further word, he crammed his shabby soft felt hat upon his head and hurried out.

"The mystery of that room is most extraordinary," I remarked to her ladyship when we were alone. "Has the influence ever been felt there before?"

"Not to my knowledge," she responded. "Never before to-night."

"Never before the entrance of that strange woman?" I suggested.

"Exactly! It is an absolute mystery."

"And you have no knowledge of whom that person was?"

"None whatever."

"Not even a surmise?" I inquired rather dubiously.

My thoughts reverted to what I had overheard regarding the unwelcome presence in London of that woman known as "La Gioia."

"No, not even a surmise," she answered.

Should I tell her of my own suspicions? No. To keep my knowledge to myself and seek to discover the key to the problem was my best course.

"And your cousin was with her for twenty minutes, you say?"

"Yes, about that time," she replied. "I did not hurry to finish my dinner as I believed Beryl was talking with the dressmaker regarding some alterations to an evening bodice which she had mentioned to me. They did not interest me, therefore I sat awaiting her return."

"And by that time this woman, whoever she was, had already slipped out of the house."

"She must have done so. No one heard her leave."

"Let us hope that Hoefer will solve the enigma. If any one is able, he is."

"But first urge him to bring poor Beryl back to consciousness," she said, turning to gaze upon the still inanimate form of the woman I adored.

At that moment the German returned, puffing and grunting, for he had hurried, and the perspiration was rolling off his brow.

He took several little packets from his pocket, and, seating himself at the table, commenced to carefully prepare another solution, the ingredients of which were unknown to me. Some of the drugs I knew by their appearance, of course, but others were white powders, impossible to recognise.

Again he administered an injection into the arm of my prostrate loved one, and then we all three stood in silence watching for the effect.

Hoefer gave vent to a further grunt of confidence, glanced at his watch, and turned back to the table to rearrange his array of drugs. I saw that the little pocket-case lying on the table contained about twenty tiny tubes about an inch and a half long; each contained very small pilules of tabloids, coloured brightly to render them more easily distinguishable, and not much larger than ordinary shot. Each tube was marked, but by mysterious signs unknown in British pharmacology.

The action of this last prophylactic was slow, but signs were nevertheless not wanting that its effect was to reanimate, for by degrees the deathly pallor of the sweet face I adored became less marked, and the lips showed red instead of that ashen hue which had told us of her nearness to death.

The German returned to her, and, feeling her pulse, counted the seconds upon his watch, while at the same time I listened to the respiration.

"Good?" exclaimed the old fellow, beaming through his glasses. "The diagnosis is correct, and the refocillation is more rapid than I should have expected. She will recover."

Suddenly the pallid cheeks became flushed. Life was returning. The liquid injected into the blood bad at last neutralised the effect, stimulated the circulation, reanimated the whole system, and revived the flickering spark of life. The hand I held grew warmer, the pulse throbbed more quickly, the breathing became regular, and a few minutes later, without warning, she opened her eyes and looked wonderingly around. A loud cry of joy escaped my lips. My love was saved.

"You know me, I think?" I said, bending down to her. "My name is Colkirk."

"Yes, I know you quite well," she responded very faintly. "But what has happened? Where is she?"

"Whom do you mean? Your visitor?"

"Yes," she responded eagerly.

"We have no idea," I replied. "You have been taken ill, and my friend here. Doctor Hoefer, has been attending you."

"How do you feel?" the old German asked in his brusque manner.

"I am very thirsty," she answered.

He took the decanter, and, mixing a little brandy and water, gave it to her.

Then just at that moment her ladyship re-entered, and, falling on her knees, clasped her cousin around the neck and shed wild tears of joy.

Liquid beef and other restoratives having been administered, the woman whose appearance had been identical in every respect with that of the dead was, ere long, able to sit up and talk with us. Her recovery had been almost as rapid as her attack.

We questioned her regarding her symptoms, and found them exactly similar to those we had ourselves experienced.

"I felt as though my whole body were frozen stiff and rigid," she explained. "At first I heard a strange voice about me—the voice of Doctor Colkirk, I suppose it must have been—speaking with Nora; but I was unable to make any sign. It was just as though I were in a kind of trance, yet half-conscious of things about me. My muscles were paralysed, and I knew that you believed me to be dead. The one horrible thought that possessed me was that I might, perhaps, be buried alive."

"But you were not conscious the whole time?" Hoefer asked.

"No; I think I slept during the latter part of the seizure. How long have I been lying here?"

"About two hours and a half," answered her cousin. "Do you feel able to talk any more now?" I inquired.

"I feel much better," she responded. "The draught that your friend has given me has had a wonderful effect. I'm quite restored." And she rose to her feet and stood before us, little the worse for her experience, save, perhaps, that the dark rings about her beautiful eyes showed that her system had received a terrible shock.

"We want you to relate to us in detail what occurred when you entered the morning-room to see the woman who called upon you."

She glanced inquiringly at her cousin, as though to obtain her permission to speak.

"Nothing occurred," she answered; "she was sitting there awaiting me."

"She had sent in a message, and you thought it—as your dressmaker, did you not?"

"Yes. And I was very much surprised to find that it was not."

"Was it some other person whom you knew?"

"I had never seen her before," answered the woman who was my wedded wife. "She was tall, thin and dressed in black which seemed much the worse for wear."

"Dark or fair?"

"Dark. But I could not see her features well because of her thick black veil."

"She was young, I suppose?"

"Not very, I think. Her voice was low and rather refined."

"And how did she explain her reason for sending in a message that she was your dressmaker? She must have been aware that you expected the woman to call on you."

"She explained that the ruse was necessary, as she did not wish her visit to be known, either to my cousin or to the servants."

"Why?"

"Because she had brought me a message."

"A message?" I exclaimed. "From whom?"

"A verbal message from—from a friend."

"And may we not know the name of that friend?" I asked. "There is a most remarkable mystery connected with that room into which she was shown, and, in order to solve the problem, we must be in possession of the whole truth."

"What mystery?" Beryl inquired quickly, opening her eyes widely.

"Any person who enters is, on leaving, attacked just as you were. Your cousin here, Doctor Hoefer, and myself, had all three experienced exactly similar symptoms."

"That's most extraordinary!" she declared, in an incredulous tone. "When I was seized it was not until I had left the room. I went out with the object of obtaining a sheet of note-paper from the library in order to write a reply to the message, but on emerging into the hall I was suddenly seized, and returned to the morning-room at once. I stood holding on to the table; but my limbs failed me, and I fell to the ground."

"And then the woman who had called upon you slipped along the hall and out into the street."

"I suppose she must have done, for I did not see her again. I tried to call out, but could not. The electric light was suddenly switched off. She must have done that on her way out."

"Cannot you tell us either of the nature of the message or from whom it came?" I asked earnestly.

She was silent for a moment, glancing at her cousin. "No," she answered; "I am unable to do that."

Chapter Twenty.

The Chill Hand.

Was the message from her lover or from that villain Tattersett?

Her refusal piqued me, and I was half inclined to suggest that it was from the one or the other. Still, in this marvellous maze of mystery, I saw that it was not at all a judicious proceeding to show my hand. What I already knew was of value to me in my efforts to piece together this bewildering puzzle.

The more I reflected the more convinced I became that the visitor in black was none other than the dreaded woman whose threatened vengeance was known to be imminent—La Gioia the mysterious.

"The visitor did not touch you?" I asked. "Neither did she give you any note?"

"No; the message was verbal. I went once to the library and obtained a sheet of note-paper, but on returning found it to be soiled. Therefore I went out again to get a second, sheet, and it was then that I felt a sudden grip, just as though an icy breath had touched me. In an instant I went cold all over, and my limbs became so benumbed that I could not feel them."

"You did not suspect this woman of producing this effect upon you?" Hoefer asked, grunting dubiously.

"Certainly not. How could she?"

"But her actions afterwards, in switching off the light and stealing out, were suspicious."

"That's so; but how do you account for your own seizure nearly two hours after her departure?"

"Ach!" he cried; "it is extraordinary—that is all we can say."

"The room is nothing less than a death-trap," I remarked. "And yet the baneful influence is a mysterious one. I wish you could tell us the name of the sender of the message, Miss Wynd. It would materially assist us in our researches."

"I tell you that it was a friend who could have no object whatever in making any attack upon my life," she answered, ambiguously.

"But this woman," I continued. "Are you certain that you do not know her—that you have never met her before?"

"Quite certain," she responded without hesitation. "She was an utter stranger."

I exchanged glances with Hoefer. The mystery was still inscrutable.

Again we all four went to the door of the room of mystery, and

Hoefer, still grunting in dissatisfaction, declared his intention to re-enter the place. Seen from the hall there was certainly nothing about the apartment to excite suspicion. It was bright and comfortable, with handsome substantial furniture, sage-green hangings, and a thick Turkey carpet into which one's feet sank noiselessly.

"It is a risk!" exclaimed her ladyship, when Hoefer made the announcement. "Death lurks in that place. Let us close and lock it."

"Ach! no, madame," he responded. "It is no risk now that we have the prophylactic." And, turning to me, he handed me a little of the last injection which he had given to Beryl, together with the phial of ether and the syringe.

"Use this, if necessary," he said, briefly, and then leaving us, he crossed the threshold and examined every nook of the room.

The window was still open, but he closed and fastened it. Upon a little writing-table in the corner lay the soiled sheet of note-paper that Beryl had obtained on her first visit to the library, thus proving the truth of her story. The door swung to, as before, and after about five minutes he again emerged.

Scarcely had he crossed the threshold when he gave vent to a loud cry.

"Gott!" he gasped. "The injection—quick!"

He had again been seized. The unseen hand of Death was upon him. Truly, it was an uncanny mystery.

Without a second's delay I filled the syringe, rubbed the flesh with ether, and then ran the needle beneath the skin. The effect was almost instantaneous. The sudden paralysis was arrested, and the muscles reanimated in a manner most marvellous. One fact was, therefore, plain: Hoefer had discovered the proper treatment, even if the cause of the extraordinary seizure remained unknown.

He stood for a few moments motionless, but at length declaring himself better, said—

"The thing is an absolute enigma; I can discern no cause whatever for it. There would seem to be some hidden influence at work, but of its nature we can discover absolutely nothing. The attack does not occur until one emerges here into the hall."

"Can it be out here?" I suggested, whereat both my companions turned pale with fright.

Certainly the situation was as weird and uncanny as any in which I have ever found myself. An unseen influence is always mysterious, and this chill touch of the hand of death that we had all experienced was actually appalling.

We held council, and decided that the room should be closed and locked to prevent any of the servants entering there. Our conversation had undoubtedly been overheard by them, and Hoefer was anxious that the place should remain undisturbed so that he might make further investigations, which he promised to do on the following day.

Then we entered the dining-room together, partook of some wine which her ladyship offered us, and left the house in company—not, however, before I had promised to call again on the morrow and visit my patient.

"Now, Hoefer, what is your candid opinion?" I asked my companion as we stood on the kerb, opposite the Marble Arch, awaiting the belated omnibus to take him back to Bloomsbury.

"I don't like it, my dear frient," he answered dubiously; "I don't like it." And, shaking my hand, he entered the last Holborn 'bus without further word.

On foot I returned to Bayswater utterly confounded by the curious events of the evening. By Hoefer's serious expression and preoccupied manner, I saw that the influence within or without that room of mystery was to him utterly bewildering. He had spent his life in the study of micro-organisms, and knew more of staphylococci, streptococci, and pneumococci than any other living man, while as a toxicologist he was acknowledged, even by his clever compatriots in Germany, as the greatest of them all. He had searched out many of the secrets of Nature, and I had myself at times witnessed certain, of his experiments, which were little short of marvellous. It was, therefore, gratifying that I had enlisted his aid in solving this most difficult problem.

Yet, as I lay awake that night, reflecting deeply upon the curious situation, I could not arrest my thoughts from turning back to the tragedy at Whitton and the omission of those two names from the list of visitors furnished to the police. That her ladyship was a bosom friend of Mrs Chetwode's was quite plain, and that she was present, together with Beryl, earlier in the day, I had myself seen. Somehow, I could not get rid of the conviction that Sir Henry's wife, the woman who had taken this secret journey from Atworth to London to have a clandestine interview with some person whom she declined to name, knew the truth regarding the Colonel's death.

I was plunged into a veritable sea of perplexity.

If I could but discover the identity of La Gioia! That name rang in my ears, sleeping or waking. La Gioia! La Gioia! Ever La Gioia!

Beryl held her in abject dread. Of that I knew from those words of here I had overheard at Whitton. She had declared that she would commit suicide rather than face her vengeance. What had rendered my adored one so desperate?

As I sat over my lonely breakfast on the following morning, there being already a couple of patients in the waiting-room—clerks who had come for "doctors' certificates" to enable them to enjoy a day's repose—the servant brought in the letters, among them being one for me which had been forwarded from Shrewsbury by my mother.

The superscription was in a formal hand, and, on reading it, I was surprised to find that it was from a firm of solicitors in Bedford Row, stating that my uncle George, a cotton-spinner in Bury, had died, leaving a will by which I was to receive the sum of one thousand pounds as a legacy. I read the letter, time after time, scarcely able to believe the good news.

But an hour later, when I sat in the dingy office in Bedford Row, and my uncle's solicitor read a copy of the will to me, I saw that it was a reality—a fact which was indeed, proved by the cheque for fifty pounds which he handed me for my immediate use. I drove to the Joint Stock Bank in Chancery Lane, cashed the draft, and returned to Bayswater with five ten-pound notes in my pocket. From a state of penury I had, within that single hour, become possessed of funds. True, I had always had expectations from that quarter; but I had, like millions of other men, never before been possessor of a thousand pounds. In a week or two the money would be placed to my credit. To a man with only half a crown in his pocket a thousand pounds appears a fortune.

I counted the crisp new notes in the privacy of the doctor's sitting-room, then, locking three of them in my portmanteau, took a cab down to Rowan Road to receive Bob's congratulations. He was delighted. He sent Mrs Bishop out for a bottle of the best champagne procurable in the neighbourhood, and we drank merrily to my future success. Then, while smoking a cigarette over what remained of the wine, I related to him my strange adventure of the previous night.

He sat listening to my story open-mouthed. Until I had concluded, he uttered no word. Then gravely he exclaimed—

"The affair grows more and more amazing. But now, look here, Dick! Why don't you take my advice, and drop the affair altogether?"

"Drop it? What do you mean? Remember Beryl!"

"I know," he answered. "But I can't help feeling that association with those people is dangerous. They're a queer lot—a devilishly queer lot!"

"Of course they're a queer lot," I said; "but I can't leave her to their mercy. She's in deadly peril of her life; they intend to kill her."

A grave expression was on his face. "Do you think that last night's curious phenomenon was actually an attempt to kill her?" he inquired.

"Without a doubt."

"Then, if so, how was it that you all experienced similar symptoms? What's old Hoefer's theory?"

"He has none."

"He never has—or, at least, he pretends that he hasn't; he keeps all his discoveries to himself. That's why he has always refused to write any books. When he lectures he's always careful to keep his secrets to himself."

"Yes; he's a queer old boy," I remarked, for his eccentricities were many, and had often caused us much amusement at Guy's.

"I only wish, Dick, that you'd try to forget all about this tangled affair," Bob said earnestly. "You're worrying yourself to death all to no purpose."

"Why 'all to no purpose'?" I echoed. "I am patient, and I shall discover something one day."

"No," he said confidently. "You'll never discover anything—mark my words."

"What makes you think that?"

"Because you are watched far too closely."

"Watched!" I cried in surprise. "Who watches me?"

"Several persons. Among them your wife herself."

"How do you know?"

"Because I saw her in this street, on the evening before last, evidently in search of you. She passed several times, and glanced across here. Yet she tells you—or, rather, her cousin tells you—that they were not in London at that time."

"Are you certain?"

"Absolutely."

"But how did you recognise her?" I demanded eagerly. "Why, you've never seen her!"

He started quickly. By the expression on his face I recognised in an instant, that he had inadvertently betrayed to me the fact that they were not strangers.

He knew her! And he had tried to dissuade me from following up the slight clue I had obtained. With what motive? This man, whom I had believed was my friend, had played me false.

The discovery was as a blow that staggered me.

Chapter Twenty One.

Two Hearts.

The truth was plain. Bob Raymond, the man whom I had believed to be my friend, had endeavoured to dissuade me from following up the clue I had obtained, fearing lest I should discover the whole of the strange conspiracy.

I pressed him for an explanation of how he had been able to recognise her, but with marvellous tact he answered—

"Oh, I recognised her from your descriptions, you know."

Frankly I did not believe it. Whether he had a personal acquaintance with her or not, it was nevertheless manifest that she was actually in London at a time when she was believed to be at Atworth; and further, that not knowing of my change of address, had been in search of me.

Why had she not rung the bell and inquired? There seemed but a single answer to that question; because she feared to meet Bob!

I scented suspicion. In our conversation that followed I detected, on his part, a strenuous determination to evade any explanation. That he was actually acquainted with Beryl was apparent. Perhaps, even, he knew the truth regarding my strange marriage, and, from motives of his own, refused to tell me.

Anger arose within me, but I preserved a diplomatic calm, striving to worm his secret from him. Either he would not or could not tell me anything. In that hour of affluence, after all the penury of past years, I was perhaps a trifle egotistical, as men who suddenly receive an unexpected legacy are apt to be. Money has a greater influence upon our temperament or disposition than even love. A few paltry pounds can transform this earth of ours from a hell into a paradise.

I drained my glass, flung my cigarette end into the empty grate, and left my friend with a rather abrupt farewell.

"You'll let me know if you elicit anything further?" he urged.

"Of course," I answered, although such was not my intention. Then I went forth walking out to the Hammersmith Road.

The noon was stifling—one of those hot, close, oven-cast days of the London summer—when I was shown into the drawing-room of Gloucester Square, and, after the lapse of a few minutes, my love came forward gladly to meet me.

"It's awfully kind of you to call, Doctor," she exclaimed, offering her thin little hand—that hand that on the previous night had been so stiff and cold. "Nora is out, but I expect her in again every moment. She's gone to the Stores to order things to be sent up to Atworth."

"And how do you feel?" I inquired, as she seated herself upon a low silken lounge-chair and stretched out her tiny foot, neat in its patent leather slipper with large steel buckle.

She looked cool and fresh in a gown of white muslin relieved with a dash of Nile-green silk at the throat and waist.

"Oh, I am so much better," she declared. "Except for a slight headache, I feel no ill effects of last night's extraordinary attack."

I asked permission to feel her pulse, and found it beating with the regularity of a person in normal health.

As I held her white wrist, her deep clear eyes met mine. In her pure white clinging drapery, with her gold-brown hair making the half-darkened room bright, with her red lips parted in a tender and solemn smile, with something like a halo about her of youth and ardour, she was a vision so entrancing that, as I gazed at her, my heart grew heavy with an aching consciousness of her perfection. And yet she was actually my wife!

I stammered satisfaction that she had recovered so entirely from the strange seizure, and her eyes opened widely, as though in wonder at my inarticulate words.

"Yes," she said, "the affair was most extraordinary. I cannot imagine what horrid mystery is concealed within that room."

"Nor I," I responded. "Has Doctor Hoefer been here yet?"

"Oh yes," she laughed; "he came at nine o'clock, opened the room, entered, and was seized again, but only slightly. He used the same drug as last night, and quickly recovered. For about an hour he remained, and then left. He's such a queer old fellow," she added, with a laugh; "I don't think he uttered a dozen words during the whole time."

"No," I said; "his habit is to give vent to those expressive grunts. When interested his mind seems always so actively centred upon the matter under investigation that to speak is an effort. But tell me," I urged, glancing into those pure, honest eyes, "have you ever experienced before such a seizure as that last night?"

She turned rather pale, I thought: this direct question seemed not easy to answer.

"I was ill once," she responded, with hesitation, yet with sweet, simple, girlish tenderness. "One day, some little time ago, I suddenly fell unconscious, and seemed to dream all sorts of absurd and grotesque things."

Did she refer to the fateful day of our marriage?

"Were you quite unconscious on that occasion?" I asked quickly, "or were you aware, in a hazy manner, of what was going on around you, as you were last night?"

A wild hope sprang up in my heart. Was it possible that she would reveal to me her secret?

"I think," she answered, "that my condition then was very similar to that of last night; I recollect quite well being unable to move my limbs or to lift a finger. Every muscle seemed paralysed, while, at the same time, I went as cold as ice, just as though I were frozen to death. Indeed, a horrible dread took possession of me lest my friends should allow me to be buried alive."

"You were in a kind of cataleptic state," I remarked. "Who were these friends?"

Her great eyes were lifted. They were full of depths unfathomable even to my intense love.

"I was practically unconscious, therefore I do not know who was present; I only heard voices."

"Of whom?"

"Of men talking."

"Could you not recognise them?"

"No," she answered, in a low tone; "they were dream-voices, strange and weird—sounding afar off."

"What did they say?"

"I cannot tell, only I recollect that I thought I was in church; I had a curious dream."

Again she hesitated. Her voice had suddenly fallen so that I could scarcely make out the sound of the last word.

"What did you dream? The vagaries of the brain sometimes give us a clue to the nature of such seizures."

"I dreamed that I was wedded," she responded, in a low, unnatural voice.

The next instant she seemed to realise what she had said. With a start of terror she drew herself away from me.

"Wedded? To whom?"

"I do not know," she replied, with a queer laugh. "Of course, it was a mere dream; I saw no one."

"But you heard voices?"

"They were so distorted as to be indistinguishable," she replied readily.

"Are you absolutely certain that the marriage was only a dream?" I asked, looking her straight in the face.

A flash of indignant surprise passed across her features, now pale as marble; her lips were slightly parted, her large full eyes were fixed upon me steadfastly, and her fingers pressed themselves into the palms of her hands.

"I don't understand you, Doctor!" she said at length, after a pause of the most awkward duration. "Of course I am not married?"

"I regret if you take my words as an insinuation," I said hastily.

"It was a kind of dream," she declared. "Indeed, I think that I was in a sort of delirium and imagined it all, for when I recovered completely I found myself here, in my own room, with Nora at my side."

"And where were you when you were taken ill?"

"In the house of a friend."

"May I not know the name?" I inquired.

"It is a name with which you are not acquainted," she assured me. "The house at which I was visiting was in Queen's-gate Gardens."

Queen's-gate Gardens! Then she was telling the truth!

"And you have no knowledge of how you came to be back here in your cousin's house?"

"None whatever. I tell you that I was entirely unconscious."

"And you are certain that the symptoms on that day were the same as those which we all experienced last night? You felt frozen to death?"

"Yes," she responded, lying back in her chair, sighing rather wearily and passing her hand across her aching brow.

There was a deep silence. We could hear the throbbing of each other's heart. At last she looked up tremblingly, with an expression of undissembled pain, saying—

"The truth is, Doctor, it was an absolute mystery, just as were the events of last night—a mystery which is driving me to desperation."

"It's not the mystery that troubles you," I said, in a low earnest voice, "but the recollection of that dream-marriage, is it not?"

"Exactly," she faltered.

"You do not recollect the name announced by the clergyman, as that of your husband?" I inquired, eagerly.

"I heard it but once, and it was strange and unusual; the droning voice stumbled over it indistinctly, therefore I could not catch it."

She was in ignorance that she was my bride. Her heart was beating rapidly, the lace on her bosom trembled as she slowly lifted her eyes to mine. Could she ever love me?

A thought of young Chetwode stung me to the quick. He was my rival, yet I was already her husband.

"I have been foolish to tell you all this," she said presently, with a nervous laugh. "It was only a dream—a dream so vivid that I have sometimes thought it was actual truth."

Her speech was the softest murmur, and the beautiful face, nearer to mine than it had been before, was looking at me with beseeching tenderness. Then her eyes dropped, a martyr pain passed over her face, her small hands sought each other as though they must hold something, the fingers clasped themselves, and her head drooped.

"I am glad you have told me," I said. "The incident is certainly curious, judged in connexion with the unusual phenomena of last night."

"Yes, but I ought not to have told you," she said slowly. "Nora will be very angry."

"Why?"

"Because she made me promise to tell absolutely no one," she answered, with a faint sharpness in her voice. There were loss and woe in those words of hers.

"What motive had she in preserving your secret?" I asked, surprised. "Surely she is—"

My love interrupted me.

"No, do not let us discuss her motives or her actions; she is my friend. Let us not talk of the affair any more, I beg of you."

She was pale as death, and it seemed as though a tremor ran through all her limbs.

"But am I not also your friend, Miss Wynd?" I asked in deep seriousness.

"I—I hope you are."

Her voice was timid, troubled; but her sincere eyes again lifted themselves to mine.

"I assure you that I am," I declared. "If you will but give me your permission I will continue, with Hoefer, to seek a solution of this puzzling problem."

"It is so uncanny," she said. "To me it surpasses belief."

"I admit that. At present, to leave that room is to invite death. We must, therefore, make active researches to ascertain the truth. We must find your strange visitor in black."

"Find her?" she gasped. "You could never do that."

"Why not? She is not supernatural; she lives and is in hiding somewhere, that's evident."

"And you would find her, and seek from her the truth?"

"Certainly."

She shut her lips tight and sat motionless, looking at me. Then at last she said, shuddering—

"No. Not that."

"Then you know this woman—or at least you guess her identity," I said in a low voice.

She gazed at me with parted lips.

"I have already told you that I do not know her," was her firm response.

"Then what do you fear?" I demanded.

Again she was silent. Whatever potential complicity had lurked in her heart, my words brought her only immeasurable dismay.

"I dread such an action for your own sake," she faltered.

"Then I will remain till your cousin comes, and ask her what it is."

"Ask her?"

Chapter Twenty Two.

A Savant at Home.

"Why should I not ask your cousin?" I inquired earnestly. "I see by your manner that you are in sore need of a friend, and yet you will not allow me to act as such."

"Not allow you!" she echoed. "You are my friend. Were it not for you I should have died last night."

"Your recovery was due to Hoefer, not to myself," I declared.

I longed to speak to her of her visit to Whitton and of her relations with the Major, but dare not. By so doing I should only expose myself as an eavesdropper and a spy. Therefore, I was held to silence.

My thoughts wandered back to that fateful night when I was called to the house with the grey front in Queen's-gate Gardens. That house, she had told me, was the home of "a friend." I remembered how, after our marriage, I had seen her lying there as one dead, and knew that she had fallen the victim of some foul and deep conspiracy. Who was that man who had called himself Wyndham Wynd? An associate of the Major's, who was careful in the concealment of his identity. The manner in which the plot had been arranged was both amazing in its ingenuity and bewildering in its complications.

And lounging before me there in the low silken chair, her small mouth slightly parted, displaying an even set of pearly teeth, sat the victim—the woman who was unconsciously my wedded wife.

Her attitude towards me was plainly one of fear lest I should discover her secret. It was evident that she now regretted having told me of that strange, dreamlike scene which was photographed so indelibly upon her memory, that incident so vivid that she vaguely believed she had been actually wedded.

"So you are returning to Atworth again?" I asked, for want of something better to say.

"I believe that is Nora's intention," she responded quickly, with a slight sigh of relief at the change in our conversation.

"Have you many visitors there?"

"Oh, about fifteen—all rather jolly people. It's such a charming place. Nora must ask you down there."

"I should be delighted," I said.

Now that I had money in my pocket, and was no longer compelled to toil for the bare necessities of life, I was eager to get away from the heat and dust of the London August. This suggestion of hers was to me doubly welcome too, for as a visitor at Atworth I should be always beside her. That she was in peril was evident, and my place was near her.

On the other hand, however, I distrusted her ladyship. She had, at the first moment of our meeting, shown herself to be artificial and an admirable actress. Indeed, had she not, for purposes known best to herself, endeavoured to start a flirtation with me? Her character everywhere was that of a smart woman—popular in society, and noted for the success of her various entertainments during the season; but women of her stamp never commended themselves to me. Doctors, truth to tell, see rather too much of the reverse of the medal—especially in social London.

"When did you return from Wiltshire?" I inquired, determined to clear up one point.

"The day before yesterday," she responded.

"In the evening?"

"No, in the morning."

Then her ladyship had lied to me, for she had said they had arrived in London on the morning of the day when the unknown woman in black had called. Beryl had told the truth, and her words were proved by the statement of Bob Raymond that he had seen her pass along Rowan Road.

Were they acquaintances? As I reflected upon that problem one fact alone stood out above all others. If I had been unknown to Wynd and that scoundrel Tattersett, how was it that they were enabled to give every detail regarding myself in their application for the marriage licence? How, indeed, did they know that I was acting as Bob's locum tenens? Or how was the Tempter so well aware of my penury?

No. Now that my friend had betrayed himself, I felt convinced that he knew something of the extraordinary plot in which I had become so hopelessly involved.

"The day before yesterday," I said, looking her straight in the face, "you came to Hammersmith to try to find me."

She started quickly, but in an instant recovered herself.

"Yes," she admitted. "I walked through Rowan Road, expecting to find your plate on one of the doors, but could not."

"I have no plate," I answered. "When I lived there I was assistant to my friend. Doctor Raymond."

"Raymond!" she exclaimed. "Oh yes, I remember I saw his name; but I was looking for yours."

"You wished to see me?"

"Yes; I was not well," she faltered.

"But your cousin knew that I had lived with Raymond. Did you not ask her?"

"No," she answered, "it never occurred to me to do so."

Rather a lame response, I thought.

"But last night she found me quite easily. She called upon Doctor Raymond, who gave her my new address." And, continuing, I told her of my temporary abode.

"I know," she replied.

"Have you ever met my friend Raymond?" I inquired with an air of affected carelessness.

"Not to my knowledge," she answered quite frankly.

"How long ago did Hoefer leave?" I asked.

"About an hour, I think. He has locked the door of the morning-room and taken the key with him," she added, laughing.

She presented a pretty picture, indeed, in that half-darkened room, leaning back gracefully and smiling upon me.

"He announced no fresh discovery?"

"He spoke scarcely a dozen words."

"But this mystery is a very disagreeable one for you who live here. I presume that you live with your cousin always?"

"Yes," she responded. "After my father's death, some years ago, I came here to live with her."

So her father was dead! The Tempter was not, as I had all along suspected, her father.

I longed to take her in my arms and tell her the truth, that I was actually her husband and that I loved her. Yet, how could I? The mystery was so complicated, and so full of inscrutable points, that to make any such declaration must only fill her with fear of myself.

We chatted on while I feasted my eyes upon her wondrous beauty. Had she, I asked myself, ever seen young Chetwode since her return to London? Did she really love him, or was he merely the harmless but necessary admirer which every girl attracts towards herself as a sort of natural instinct? The thought of him caused a vivid recollection of that night in Whitton Park to arise within me.

Where was Tattersett—the man who had laughed at her when she had declared her intention of escaping him by suicide? Who was he? What was he?

It occurred to me, now that I had learned some potent facts from her own lips, that my next course should be to find this man and investigate his past. By doing so I might elucidate the problem.

Her ladyship, with a cry of welcome upon her lips, entered the room and sank, hot and fatigued, into a cosy armchair.

"London is simply unbearable!" she declared. "It's ever so many degrees hotter than at Atworth, and in the Stores it is awfully stuffy. In the provision department butter, bacon, and things seem all melting away."

"You'll be glad to get back again to Wiltshire," I laughed.

"Very. We shall go by the night-mail to-morrow," she answered. "Why don't you come up and visit us, Doctor? My husband would be charmed to meet you I'm sure."

"That's just what I've been saying, dear," exclaimed Beryl. "Do persuade Doctor Colkirk to come."

"I am sure you are both very kind," I replied, "but at present I am in practice."

"You can surely take a holiday," urged Beryl. "Do come. We would try to make it pleasant for you."

Her persuasion decided me, and, after some further pressing on the part of her ladyship, I accepted the invitation with secret satisfaction, promising to leave in the course of a week or ten days.

Then we fell to discussing the curious phenomena of the previous night, until, having again exhausted the subject, I rose to take my leave.

"Good-bye, Doctor Colkirk," Beryl said, looking into my eyes as I held her small hand. "I hope we shall soon meet down in Wiltshire, and, when we do, let us forget all the mystery of yesterday."

"I suppose you have given Hoefer permission to visit, the room when he wishes to pursue his investigations?" I said, turning to her ladyship.

"Of course. The house is entirely at his disposal. One does not care to have a death-trap in one's own house."

"He will do his best—of that I feel quite sure," I said.

And then again promising to visit her soon, I shook her hand, bade them both adieu, and with a last look at the frail, graceful woman I loved, went out into the hot, dusty street.

In order to celebrate my sudden accession to wealth I lunched well at Simpson's, and then took a hansom to old Hoefer's dismal rooms in. Bloomsbury. To me, so gloomy and severe is that once-aristocratic district that, in my hospital days, I called it Gloomsbury.

Hoefer occupied a dingy flat in Museum Mansions, and, as I entered the small room which served him as laboratory, I was almost knocked back by the choking fumes of some acid with which he was experimenting. A dense blue smoke hung over everything, and through it loomed the German's great fleshy face and gold-rimmed spectacles. He was in his shirt-sleeves, seated at a table, watching some liquid boiling in a big glass retort. Around his mouth and nose a damp towel was tied, and as I entered he motioned me back.

"Ach! don't come in here, my tear Colkirk! I vill come to you. Ze air is not good just now. Wait for me there in my room."

Heedless of his warning, however, I went forward to the table, coughing and choking the while. I took out my handkerchief, when suddenly he snatched it from me, and steeped it in some pale yellow solution. Then, when I placed it before my mouth, inhaling it, I experienced no further difficulty in respiration.

The nature of the experiment on which he was engaged I could not determine. From the retort he was condensing those suffocating fumes, drop by drop, now and then dipping pieces of white, prepared paper into the liquid thus obtained. I stood by watching in silence.

Once he placed a drop of that liquid upon a glass slide, dried it for crystallisation, and, placing it beneath the microscope, examined it carefully.

He grunted. And I knew he was not satisfied.

Then he added a few drops of some colourless liquid to that in the retort, and the solution at once assumed a pale green hue. He boiled it again for three minutes by his common, metal watch, then, having drained it off into a shallow glass bowl to cool, blew out his lamp, and I followed him back into his small, cosy, but rather stuffy little den.

"Well?" he inquired. "You have called at her ladyship's—eh?"

"Yes," I replied, stretching myself in one of his rickety chairs; "but you were there before me. What have you discovered?"

"Nothing."

"But that experiment I have just witnessed? Has it no connexion with the mystery?"

"Yes, some slight connexion. It was, however, a failure," he grunted, still speaking with his strong accent.

"You experienced the same sensation there to-day, I hear?" I said.

"H'm, yes; but not so strong."

"And the same injection cured you?"

"Of course. That, however, tells us nothing. We cannot yet ascertain how it is caused."

"Or find out who was that unknown woman in black," I added.

"If we could discover her we might obtain the key to the situation," he responded.

"I have been invited by her ladyship to visit them in Wiltshire," I said suddenly, as I lit a cigarette, "and I have accepted. Have I done right, do you think?"

"You would have done far better to stay here in London," grunted the old man. "If we mean to get at the bottom of this mystery we must work together."

"How?"

"In this affair, my dear Colkirk," he exclaimed, with a sudden burst of confidence, "there is much more than of what we are aware. There is some motive in getting rid of Miss Wynd secretly and surely. I feel certain that she knows who her mysterious visitor was, but dare not tell us."

"I am going down to Atworth," I said. "Perhaps I shall discover something."

"Perhaps?" he sniffed dubiously. "But, depend upon it, the key to this problem lies in London. You haven't yet told me who this Miss Wynd is."

"A lady who, her father being dead, went to live with Sir Henry Pierrepoint-Lane and his wife."

"Ach! then she has no home? I thought not."

"Why? What made you think that?"

"I fancied so," he said, continuing to puff at his great pipe. "I fancied, too, that she had a lover—a young lover—who is a lieutenant in a cavalry regiment."

"How did you know?"

"Merely from my own observations. It was all plain last night."

"How?"

But he grinned at me through his great ugly spectacles without replying. I knew that he was a marvellously acute observer.

"And your opinion of her ladyship?" I inquired, much interested.

"She, like her charming cousin, is concealing the truth," he answered frankly. "Neither are to be trusted."

"Not Beryl—I mean Miss Wynd?"

"No; for she knows who her visitor was, and will not tell us."

Then he paused. In that moment I made a sudden resolve; I asked him whether he had read in the newspapers the account of the Whitton tragedy.

"I read every word of it," he responded—"a most interesting affair. I was not well at the time, otherwise I dare say I might have gone down there."

"Yes," I said, "from our point of view it is intensely interesting, the more so because of one fact, namely, that her ladyship was among the visitors when the Colonel was so mysteriously assassinated."

"At Whitton!" he exclaimed, bending forward. "Was she at Whitton?"

"Yes," I answered.

"And her cousin, Miss Wynd?"

"Of that I am not quite sure. All I know is that she was there on the afternoon previous to the tragedy. Sir Henry's wife is Mrs Chetwode's bosom friend."

The old fellow grunted, closed his eyes, and puffed contentedly at his pipe.

"In that case," he observed at last, "her ladyship may know something about that affair. Is that your suspicion?"

"Well, yes; to tell the truth, that is my opinion."

"And also mine," he exclaimed. "I am glad you have told me this, for it throws considerable light upon my discovery."

"Discovery?" I echoed. "What have you discovered?"

"The identity of the woman in black who visited Miss Wynd last night."

"You've discovered her—already?" I cried. "Who was she?"

"A woman known as La Gioia," responded the queer old fellow, puffing a cloud of rank smoke from his heavy lips.

"La Gioia?" I gasped, open-mouthed and rigid. "La Gioia! And you have found her?"

"Yes; I have found her."

Chapter Twenty Three.

A Counter-Plot.

"I have no knowledge yet of who the woman is," responded Hoefer, in answer to my question. "I only know that her name is La Gioia. But you are aware of her identity, it seems."

"No; like yourself, I only know her name."

He glanced at me rather curiously through his big spectacles, and I knew that he doubted my words. I pressed him to explain by what means he had made the discovery, but his answers were ambiguous. In brief, he believed that I knew more than I really did, and therefore declined to tell me anything. He was extremely eccentric, this queer old dabbler in the occult, and I well knew that, having once adopted a plan in the pursuit of an inquiry, no power on earth would induce him to deviate from it.

Fully an hour I remained in that atmosphere full of poisonous fumes, watching a further but futile analysis that he made, and afterwards took my leave of him.

I went back to Bayswater, wrote a letter of resignation to the doctor who had employed me, and then went forth again upon my round of visits. The practice was large and scattered, and several cases were critical ones, therefore it was not until nearly eight o'clock that I returned again, fagged and hungry, only to find the waiting-room filled with club patients and others.

The irregularity of meals is one of the chief discomforts of a busy doctor's life. I snatched a few moments to swallow my soup, and then entered the surgery and sat there until past nine ere I could commence dinner.

Then, over my coffee and a pipe, I sat at ease, thinking over the many occurrences of the day. Truly it had been an eventful one—the turning-point of my life. I had telegraphed to my mother, telling her of my good fortune, and, in response, received her hearty congratulations. One of the chief gratifications which the thousand pounds had brought to me was the fact that, for a year or so, she would not feel the absolute pinch of poverty as she had done through so long past.

And I was invited to Atworth! I should there have an opportunity of being always at the side of the woman I loved so madly, and perhaps be enabled to penetrate the veil of mystery with which she was surrounded. I was suspicious of the baronet's wife—suspicious because she had made her first call upon me under such curious circumstances. How did she know me? and for what reason had she sought my acquaintance?

She had endeavoured to flirt with me. Faugh! Her beauty, her smartness, and her clever woman's wiles might have turned the heads of the majority of men. But I loved Beryl, and she was mine—mine!

Reader, I have taken you entirely into my confidence, and I am laying bare to you my secret. Need I tell you how maddening the enigma had now become, how near I always seemed to some solution and yet how far off the truth? Place yourself in my position for a single moment—adoring the woman who, although she was actually my wife, was yet ignorant of the fact; and I dare not tell her the truth lest she might hold me in suspicion as one of those who had conspired against her. So far from the problem being, solved, each day rendered it more intricate and more inscrutable, until the continual weight upon my mind drove me to despair. Hence my anxiety for the days to pass in order that I might journey down to Atworth.

At last, on a close, overcast afternoon in the middle of September, when the hot sun seemed unable to penetrate the heavy veil of London smoke and the air was suffocating, I left Paddington, and, in due course, found myself upon the platform of the wayside station of Corsham, close to the entrance to the Box tunnel, where Sir Henry and his wife awaited me. The former was a tall, smart-looking, elderly man with grey hair and a well-trimmed grey beard, who, on our introduction, greeted me most cordially, expressing a hope that I should have "a good time" with them. I liked him at once; his face was open and honest, and his hand-grip was sincere.

We mounted the smart dogcart, and, leaving my baggage to the servant, drove out into the high-road which ran over the hills, looming purple in the golden sunset haze, to Trowbridge. Five miles through that picturesque, romantic district—one of the fairest in England—skirting the Monk's Park, crossing the old Roman Road between Bath and London, and having ascended the ridge of the steep known as Corsham Side, we descended again through the little old-fashioned village of Atworth by a road which brought us, at last, to the lodge of the Hall. Then, entering the drive, we drove up to the fine old Tudor mansion, low and comfortable looking, with its long façade almost overgrown with ivy. One of "the stately homes of England," it stood commanding a view of the whole range of the Wiltshire hills, the trees and park now bathed in the violets of the afterglow.

From the great hall the guests came forth to meet us in old English welcome, and, as I descended, Beryl herself, fresh in a pink cotton blouse and short cycling skirt, was the first to take my hand.

"At last, Doctor Colkirk!" she cried. "We're all awfully delighted to see you."

Our eyes met, and I saw in hers a look of genuine welcome.

"You are very kind," I answered. "The pleasure is, I assure you, quite mutual."

Then my host introduced me to all the others.

The house, built in the form of a square, with a large courtyard in the centre, was much larger than it appeared from the exterior. The hall, filled as it was with curios and trophies of the chase—for the baronet was a keen sportsman, and his wife, too, was an excellent shot—formed a comfortable lounge. My host and hostess had travelled widely in India and the East, and most of the Atworth collection had been acquired during their visits to the Colonies. The room assigned to me was a bright pleasant one, clean, with old-fashioned chintzes, while from the deep window I could see across the lawn and the deep glen beyond, away over the winding Avon to the darkening hills.

At dinner I was placed next my hostess, with Beryl on my left. The latter wore a striking gown of turquoise blue, which, cut low at the neck, suited her admirably. Her wonderful gold-brown hair had evidently been arranged by a practised maid; but, as I turned to her, before she seated herself, I saw, at her throat, an object which caused me to start in surprise; suspended by a thin gold chain around her neck, a small ornament in diamonds, an exact replica of that curious little charm, shaped like a note of interrogation, which I had taken from her on the fateful day of our marriage, which I wore around my own neck at the moment. As I looked it sparkled and flashed with a thousand brilliant fires. Could that strange little device convey any hidden meaning? It was curious that, having lost one, she should wear another exactly similar.

We sat down together chatting merrily. The baronet's wife was in black lace, her white throat and arms gleaming through the transparency, while her corsage was relieved by crimson carnations. Around the table, too, were several other striking dresses, for the majority of the guests were young, and the house-party was a decidedly smart one. The meal, too, was served with a stateliness which characterised everything in the household of the Pierrepoint-Lanes.

I watched my love carefully, and saw, by her slightly flushed cheeks, that my arrival gave her the utmost satisfaction.

It was in the drawing-room afterwards, when we were sitting together, that I inquired if she had entirely recovered.

"Oh, entirely," she replied. "It was extraordinary, was it not? Do you know whether Doctor Hoefer has visited the house again?"

"I don't know," I responded. "He's so very secret in all his doings. He will tell me nothing—save one thing."

"One thing—what is that?"

"He has discovered the identity of your visitor in black."

"He has?" she cried quickly. "Who was she?"

"A woman whom he called by a curious foreign name," I said, watching Beryl's face the while. "I think he said she was known amongst her intimates as La Gioia."

The light died in an instant from her face.

"La Gioia!" she gasped. "And he knows her?"

"I presume that, as a result of his inquiries, he has made this discovery. His shrewdness is something marvellous; he has succeeded in many cases where the cleverest detectives have utterly failed."

"But how can he have found her?" she went on, greatly agitated by my statement.

"I have no idea. I only tell you this just as he made the announcement to me—without any explanation."

She was silent, her eyes downcast. The ornament at her throat caught the light and glittered. My words had utterly upset her.

"I must tell Nora," she said briefly, at last.

"But I presume that you know this person called La Gioia?" I remarked.

"Know her?" she gasped, looking up at me quickly. "Know her? How should I know her?"

"Because she visited you as a messenger from the friend whose name you refused to tell me."

"I did not know it was her?" she declared wildly. "I cannot think that it was actually that woman."

"You have, then, a reason for wishing not to meet her?"

"I have never met her," she declared in a hard voice. "I do not believe she was actually that woman?"

"I have merely told you Hoefer's statement," I answered. "I know nothing of who or what she is; the name sounds as though she were an actress."

"Did he tell you anything else?" she demanded. "Not another word beyond what you have already said?"

"He only told me that he had discovered her identity."

"He has not found out her motive in visiting me?" she cried quickly.

"Not yet—as far as I am aware."

She breathed more freely. That she desired to preserve the secret of this woman, whom she feared, was plain, but for what reason it was impossible to guess. Indeed, from her attitude, it seemed very much as though she were actually aware that her visitor and La Gioia were one and the same person. I saw by the twitching of her lips that she was nervous, and knew that she now regretted allowing Hoefer to prosecute his inquiries into the curious phenomena.

As I sat there with her, feasting my eyes upon her peerless beauty, I thought it all over, and arrived at the conclusion that, to discover the truth, I must remain patient and watchful, and never for a single instant show "my hand."

I was suspicious of the baronet's wife, and regarded her rather as an enemy than as a friend. She had forced herself upon me with some ulterior motive, which, although not yet apparent, would, I felt confident, be some day revealed.

Fortunately, at that moment, a smart woman in a cream gown went to the piano and began to play the overture from Adams' Poupée de Nuremburg, rendering silence imperative. And afterwards, at my suggestion, my wife and I strolled along to the billiard-room, where we joined a party playing pool. She handled her cue quite cleverly, for a woman, and was frequently applauded for her strokes.

Of the agitation caused by my words not a single trace now remained. She was as gay, merry, and reckless as the others; indeed, she struck me as the very soul of the whole party. There was a smartness about her, without that annoying air of mannishness, which has, alas! developed among girls nowadays, and all that she did was full of that graceful sweetness so typically English.

The billiard-room echoed with laughter, again and again, for the game proved an exciting one, and the men of the party were, of course, gallant to the ladies in their play. There was a careless freedom in it all that was most enjoyable. The baronet was altogether an excellent fellow, eager to amuse everybody. What, I wondered, would he say if he knew of the vagaries of his smart wife, namely, that instead of visiting her relatives, she had run up to London for some purpose unknown? One fact was plain to me before I had been an hour in his house: he allowed her absolute and complete liberty.

We chatted together, sipping our whiskies between our turns at the game, and I found him a true type of the courteous, easy-going English gentlemen. I cannot, even to-day, tell what had prejudiced me against his wife, but somehow I did not like her. My distrust was a vague, undefined one, and I could not account for it.

She was eager to entertain me, it was true, anxious for my comfort, merry, full of smart sayings, and altogether a clever and tactful hostess. Nevertheless, I could not get away from the distinct feeling that I had been invited there with some ulterior motive.

The thought was a curious one, and it troubled me, not only that evening, but far into the silent night, as I lay awake striving to form some theory, but ever in vain.

Of one thing alone I felt absolutely assured—I am quick to distinguish the smallest signs, and I had not failed to become impressed by the truth I had read in her eyes that night—she was not sincere, she was plotting against me. I knew it, and regretted that I had accepted her invitation.

Chapter Twenty Four.

Face to Face.

The days passed merrily until the end of September. There was never a dull moment, for Sir Henry's wife was one of those born hostesses who always gauge accurately the tastes of her guests, and was constantly making arrangements for their pleasure.

All the young ladies—save one young widow—and several of the men had brought their cycles, and many were the enjoyable spins we had in the vicinity. The fashion of cycling nowadays relieves a hostess of much responsibility, for on fine days guests can always amuse themselves, providing that the roads are good. I obtained a very decent machine from Bath, and, at Beryl's side, accompanied the others on excursions into Bath or Chippenham, or, on longer journeys, to Malmesbury, Stroud, and Trowbridge. In her well-cut cycling skirt, cotton blouse, and straw hat, her wealth of hair dressed tightly by her maid, and her narrow waist girdled by a belt of grey chamois leather, she looked smart and lithe awheel. As a rule there is not much poetry in the cycling skirt, for it is generally made in such a manner as to hang baggy at the sides, which become disturbed by every puff of wind, and give the wearer the greatest amount of unnecessary annoyance. The French culottes are practical, if not altogether in accordance with our British view of feminine dress, and that they impart to a woman a considerable chicness, when in the saddle, cannot be denied. Yet there is nothing more graceful, nor more becoming to a woman than the English cycling skirt when cut by an artist in that form.

Sometimes alone, but often accompanied by our hostess, Sir Henry, or some of the guests. Beryl and I explored all the roads in the vicinity. My love constituted herself my guide, showing me the Three Shire Stones (the spot where the counties of Gloucester, Somerset, and Wilts join), the old Abbey of Lacock, the ancient moat and ruins at Kington Langley, the Lord's Barn at Frogwell, the Roman tumuli at Blue Vein, and other objects of interest in the neighbourhood.

After my hard, laborious life in London these bright hours—spent in the fresh air by day, and in dancing and other gaieties at night—were indeed a welcome change. But it was not of that I reflected; my every thought was of her.

A score of times, during the week that had passed since my arrival at Atworth, I had been on the point of declaring my love for her and relating to her all I knew. Yet I hesitated. By so doing I might arouse her indignation. I had spied upon her; I was endeavouring to learn her secret.

Thus, from day to day I lingered at her side, played tennis, walked in the park, danced after dinner, and played billiards in the hour before we parted for the night, with eyes only for her, thoughts only of her, my life was hers alone. Perhaps I neglected the other guests. I think I must have done. Yet, well aware how quickly gossip arises among a house-party, I was always careful to remain sufficiently distant towards her to avoid any suspicion of flirtation. With a woman's natural instinct she sometimes exerted her coquetry over me when we were alone, and by that I felt assured she was by no means averse to my companionship.

Often I gave young Chetwode a passing thought. I hated the prig, and thanked the Fates that he was not there. Sometimes his name was mentioned by one or other of the guests, and always in a manner that showed how her engagement to him was accepted by all her friends. Thus any mention of him caused me a sharp twinge.

During those warm, clear August days, spent with my love, I became somehow less suspicious of her ladyship's actions. Hers was a complex nature; but I could not fail to notice her extreme friendliness towards me, and more than once it struck me that she contrived to bring Beryl and myself together on every possible occasion. The motive puzzled me.

Little time, however, was afforded for rumination, save in the privacy of one's room at night. The round of gaiety was unceasing, and as one guest left another arrived, so that we always had some fresh diversion and merriment. It was open house to all. We men were told that no formalities would be permitted. The tantalus was ever open, the glasses ready, the soda in the ice, and the cigars of various brands placed invitingly in the smoking-room. Hence, every one made himself thoroughly at home, and helped himself, at any hour, to whatever he pleased.

The phantasmagoria of life is very curious. Only a fortnight before I was a penniless medico, feeling pulses and examining tongues in order to earn a shilling or two to keep the wolf from the door, yet, within eight days, I had entered into the possession of a thousand pounds, and was, moreover, the guest of one of the smartest hostesses in England.

I had been at Atworth about a fortnight, and had written twice to Hoefer, but, as yet, had received no response. He was a sorry correspondent, I knew, for when he wrote it was a painful effort with a quill.

Bob Raymond had written me one of those flippant notes characteristic of him; but to this I had not replied, for I could not rid myself of the belief that he had somehow played me false.

One evening, while sitting in the hall with my hostess, in the quiet hour that precedes the dressing-bell, she, of her own accord, began to chat about the curious phenomena in Gloucester Square.

"I have told my husband nothing," she said. "I do hope your friend will discover the cause before we return to town."

"If he does not, then it would be best to keep the door locked," I said. "At present the affair is still unexplained."

"Fortunately Beryl is quite as well as ever—thanks to you and to him."

"It was a happy thought of yours to call me," I said. "Hoefer was the only man in London who could give her back her life, and, if ever the mystery is solved, it is he who will solve it."

I noticed that she was unusually pale, whether on account of the heat, or from mental agitation, I could not determine. The day had been a blazing one—so hot, indeed, that no one had been out before tea. At that moment every one had gone forth except ourselves, and, as she sat in a cane rocking-chair, swinging herself lazily to and fro, she looked little more than a girl, her cream serge tennis-dress imparting to her quite a juvenile appearance.

"I hope you are not bored here, Doctor," she said presently, after we had been talking for some time.

"Bored?" I laughed. "Why, one has not a moment in which to be bored. This is the first half-hour of repose I've had since I arrived here."

She looked at me strangely, and, with a curious smile, said—

"Because you are always so taken up with Beryl."

"With Beryl!" I echoed, starting quickly. "I really did not know that—" I hastened to protest.

"Ah, no," she laughed, "To excuse yourself is useless. The truth is quite patent to me if not to the others."

"The truth of what?" I inquired, with affected ignorance.

"The truth that you love her."

I laughed aloud, scouting the idea. I did not intend to show my hand, for I was never certain of her tactics.

"My dear Doctor," she said presently, "you may deny it, if you like, but I have my eyes open, and I know that in your heart you love her."

"Then you know my feelings better than myself," I responded, inwardly angry that I should have acted in such a manner as to cause her to notice my infatuation.

"One's actions often betray one's heart. Yours have done," she replied. "But I would warn you that love with Beryl is a dangerous game."

"Dangerous! I don't understand you."

"I mean that you must not love her. It is impossible."

"Why impossible?"

"For one simple and very good reason," she responded. Then, looking straight in my face, she added, "Could you, Doctor, keep a secret if I told you one?"

"I think I could. It would not be the first one I've kept."

"Well, it is for the sake of your own happiness that I tell you this," she said. "You will promise never to breathe a word to her if I tell you."

"I promise, of course."

She hesitated, with her dark eyes fixed upon mine. Then she said, in a low voice—

"Beryl is already married."

"To whom?" I asked, so calmly that I think I surprised her.

"To whom I cannot tell you."

"Why not? Surely it is no secret."

"Yes, it is a secret. That is why I dare not tell you her husband's name."

"Is she actually the wife of young Chetwode?"

"Certainly not."

"But she is engaged to him," I observed.

"She is believed to be," my hostess announced, "but such is not really the case."

"And her husband? Where is he?"

It was strange that I should be asking such a question about my own whereabouts.

"In London, I think."

"Then he is quite content that his wife should pose as the affianced bride of young Chetwode? Such an arrangement is certainly rather strange."

"I know nothing of the whys and wherefores," she replied. "I only know that she is already married, and I warn you not to lose your heart to her."

"Well, what you have told me is curious, but I think—"

The remainder of the sentence died upon my lips, for at that moment Beryl burst gaily into the hall, dusty and flushed after cycling, exclaiming—

"We've had such an awfully jolly ride. But the others came along so slowly that Connie and I scorched home all the way from Monkton. How stifling it is to-night!" And she drew the pins from her hat, and, sinking into a chair, began fanning herself, while, at the same moment, her companion, Connie Knowles, a rather smart girl who was one of the party, also entered.

Hence our conversation was interrupted—a fact which for several reasons I much regretted. Yet from her words, it seemed plain that she did not know that I was actually her cousin's husband. She knew Beryl's secret, that she was married, but to whom she was unaware.

There is an old saying among the contadinelli of the Tuscan mountains, "Le donne dicono semure i vero; ma non lo dicono tutto intero." Alas, that it is so true!

That same evening when, after dressing, I descended for dinner, I found Beryl in the study, scribbling a note which, having finished, she gave to the servant.

"Is he waiting?" she inquired.

"Yes, miss."

"Then give it to him—with this;" and she handed the girl a shilling.

When, however, she noticed me standing in the doorway she seemed just a trifle confused. In this message I scented something suspicious; but, affecting to take no notice, walked at her side down the corridor into the hall to await the others. She wore a toilette that night which bore the cut of a first-class couturier. It was a handsome heliotrope gown with a collar of seed pearls. After dining we danced together, and, in so doing, I glanced down at her white, heaving chest, for her corsage was a trifle lower than others she had hitherto worn. I found that for which my eyes were searching—a tiny dark mark low down, and only just visible above the lace edging of the gown—the tattoo-mark which I had discovered on that fateful day, the mark of the three hearts entwined.

What, I wondered, did that indelible device denote?

That it had some significance was certain. I had been waltzing with her for perhaps five minutes, when suddenly I withdrew my hand from her waist, and halting, reeled and almost fell.

"Why, Doctor," she cried, "what's the matter? How pale you are?"

"Nothing," I gasped, endeavouring to reassure her. "A little faintness, that is all. I'll go out into the night." And, unnoticed by the others, I staggered out upon the broad, gravelled terrace which ran the whole length of the house.

She had walked beside me in alarm, and, when we were alone, suggested that she should obtain assistance.

"No," I said; "I shall be better in a moment."

"How do you feel?" she inquired, greatly concerned.

"As though I had suddenly become frozen," I answered. "It is the same sensation as when I entered that room at Gloucester Square."

"Impossible!" she cried in alarm.

"Yes," I said; "it is unaccountable—quite unaccountable."

The circumstance was absolutely beyond credence. I stood there, for a few minutes, leaning upon her arm, which she offered me, and slowly the curious sensation died away, until a quarter of an hour afterwards I found myself quite as vigorous as I had been before. Neither of us, however, danced again, but lighting a cigar, I spent some time strolling with her up and down the terrace, enjoying the calm, warm, starlit night.

We discussed my mysterious seizure a good deal, but could arrive at no conclusion.

After some hesitation I broached the subject which was very near my heart.

"I have heard nothing of late of Chetwode," I said. "Where is he?"

"I don't know," she responded. "His regiment has left Hounslow for York, you know."

"And he is in York?"

"I suppose so."

"Suppose! And yet you are to be his wife!" I exclaimed.

"Who told you that?" she asked quickly, halting and looking straight at me.

"Every one discusses it," I answered. "They say he is to be your husband very shortly. What would he say, I wonder, if he knew that you and I frivol so much together?"

"What right has he to say anything regarding my actions? I am quite free."

"Then he is not your lover?" I inquired in deep earnestness. "Tell me the truth."

"Of course not. We have danced together and walked together, just as you and I have done; but as for love—why, the thing is absurd."

"You do not love him?" I asked.

"Certainly not," she laughed. Then she added, "I never love. That is why I am not like other women."

"Every woman denies the tender passion," I said, smiling.

"Well, I only tell you the truth," she responded, with a slight sigh. "If every woman must love at one time in her life, there must of course be some exceptions. I am one of them."

"Ah, you do yourself an injustice?" I declared. "Every woman has a heart."

She was silent. Then, in a hard strained voice, she answered—

"True; but mine is like stone."

"Why? What has hardened it?"

"Ah, no!" she cried quickly. "You are always, trying to learn my secret, but I can never tell you—never! Let us go in." And, without another word, she passed through the French windows into the billiard-room, where the usual game of pool was in progress and the merry chatter was general.

Like that of her cousin, her nature was a complex one. The more I strove to understand her the more utterly hopeless the analysis became. I loved her—nay, in all the world there was but one woman for my eyes. Superb in beauty and in grace, she was incomparable—perfect.

That night, when the household was at rest, I still sat smoking in my room, puzzled over the curious recurrence of the sensation which seized all who entered the lethal chamber in London. The turret-clock over the stables had chimed half-past one, yet I felt in no mood to turn in. The writing of that hasty note by Beryl was an incident which I had forgotten, but which now came back to me. What if I could discover its nature? She had written it upon the blotting-pad in Sir Henry's study, and the thought occurred to me that I might, perhaps, discover the impression there.

With that object I placed a box of matches in my pocket, switched off my light, and crept in the darkness noiselessly along the corridor. The carpeting was thick, and, being without slippers, I stole along without a sound past the door of Beryl's room, and down the great oaken staircase into the hall.

I had crossed the latter, and had my hand upon the green baize door which kept out the draught of the corridors, and was about to open it, when of a sudden my quick ear caught a sound. In an instant I halted, straining my ears to listen. In the stillness of the night, and especially in the darkness, every sound becomes exaggerated and distorted. I stood there not daring to breathe.

Through the great high windows of the hall, filled with diamond panes like the windows of an ancient church, the faint starlight struggled so that the opposite side of the place was quite light. I glanced around at the shining armour standing weird in the half-light, with visors down and pikes in hand—a row of steel-clad warriors of the days gone by when Atworth was a stronghold. They looked a ghostly lot, and quite unnerved me.

But, as I listened, the suspicious sound again greeted my quick ear, and I heard in the door on the opposite side of the hall, straight before me, a key slowly turn. Even in that dead silence it made but little noise; the lock had evidently been well oiled.

Then cautiously the door gradually opened, and I was no longer alone. The dark figure of a woman advanced, treading so silently that she seemed to walk on air. She came straight towards the spot where I stood watching in the darkness, and I saw that she was dressed in black.

As she reached the centre of the hall the pale light fell upon her face, and, although uncertain, it was sufficient to reveal to me the truth; I was face to face with the woman who had been described by Beryl—the mysterious La Gioia!

Chapter Twenty Five.

The Woman in Black.

The encounter was unexpected and startling. I stood glaring at the dark figure, unable for the moment to move. The dark face, with its keen black eyes, fascinated me; there was a look of evil there. What business could bring her there, stealthily, like a thief?

She had halted in the centre of the hall, and seemed to be examining some object upon the Indian table, whereon tea was always served in the afternoon. The light was just sufficient to reveal that she held something small and white in her hand, but what it was I was unable to distinguish.

The "partial aboulia," as we doctors term the lack of ability to perform intentional acts, which had seized me on discovering the intruder, quickly gave place to an endeavour to conceal myself; and this I accomplished by crouching down behind a large square pedestal whereon stood a giant palm. As I watched I saw her make a tour of the place, examining every object as though in search of something. Then, with deliberation, she passed through the door by which I had entered, and crept noiselessly up the stairs.

She was ascending to the room of the woman who feared her! I stole along after her. It was an adventurous piece of spying, for the slightest creak of the stairs would betray my presence, and oaken stairs creak horribly.

At last I gained the top, and, as I stood, watched her steal noiselessly along the corridor, past Beryl's room, to my own room. She tried the door cautiously, opened it, and entered. As though in disappointment that I was not there she quickly came forth, stood in hesitation listening in the corridor, and then, creeping back, stopped before Beryl's room. Evidently, she was well acquainted with the geography of the house, and knew who occupied the various chambers.

In the corridor it was much lighter than in the hall, and, as she came to a standstill before Beryl's door, I was quite close to her, crouching on the dark stair, my head only on a level with the floor of the corridor. It was then I made a discovery which was somewhat puzzling: while her right hand was free, on the left she wore a black glove.

She bent at the door, peered into the keyhole, and, having listened in order to satisfy herself that Beryl was asleep, slowly turned the handle to try if it were locked.

Would she enter? I stood watching her actions with bated breath. That she was there with evil intent was absolutely certain.

The lock yielded, and, pushing open the door very slowly, she stole in on tiptoe, closing it after her.

What should I do? My love was in deadly peril—of that I felt certain. She had defied the Major, and the revenge of that all-powerful but unknown person, La Gioia, was upon her. She was alone—asleep, and at her mercy!

To dash in and seize her would be to alarm the house and, perhaps, compromise my loved one. Yet what could I do to save her? I had seen by the evil glint in her eyes that she was there with fell intent, and I knew by the cautious manner in which she moved, without hesitation or fear, that she was no amateur at such nocturnal visits. Indeed, she moved like a dark shadow, gliding without the slightest noise until one might almost have believed her to be some supernatural visitant.

It was my duty, however, to protect my love, no matter at what cost. I had come there for that purpose, having a distinct foreboding that some deadly peril surrounded her; therefore, now was my time to act, to meet that woman face to face and to demand an explanation.

Upon this decision I acted without further delay, for creeping as noiselessly as she had done, I reached the door and slowly turned the handle in order to burst in unexpectedly upon her. The handle turned, but the door would not open; she had locked it behind her.

I bent to the keyhole. All was dark within. There was no sound. The noise I had made by trying the door had, no doubt, alarmed her, and she was standing within preparing to make a sudden dash for liberty.

I drew myself up at the door prepared. Those moments were full of excitement. I held my breath, straining my ears to listen. There was no sound. The silence was like that of the grave.

My love was within that room, and her enemy was at her side!

Should I arouse the household? Again I hesitated, fearing lest I should compromise Beryl. Of a sudden, however, I recollected that in many houses the doors of the bedrooms frequently bear similar locks, and finding that the key had been removed by the intruder—possibly for the purpose of watching my movements from the inside—it occurred to me that I might try the key of my own room.

Yet if I left my post she might escape; she was evidently watching her opportunity.

Fully ten minutes passed, each second ticked out loudly by the long grandfather's clock at the end of the corridor, until I could stand the tension no longer, and, receding slowly backwards, with my eyes still upon the door, ready for La Gioia's dash for liberty, I reached my own room and secured the key.

Then, slipping back again, I placed the key swiftly in the lock, heedless of the noise it made, and turned it. The lock yielded, and a second later I stood within the room.

An involuntary cry of amazement escaped me, and I drew back. I dashed towards the bed, but it had not been slept in. The room, with its great mirror draped with silk, and its silver toilet-set catching the pale light, was empty! The window stood open, and, springing towards it, I saw to my dismay a rope-ladder reaching to the ground. Both La Gioia and my well-beloved had disappeared.

I looked out, but all was dark across the park. The night wind rustled in the trees, and a dog was howling dismally in the kennels. Could Beryl have been awaiting La Gioia, and have left in her company? The discovery utterly dismayed me.

I ran to my room, obtained a cap and boots, and, returning, passed through the open window, descending by the ladder to the terrace.

Around the house I dashed like a madman, and down the drive towards the lodge-gates, halting suddenly now and then with my ear to the wind, eager to distinguish any sound of movement. I was utterly without clue to guide me as to the direction the fugitives had taken. Four or five roads and paths led from the house, in various directions, to Atworth village, to Corsham, and to Lacock, while one byway through the wood led out upon the old high-road to, Bath. The latter went straight into a dark copse at the rear of the house, and would afford ample concealment for any one wishing to get away unobserved. All the other roads cut across the park, and any one travelling along them would be visible for some distance. Therefore, I started down the byway in question, entering the wood and traversing it as noiselessly as I could, and emerged at last into the broad, white high-road which I knew so well, having cycled and driven over it dozens of times.

I calculated that the fugitives had about ten to twelve minutes' start, and if they had really taken the road, I must be close upon them. The road ascended steadily all the way from the Wormwood Farm to Kingsdown, yet I slackened not my pace until I gained the crest of the hill. The moon had come out from behind the clouds, and the night was so light that any object upon that white open road could be seen for a long distance. Having gained the hilltop at the junction of the road to Wraxall, I stood and strained my eyes down both highways, but to my disappointment saw no one. Either I had passed them while they had hidden themselves in the wood, or I had mistaken the direction they had taken.

The presence in the house of that sinister woman in black, her mode of exit, and the startling fact that Beryl was missing, had, I think, unnerved me. As I stood reflecting I regretted that I had relied too much upon my own strategy, and had not aroused the household. In my constant efforts to preserve the secret of my well-beloved I had made a fatal mistake.

My mind had become confused by these constantly recurring mysteries. As a medical man I knew that all mental troubles involve diseases of the brain. The more complex troubles, such as my own at that moment, are still wrapped in obscurity. To the psychologist there are, of course, certain guiding principles through the maze of facts which constitute the science of the mind; but, after all, he knows practically nothing about the laws which govern the influence of mind over body. I had acted foolishly and impulsively. Both the women had fled.

I took the road down the hill to Wraxall, and thence, by a circular route by way of Ganbrook Farm and the old church at Atworth, back to the Hall. I hoped that they might take that road to Bath, but, although I walked for more than an hour, I met not a soul. A church clock chimed three as I came down the hill from Kingsdown, and it was already growing light ere I gained the terrace of the Hall again. I climbed back into Beryl's room by the ladder still suspended there. Her absence was as yet undiscovered. Everything was just as I had left it an hour and a half before. I was undecided, at that moment, whether to alarm the household or to affect ignorance of the whole thing and await developments of the strange affair. Judged from all points the latter course seemed the best; therefore, still in indecision, I crept back to my room, and, entering there, closed the door.

I sank into a chair, exhausted after my walk, when a sudden pain shot through me from head to foot, causing me to utter an involuntary cry. The next instant the same sensation of being frozen crept over me, as it had done outside that room in Gloucester Square, and again on the previous night when dancing with my beloved. The same rigidity of my muscles, the same aphasia and amnesia, the same complex symptoms that I had before experienced, and so well remembered, were again upon me. My lower limbs seemed frozen and lifeless, my heart was beating so faintly that it seemed almost imperceptible, and my senses seemed so utterly dulled that I was unable either to cry out or to move.

If I had but a little of that curious liquid which Hoefer had injected! I blamed myself for not asking him to give me some in case of emergency. The unknown woman in black had left again behind her the curious unseen influence that so puzzled the greatest known medico-legist.

The sensation was much sharper, and of far longer duration, than that which had so suddenly fallen upon me when dancing. Reader, I can only describe it, even now, I sit recounting to you the curious story, as the icy touch of the grim Avenger. The hand of Death was actually upon me.

I think that the automatic processes of my brain must have ceased. Without entering into a long description, which the majority of the laity would not properly understand, it is but necessary to say that the lowest, or "third level" of the brain includes all the functions which the spinal cord and its upper termination, which we call the "medulla," are able to perform alone—that is, without involving necessarily the activity of the nervous centres and brain areas which lie above them. The "third level" functions are those of life-sustaining processes generally—breathing, heart-beat and vaso-motor action—which secure the circulation of the blood. It was this portion of the brain, controlling the automatic processes, which had become paralysed. I needed, I knew, an artificial stimulation—some agent by which the physiological processes might be started again. What if they would not start again normally!

I sat in my chair, rigid as a corpse, unable to move or to utter a sound—cold, stiff, and as I well knew, resembling in every way a person lifeless. Slight consciousness remained to me, but, after a while, even that faded, and I knew not then what followed.

The period of blank unconsciousness appeared to me but a few minutes, but it must have been hours, for when I awoke the morning sun was high and was shining full in my face as I sat there. My limbs were cramped and my head was heavy, but there was no pain with my returning sensibility, as is generally the case after a period of insensibility. I rose with difficulty, and, staggering unevenly to the window, looked out. Upon the terrace two men were idly strolling as was the habit of those who came down early, awaiting the breakfast bell. I glanced at the timepiece and saw that it was about nine o'clock.

Had Beryl's absence yet been discovered?

I glanced over to my bed, and then recollected that I had not undressed. Truly that night had been an eventful one. La Gioia had actually been in that room. In an instant, recollections of my midnight vigil and my chase crowded upon me. Surely, if that rope-ladder were still suspended from the window of the room occupied by my love, those two men strolling there must have noticed it!

I opened my own window and leaned out to look. No, it had been removed. My loved one's absence had been discovered.

The breakfast bell rang and aroused me to a sense of responsibility. I knew of the secret visit of La Gioia, and it was my duty to reveal it so that the truth might be ascertained. Therefore, I shaved quickly, changed my clothes, and tossed about my bed so that the maids should not suspect my wakefulness.

There was merry chatter outside in the corridor as the guests descended, but, although I listened, I could hear no mention of Beryl's disappearance. On completion of my toilet I opened my door and followed them down. Yet scarcely had I got to the head of the stairs when that same now-familiar sensation came upon me, like the touch of an icy hand. I gripped the old oaken banisters and stood cold and dumb. The same phenomena had occurred in my room as in that room of mystery at Gloucester Square. The thing utterly staggered belief.

Nevertheless, almost as swiftly as the hand of Death touched me was it withdrawn, and, walking somewhat unsteadily, I went down and along the corridor to the breakfast room.

The chatter was general before I entered, but there was a sudden silence as I opened the door.

"Why, Doctor Colkirk?" cried a voice, "this isn't like you to be late. You're an awful sluggard this morning!"

I glanced quickly across at the speaker and held my breath in amazement. It was Beryl! She was sitting there, in her usual place looking fresh in her pale blue cotton blouse, the merriest and happiest of the party.

What response I made I have no idea; I only know that I saluted my hostess mechanically and then walked to my chair like a man in a dream.

Chapter Twenty Six.

Husband and Wife.

Personally, I am one of those who pay no tribute of grateful admiration to those who have oppressed mankind with the dubious blessings of the penny post. Just as no household, which is adorned with the presence of pen-propelling young ladies, is ever without its due quantity of morning letters, so no breakfast table is quite complete if the post-bag has been drawn blank. The urn may hiss, eggs may be boiled to the precise degree of solidity, frizzling strips of "home-cured" may smile upon you from dish of silver, or golden marmalade may strive to allure you with the richness of its hue, but if the morning letters are not present the picture is incomplete. They are the crowning glory of the British breakfast table.

For a good many days my correspondents had happily left me in the lurch, but as I sank into my seat I saw upon my plate a single letter, and took it up mechanically. As a rule the handwriting of the envelope betrayed the writer, but this possessed the additional attraction of unfamiliar penmanship. It had been addressed to Rowan Road, and Bob had forwarded it.

The communication was upon paper of pale straw-colour, headed "Metropolitan Police, T. Division, Brentford," and signed "J. Rowling, sub-divisional inspector." There were only two or three lines, asking whether I could make it convenient to appoint an hour when he could call upon me, as he wished to consult me upon "a matter of extreme importance." The matter referred to was, of course, the tragedy at Whitton. Truth to tell, I was sick at heart of all this ever-increasing maze of circumstances, and placed the letter in my pocket with a resolve to allow the affair to rest until I returned to London on the conclusion of my visit.

The receipt of it, however, had served one purpose admirably: it had given me an opportunity to recover my surprise at discovering Beryl sitting there opposite me, bright and vivacious, as though nothing unusual had occurred. The letter which I had seen her writing in the study on the previous evening had been, I now felt convinced, to make an appointment which she had kept.

But with whom?

I glanced at my hostess, who was busily arranging with those near her at table for a driving party to visit the Haywards at Dodington Park, and wondered whether she could be aware of the strange midnight visitant. I contrived to have a brief chat with her after breakfast was finished, but she appeared in entire ignorance of what had transpired during the night. I lit a cigarette, and as usual strolled around for a morning visit to the kennels with Sir Henry. On returning I saw my well-beloved seated beneath one of the great trees near the house, reading a novel. The morning was hot, but in the shade it was delightful. As I crossed the grass to her she raised her head, and then, smiling gladly, exclaimed—

"Why, I thought you'd gone to Dodington with the others, Doctor Colkirk?"

"No," I answered, taking a chair near her; "I'm really very lazy this hot weather."

How charming she looked in her fresh cotton gown and large flop-hat of Leghorn straw trimmed with poppies.

"And I prefer quiet and an interesting book to driving in this sun. I wonder they didn't start about three, and come home in the sunset. But Nora's always so wilful."

Though as merry as was her wont, I detected a tired look in her eyes. Where had she been during the long night—and with whom? The silence was only disturbed by the hum of the insects about us and the songs of the birds above. The morning was a perfect one.

"I found it very oppressive last night," I said, carefully approaching the subject upon which I wanted to talk to her. "I couldn't sleep, so I came out here into the park."

"Into the park?" she echoed quickly, and I saw by her look that she was apprehensive.

"Yes. It was a beautiful night—cool, refreshing, and starlit."

"You were alone?"

I hesitated. Then, looking her straight in the face, answered—

"No, I was not. I had yourself as company."

The colour in an instant left her cheeks.

"Me?" she gasped.

"Yes," I replied, in a low, earnest voice. "You were also in the park last night."

She was silent.

"I did not see you," she faltered. Then, as though recovering her self-possession, she added, with some hauteur, "And even if I chose to walk here after every one had gone to rest, I really don't think that you have any right to question my actions."

"Forgive me," I said quickly. "I do not question you in the least; I have no right to do so. You are certainly free to do as you please, save where you neglect your own interests or place yourself in peril—as you did last night."

"In peril of what?" she demanded defiantly.

"In peril of falling a victim to the vengeance of an enemy."

"I don't understand you."

"Then I will speak more frankly, Miss Wynd, in the hope that you will be equally frank with me," I said, my eyes fixed upon her. "You were last night, or, rather, at an early hour this morning, with a person whom you have met on a previous occasion."

"I admit that. It is, indeed, useless to deny it," she answered.

"And yet, on the last occasion that you met, you nearly lost your life! Was it wise?"

"Nearly lost my life?" she echoed. "I do not follow you."

"The woman in black who called at Gloucester Square on that evening not so many days ago. You surely remember her? Was it not after her departure that her unaccountable, evil influence remained?"

"Certainly. But what of her?"

"You were with her last night."

"With her?" she gasped, surprised. "I certainly was not."

"Do you deny having seen her?" I demanded.

"Most assuredly," she responded promptly. "You certainly did not see us together."

"And your companion was not a woman?"

"No; it was a man."

"Who?"

"I have already told you that I object to any one interfering in my private affairs."

"A lover?" I said, with some asperity perhaps. "You are entirely at liberty to think what you please. I only deny that I have set eyes upon my mysterious visitor since that evening in Gloucester Square."

"Well, she was in the house last night," I answered decisively. "She was in your room."

"In my room?" gasped my well-beloved, in alarm. "Impossible?"

"I watched her enter there," I replied; and then continuing, gave her an exact account of all that transpired—how she had first entered my room, and how the strange evil of her presence had so strangely affected me afterwards.

"It's absolutely astounding," she declared. "I was utterly ignorant of it all. Are you absolutely certain that it was the same woman?"

"The description given of her by yourself and your cousin's servant is exact. She came here with some distinctly sinister purpose, that is quite evident."

"But she must have entered by the servants' quarters if she passed through the hall as you have described. She seemed to have been in search of us both."

"No doubt," I answered. "And if, as you say, you were absent from the room at the time, it is evident that she went straight out into the park in search of you. In that case she would have left the room before I tried the door, and would be ignorant of the fact that I had detected her presence in the house."

"But what could she want with us?" she asked in a voice which told me that this unexpected revelation had unnerved her.

"Ah, that I cannot tell," I responded. "She came here with an evil purpose, and fortunately we were both absent from our rooms."

She knit her brows in thought. Possibly she was recalling some event during her midnight walk.

"And you say that you actually experienced in your own room, on returning there, an exactly similar sensation to that which we all felt at Gloucester Square?"

"Exactly."

"Do you know," she faltered, "I felt the same sensation in my own room this morning—very faintly, but still the same feeling of being chilled. What is your private opinion about it, Doctor?"

"My opinion is that there is a conspiracy afoot against both of us," I responded very earnestly. "For some unaccountable reason we are marked down as victims—why, I cannot tell. You will forgive me for speaking plainly, but I believe that you alone hold the key to the mystery, that you alone know the motive of this vengeance—if vengeance it be—and if you were to tell me frankly of the past we might unite to vanquish our enemies."

"What do you mean by the past?" she inquired, with just a touch of indignation.

"There are several questions I have put to you which you have refused to answer," I replied. "The light which you could throw upon two or three points, now in obscurity, might lead me to a knowledge of the whole truth."

She sighed, as though the burden of her thoughts oppressed her.

"I have told you all I can," she answered.

"No; you have told me all you dare. Is not that a more truthful way of putting it?"

She nodded, but made no response.

"You have feared to tell me of the one fact concerning yourself which has, in my belief, the greatest bearing upon your perilous situation."

"And what is that?"

"The fact that you are married!"

Her face blanched to the lips, her hands trembled and for a moment my words held her dumb.

"Who told you that?" she gasped, in a low voice.

"I knew it long ago," I replied.

"Nora has betrayed my secret," she observed in a hard voice.

"No," I declared; "your cousin has told me nothing. I have known the fact for months past."

"For months past! How?"

"You are not frank with me," I replied; "therefore I may be at liberty to preserve what secrets I think best."

"I—I do not deny it," she faltered. Then, in a voice trembling with emotion, she added, "Ah, Doctor Colkirk, if you knew all that I have suffered you would quite understand my fear lest any one should discover my secret. I often wonder how it is that I have not taken my own life long, long ago."

"No," I said in deep sympathy, taking her hand. "Bear up against all these troubles. Let me assist you as your friend."

"But you cannot," she declared despairingly, tears welling in her eyes. "You can only assist me by keeping my secret. Will you promise me to do that?"

"Most certainly," I replied. "But I want to do more. I want to penetrate the veil of mystery which seems to surround your marriage. I want—"

"You can never do that," she interrupted quickly. "I have tried and tried, but have failed."

"Why?"

"Because, strange though it may seem, I am entirely unaware of the identity of my husband. I have never seen him."

I was silent. Should I reveal to her the truth? She could not believe me, if I did. What proof could I show her?

"And you do not know his name?"

"No; I do not even know his name," she answered. "All I know is that by this marriage I am debarred for ever from all love and happiness. I have nothing to live for—nothing! Each day increases the mystery, and each day brings to me only bitterness and despair. Ah! how a woman may suffer and still live."

"Have you no means by which to discover the identity of your unknown husband?" I inquired.

"None whatever," she answered. "I know that I am married—beyond that, nothing."

"And who else is in possession of this secret?" I inquired.

"Nora."

"No one else?"

"No one—to my knowledge."

"But you are, I understand, engaged to marry Cyril Chetwode," I said, anxious to get the truth. "How can you marry him if you are really a wife?"

"Ah! that's just it!" she cried. "I am the most miserable girl in all the world. Everything is so hazy, so enshrouded in mystery. I am married, and yet I have no husband."

"But is it not perhaps best that, under the circumstances, you should be apart," I said. "He may be old, or ugly, or a man you could never love."

"I dread to think of it," she said hoarsely. "Sometimes I wonder what he is really like, and who he really is."

"And, at the same time, you love Cyril Chetwode?" I said, the words almost choking me.

I saw she loved that young ape, and my heart sank within me.

"We are very good friends," she answered.

"But you love him? Why not admit it?" I said.

"And if I do—if I do, it is useless—all useless," she murmured.

"Yes," I observed, "it is useless. You are already married."

"No!" she cried, holding up her tiny hand as though to stay my words. "Do not let us talk of it. I cannot bear to think. The truth hangs like a shadow over my life."

"Does Chetwode know?" I inquired. "Is he aware that you can never be his?"

"He knows nothing. He loves me, and believes that one day we shall many. Indeed, now that he has succeeded to the estate, he sees no reason why our marriage should be delayed, and is pressing me for an answer."

Her breast heaved and fell quickly beneath her starched blouse. I saw how agitated she was, and how, with difficulty, she was restraining her tears.

"What answer can you give him?"

"Ah!" she cried, "what answer, indeed. Was there ever woman before who knew not her husband, or who suffered as I am suffering?"

"Your case is absolutely unique," I said. "Have you not endeavoured to solve the problem? Surely, from the official record of the marriage, it is possible to obtain your husband's name? You have a wedding-ring, I suppose?" I said, my thoughts running back to that fateful moment when I had placed the golden bond of matrimony upon her hand.

"Yes," she answered, and, placing her hand within her bodice, drew forth the ring suspended by a narrow blue ribbon; "it is here."

I took it in my hand with a feeling of curiosity. How strange it was! That was the very ring which I had placed upon her finger when in desperation I had sold myself to the Tempter.

"Have you no idea whatever of the circumstances of your marriage? Do you know nothing?"

"Absolutely nothing—save that I am actually married."

"The identity of the man who placed this ring upon your hand is an enigma?"

"Yes. I found it upon my finger; that is all that I am aware of. I changed my name, yet I am ignorant of what my new name really is."

A sound of wheels approaching up the drive greeted our ears, but I still held the ring in the hollow of my hand.

"Shall I tell you the true name of your husband?" I said earnestly, looking straight into those deep, clear eyes.

"What?" she cried, starting in quick surprise; "you know it? Surely, that is impossible!"

"Yes," I said in a low voice; "I know it."

At that instant the ralli-car, which had evidently been to Corsham Station, dashed past us towards the house, interrupting our conversation and causing us both to raise our heads.

At the side of Barton, the coachman, there sat a stranger, who, as he passed, turned his head aside to glance at us. Our eyes met. In an instant I recognised him. It was none other than the man for whom I had been in active search through all these weeks—the Tempter!

Chapter Twenty Seven.

The Tempter.

The small-eyed man, to whom I had sold myself that fateful day, caught sight of Beryl, and, raising his grey felt hat in recognition, pulled up, and swung himself down from the trap. I glanced at my love and saw that her face was blanched to the lips. The meeting was, to her, evidently a most unexpected one.

Beneath the seat I saw a well-worn kit-bag, and a gun-case, which showed that he had come on a visit. Smartly dressed in light grey, he wore a button-hole of pink carnations, which gave him an air of gaiety and irresponsibility scarcely in keeping with his age.

"Ah, my dear Miss Wynd!" he cried, advancing to her with outstretched hand. "I'm so delighted to find you here. It is a long time since we met."

"Yes," she answered in a voice which trembled with suppressed excitement. "But I had no idea that you were coming down," she added. "Nora told me nothing."

"I too had no idea of visiting you, until the day before yesterday," he said. "I've been abroad for nearly a year, and only arrived back in town three days ago, when I found Sir Henry's, invitation, a month old, lying at my club. I wired to ask if I might still accept it, and here I am."

He stood with his legs apart, his hat set rather jauntily upon his head, looking an entirely different person to that crabbed, strange old fellow who sat behind the bar of sunlight, with the banknotes in his claw-like fingers, every detail of that scene was as vivid in my memory as though it had occurred but yesterday. Again, I looked into his face. Yes, I had no doubt whatever that it was he.

"I—I am the first to bid you welcome to Atworth," Beryl said. "Nora has gone over with some of the people to visit the Haywards, at Dodington. There's a flower-show there."

"I quite remember," he exclaimed, "I went over there last year. Lady Dyrham drove us. Do you recollect?"

"Of course," she laughed. "And how it rained too. My new frock was quite spoilt, and I had a bad cold for a fortnight afterwards. I'm not likely to easily forget that drive home."

"Because of the spoilt frock?" he laughed, raising his small eyes to me.

"Yes, I suppose that's what has impressed itself upon my memory. We women are never forgetful where clothes are concerned."

"And who's here? Anybody I know?" he inquired.

"Oh, there are the Pirries and the Tiremans, as usual, and, of course, Lady Dyrham," she answered. Then, a moment later she added, "This is Doctor Colkirk—Mr Ashwicke. Let me introduce you, if you have not already met before."

"We have not had that pleasure," said the Tempter, turning to me and raising his hat.

He remained perfectly calm, betraying no sign whatever of recognition. In this I saw an intention on his part to deny all knowledge of our previous acquaintance.

His keen eyes glanced at me quickly, and, as though in that moment he gauged exactly my strength of character, he expressed his pleasure at our meeting, and hoped that we should all spend as pleasant a time as he had done last year.

"Here one has not an hour for leisure," he laughed. "Sir Henry and his wife are really a wonderful pair as host and hostess. You've already found them so, I've no doubt."

"Yes," I responded mechanically, his marvellous self-control staggering me. "The house-party is a very jolly one."

"I've been abroad," he went on. "But I'm pleased to be at home again. There's nothing like an English country house in summer. It is an ideal existence."

"How long have you been away?" I inquired, anxious to ascertain his tactics.

"Nearly a year. After leaving here last summer, I spent a week in London and then left for Vienna. Afterwards I went south, spending greater part of the winter in Cairo, thence to Bombay, and returned for the late spring in Florence, and afterwards wandered about France, until three days ago I found myself again back in England."

"And you did not return once during the whole year?" I asked, with affected carelessness.

His small eyes darted quickly to mine, as though in suspicion.

"No," he responded promptly. "It is almost a year to-day since I was in England."

Then, noticing Barton waiting with the trap, he ordered him to take the luggage to the house, while all three of us walked up the drive together.

A sudden change had passed over Beryl. She knew this man Ashwicke, her attitude towards him was that of fear. The looks they had exchanged at first meeting were sufficient to convince me that there was some hidden secret between them.

"Nora cannot be aware of your arrival," Beryl said, as we walked together up the sunny drive to the house. "Otherwise she would either have told me, or she certainly would have remained at home to receive you."

"Why should she?" he laughed lightly. "Surely we are old enough friends to put aside all ceremony. I'm a rolling stone, as you know, and I hate putting people out."

"Yes," she said; "you are a rolling stone, and no mistake. I don't think any one travels further afield than you do. You seem to be always travelling."

"I've only spent six months in England these last eight years," he responded. "To me, England is only bearable in August or September. A little shooting, and I'm off again."

"You only come back because you can't get decent sport on the Continent?" I said, for want of other observation to make.

"Exactly," he answered. "'La Chasse,' as the French call it, is never a success across the Channel. Some rich Frenchman started a fox-hunt down at Montigny, in the Seine and Marne, not long ago, and part of the paraphernalia was an ambulance wagon flying the red-cross flag. A fact! I went to the first meet myself."

"The French are no sportsmen," I said.

"The same everywhere, all over the Continent. Sport is chic, therefore the get-up of sportsmen must be outrageous and striking. No foreigner enjoys it. He shoots or hunts just because it's the correct thing to do. Here in England one kills game for the love of the thing. To the Frenchman in patent leather, sport is only a bore."

He had all the irresponsible air of the true cosmopolitan, yet his assertion that he had been absent from England a year was an unmitigated lie. Knowing this, I was doubtful of all his chatter.

On entering the hall, Beryl, as mistress of the house in her cousin's absence, rang for the servants and told them to take Mr Ashwicke's baggage to the same room he had occupied last year, sending Barton round to the kennels to find Sir Henry and inform him of the arrival of his guest.

In the meantime, Ashwicke had tossed his hat aside, and seated himself cross-legged, in one of the low cane-chairs, making himself thoroughly at home.

"Well," he said, stretching himself, "it is really very pleasant, Miss Wynd, to be here once again. I have so many pleasant recollections of last year—when I spent three weeks with you. What a merry time we had!"

"I hope you'll remain here longer this time," she said in a dry, unnatural voice.

"You're awfully kind—awfully kind," he answered.

"I always enjoy myself under Sir Henry's roof, both here and in town."

The baronet entered, and the greeting between the two men was a cordial one.

"You'll forgive me, Ashwicke, won't you?" Sir Henry said a moment later. "I quite forgot to tell my wife, and she's gone off to the flower-show at Dodington; must support the local things, you know."

"Of course, of course," responded the other. "I quite understand, and I know I'm welcome."

"That you certainly are," Sir Henry said, turning and ordering the man to bring whisky and sodas. "Let's see, the last letter I had from you was from Alexandria, back in the Spring. Where have you been since then?"

"Oh, knocking about here and there, as usual. I can't stay long in one place, you know. It's a bad complaint I have."

"Well, I'm glad to see you—very glad," the baronet declared

heartily. "I hope you'll stay some time. Have you brought your gun?"

"Of course," the other laughed. "I shouldn't think, of coming to Atworth without it."

While they were chatting thus, I looked at him, recalling every feature. Yes, it was the same face, scarcely perhaps the same sinister countenance as it had appeared to me on that well-remembered day, but nevertheless the face of the Tempter.

I lounged back in my chair, close to that of my well-beloved, filled with wonderment.

That the new-comer recognised me was certain, for I had been introduced by name. And that he had been unaware of my presence as guest there was equally certain. Yet he had, on encountering us together, preserved a self-control little short of marvellous.

I glanced at Beryl. She was sitting listening to the conversation of the two men, and regarding Ashwicke covertly from beneath her lashes. I knew by her manner that, although she had outwardly affected pleasure at his arrival, she, in her heart, regarded him as an enemy. He, on his part, however, was perfectly confident, and sat sipping his drink and laughing merrily with his host.

What, I wondered, was passing within Beryl's mind. She knew this man as Ashwicke, while I knew him as her own father, Wyndham Wynd. The latter were evidently a name and position both assumed, and, after all, as he sat there with the easy refined air of a gentleman, I could scarcely believe him to be an adventurer. Surely Sir Henry knew him well, or they would not be on terms of such intimate friendship.

But now I had discovered him, I meant, at all hazards, to probe the truth.

Beryl, who had spoken but little after Sir Henry's entrance, rose at last, announcing her intention of going out beneath the trees again. Her words conveyed an invitation to accompany her; therefore I strolled out at her side, anxious to learn from her what I could regarding the man to whom she had introduced me.

How curiously events occur in our lives. Many of the ordinary circumstances of everyday existence which we pass by unnoticed seem to be governed by some laws of which we have absolutely no knowledge whatever. Reader, in your own life, there has occurred some strange combinations of circumstances quite unaccountable, yet by them the whole course of your existence has been altered. You may have noticed them, or you may not. You may call it Fate, or you may be a follower of that shadowy religion called Luck, yet it remains the same—the unexpected always happens.

Who indeed would have expected that my wife herself would have introduced me to the man who had so cleverly baited the trap into which I had fallen? And yet it is always so. There is a mysterious all-ruling spirit of perversity ever at work in that complicated series of events which go to make up what we term life.

"You were telling me that you know my husband," she said quickly, as we crossed the grass together. "Our conversation was interrupted by that man's arrival."

Such reference to the new-comer showed me that she was not well-disposed towards him.

"Do you know," I said, "I believe that we've met somewhere before. I know his face."

"Possibly. But why Sir Henry should have invited him here again, I can't imagine."

"Was his company so disagreeable?" I asked.

"Disagreeable?" she echoed. "He is detestable."

"Why?"

"Oh, for many reasons," she responded ambiguously; "I have never liked him."

"He says that he is always abroad," I remarked. "But I'm confident that we have met somewhere in England."

"He did not apparently recognise you, when I introduced you."

"No. He didn't wish to. The circumstances of our meeting were not such as to leave behind any pleasant recollections."

"But you told me that you knew the identity of my husband," she said, after a pause, as we strolled together in the shadow of the great oaks. "Were you really serious?"

"No, I was not serious," I answered quickly, for the unexpected arrival of this man who called himself Ashwicke, and whose name appeared in the London Directory as occupier of the house in Queen's-gate Gardens, caused me to hesitate to tell her the truth. The manner in which they had met made it quite plain that some secret understanding existed between them. It seemed possible that this man had actually occupied the house before the present owner, Mrs Stentiford.

"Then why did you say such a thing?" she asked, in a tone of reproach. "My position is no matter for joking."

"Certainly not," I hastened to declare. "Believe me, Miss Wynd, that you have all my sympathy. You are unfortunately unique as one who is married and yet without knowledge either of her husband or his name."

"Yes," she sighed, a dark shadow of despair crossing her handsome face. "There is a shadow of evil ever upon me, just as puzzling and mysterious as the chill touch of that unseen influence which at intervals strikes both of us."

"And the presence of this man adds to your uneasiness. Is that not so?"

She nodded, but no word escaped her.

"I noticed when you met and he descended from the trap that he was not your friend."

"What caused you to suspect that?" she inquired quickly.

"The man's face betrayed his feeling towards you. He is your enemy."

"Yes," she answered slowly, as though carefully weighing each word; "he is my enemy—my bitterest enemy."

"Why?"

"Because I have a firm suspicion that he has discovered the secret of my marriage—that he alone knows who my unknown husband really is."

And turning her wonderful eyes to mine, her troubled breast slowly rose and fell.

When, oh, when should I succeed in solving the maddening problem and be free to make confession of the truth?

Chapter Twenty Eight.

Sought Out.

With untiring astuteness I watched every movement of the new-comer, but detected nothing suspicious in his actions. We lunched together, only five of us, the others being away at Dodington, and were a merry party. The man with the small eyes was excellent company, full of witty sayings and droll stories, and was really an acquisition to our party.

Yet I noticed that he spoke little with Beryl, as, though some secret understanding existed between them. And when he did address her she answered him vacantly, as though her thoughts were afar off.

That night, on the return of the party from the flower-show, his arrival was hailed with delight. At all events he was a very popular person at Atworth. He seemed rejuvenated since we had last met, and appeared fully twenty years younger than on the night when he had tempted me.

I had many chats with him. I played him at billiards, and was afterwards his partner at whist before we parted for the night. I did this in order to put him off his guard, if possible, and to induce him to believe that I had not recognised him. I had not yet decided how to act.

When at midnight I left my companions, entered my room, and closed the door, that strange, weird influence again made itself felt upon me. My lower limbs became benumbed, my blood seemed frozen in my veins.

I stood glancing around the bedroom in fear and wondering. There was nothing supernatural there, and yet this unseen influence was as the finger of Evil. The strange sensation was not of long duration, but gradually faded until I found myself in my normal state. I tested my temperature with my thermometer, and saw that I had just a slight tendency to fever—due, I supposed, to alarm and excitement.

Then, having satisfied myself that my motor nerves, which had become partially paralysed, had regained their strength, and that the sensitive portion of the spinal nervous system, that had been affected, had returned to its normal capacity, I turned in and tried to sleep.

I say I tried to sleep, but I think, if the truth were told, I did not try. My brain was too perturbed by the events of that day. Beneath that very roof the Tempter was actually sleeping. I had shaken his hand, and played billiards with him. Truly, I had been patient in my efforts to analyse and dissect the various complications of that extraordinary mystery.

At sunrise I dressed, and on stepping from my room out into the fresh air of the corridor, I again felt that bewildering influence upon me, quite distinctly; yet not so strong as to cause me any inconvenience. The feeling was a kind of cold, creepy one, without any sudden shock.

During the day I lounged at Beryl's side, endeavouring to obtain from her the truth of her midnight escapade. But she would tell me absolutely nothing. The man who had posed as her father was undoubtedly her enemy, and she held him in deadly fear. It was this latter fact that caused me at last to make a resolution, and in the idle hour before the dressing-bell went for dinner, I contrived to stroll alone with him out across the park.

With a good cigar between his lips, he walked as jauntily as a man of twenty, notwithstanding his grey hairs. He laughed and chatted merrily, recounting to me all the fun of last year's house-party, with its ill-natured chatter and its summer flirtations.

Suddenly, when we were a long way from the house, skirting the quiet lake that lay deep in a hollow surrounded by a small wood, I turned to him resolutely, saying—

"Do you know that I have a distinct recollection that we have met before?"

He started almost imperceptibly, and glanced at me quickly with his small round eyes.

"I think not," he answered. "Not, at least, to my knowledge."

"Defects of memory are sometimes useful," I replied. "Cannot you recall the twenty-fourth of July?"

"The twenty-fourth of July," he repeated reflectively. "No. There is no event which fixes the date in my memory."

His face had grown older. The light of youthfulness had gone out of it, leaving it the grey, ashen countenance of the Tempter.

"You were in London on that date," I asserted.

"No. I was in Alexandria. I sailed from there on the twenty-second."

"Then, at the outset, you deny that you were in London on the date I have mentioned? Good! Well, I will go a step further in order to refresh your memory. On that July night you met your friend, Tattersett."

"My dear fellow," he cried, laughing outright, "I have no idea of what you're driving at. Have you taken leave of your senses?"

"No," I answered angrily, "I have not, fortunately for myself. Therefore it is useless to deny the truth."

"I am not denying the truth," he replied. "I am denying the extraordinary assertion you are making."

"Because you fear to face the truth."

"I fear nothing," he responded defiantly. "What, in Heaven's name, have I to fear?"

"The consequences of the cleverly-planned conspiracy against myself."

He smiled superciliously, and answered, "I don't understand you. What conspiracy?"

"Listen!" I cried furiously. "It is useless for you to affect either ignorance or indifference. This is no case of mistaken identity. You forget that I am a medical man, and that my eye can detect a mark upon the flesh where the layman sees nothing. That crinkled depression on the inside of your wrist is a mark left in infancy. It cannot be imitated, neither can it be obliterated. You may alter your facial expression, or the outline of your figure; but you cannot alter that."

He glanced at his wrist, and I saw that he had never before noticed the indelible mark upon the flesh.

"You bore that mark on the day we met three months ago, and you bear it now," I went on. "Do you still deny your presence in London on the date I have mentioned?"

"Of course I do," he said.

"Then, you are a liar, and I will treat you as such!" I responded firmly.

We were standing facing one another, and I saw in his eyes an evil glint which told me plainly that he was no mean antagonist.

"You pay me a compliment," he said coolly. "I cannot see what motive you have in thus insulting me."

"It is no insult," I cried. "You are my enemy. You and your accomplice, Tattersett, devised an ingenious trap, and then called me in for professional consultation. The trap was well baited, and, as you intended, I fell into it. I thank God for one thing—namely, that I did not commit murder at your instigation."

He smiled again, but no word escaped him.

"You cannot think that I am in ignorance of the plot, or that I am unaware that, owing to the deception you have practised upon me, Beryl Wynd is my wife."

"And what connexion have I with all this?" he demanded. "If Beryl Wynd is your wife, what is it to do with me, pray?"

"The marriage was effected by conspiracy," I answered. "She was your victim—just as I unfortunately was. The penalty for such conspiracy is penal servitude."

"Well?" he inquired, smiling again. "And I take it that you suspect me of being implicated in the conspiracy? All I can reply is that you are entirely mistaken."

"I am not mistaken," I said hotly. "It was yourself who tempted me, holding the banknotes in your hand—"

"And if you consented, as you allege, you became equally implicated in the conspiracy," he observed, interrupting me.

I had never before looked at the matter in such a light. His words were true. I had sold myself to the conspirators—had become an accessory, and was therefore just as liable to prosecution as they were!

"You attempted to suborn me to commit murder," I added.

"It's a lie," answered the Tempter flatly.

"But I can prove it," I asserted.

"How?"

"I have proof," I replied ambiguously, for I did not intend to show my hand.

"Then you are at liberty to use it for whatever purpose you like," he answered defiantly. "But we were alone."

"Ah!" I exclaimed quickly. "Then you admit your identity?"

"I admit nothing."

"Until I can show proof positive, eh? Until I can bring those who will bear witness that, on the twenty-fourth of June, you were at number 94, Queen's-gate Gardens; that you sent for me; that on my arrival you tempted me to marry Beryl Wynd; that you accompanied me to the church of St. Ann's, and that, having accepted the promise of payment, you afterwards attempted to induce me to take her life."

"Lies—all of it."

"We shall see. You tried to take my life. Revenge is now mine," I added in a hard, distinct voice.

It may have been only my fancy, yet I could not help noticing that the word revenge caused him to shrink, and regard me with some misgiving.

"How?" he inquired.

"No," I responded firmly; "we are enemies. That is sufficient. I have discovered the whole plot, therefore rest assured that those who victimised both Beryl and myself, and have made dastardly attempts upon our lives, shall not go unpunished."

I had altered my tactics, deeming it best to assume a deeper knowledge of the affair than that which I really possessed. It was a delicate matter; this accusation must be dealt with diplomatically.

"My private opinion of you, sir, is that you are a confounded fool," he said.

"I may be," I responded. "But I intend that you, who enmeshed into your plot a defenceless woman, and who abducted me aboard so cleverly, in order to gain time, shall bear the exposure and punishment that you merit."

He nodded slowly as though perfectly comprehending my meaning.

"Then I take it that Beryl is aware of your actual alliance with her?"

he asked, his small eyes flashing at me.

But I made no satisfactory answer. I was wary of him, for I knew him to be a clever miscreant. His tone betrayed an anxiety to know the exact extent of Beryl's knowledge.

"Beryl is my wife, and my interests are hers," I replied. "It is sufficient that I am aware of the whole truth."

"You think so," he laughed with sarcasm. "Well, you are at liberty to hold your own opinion."

"The fact is," I said, "that you accepted Sir Henry's invitation here, never dreaming that you would come face to face with me. I am the last person in the world you desired to meet."

"The encounter has given me the utmost pleasure, I assure you," he replied with a sneer.

"Just as it will not only to yourself but to a certain other."

"Who?"

"A person whom you know well—an intimate friend of yours."

"I don't follow you."

"It is a woman. Think of your female friends."

"What is her name?"

"La Gioia."

"La Gioia?" he gasped glaring at me.

His face was livid and his surprise apparent. I saw that he had never dreamt that I knew of her existence.

"You see, I may be a confounded fool, as you have declared," I said. "But I have not been idle during these past months. La Gioia's revenge is mine also."

He made no response. My words had, as I intended, produced an overwhelming effect upon him. He saw, that if La Gioia's secret was out he stood in deadliest peril. I had impressed him with an intimate knowledge of the whole affair.

It was at that moment he showed himself full of resourceful villainy.

"The vengeance of La Gioia will fall upon the woman who is your wife—not upon yourself."

"And through whom?" I cried. "Why, through yourself and your accomplice, Tattersett, who betrayed Beryl into her hands. The mystery of Whitton is to me no mystery, for I know the truth."

He glared at me as though I were some evil vision, and I knew that by these words I was slowly thrusting home the truth.

"What have I to do with the affair at Whitton?" he cried. "I know nothing of it?"

"I may, perhaps, be enabled to prove differently," I said.

"Do you then allege that I am implicated in the Colonel's death?" he exclaimed furiously.

"I have my own opinion," I responded. "Remember that you once made a desperate and dastardly, attempt to kill me, fearing lest I should denounce you as having tried to bribe me to commit murder."

His eyes glittered, and I saw that his anger was unbounded. We stood there in the calm sunset near the lakeside, and I could see that he would rid himself of me, if such a course was possible. But I thought of Beryl. Ah! how I loved her. That she had fallen a victim of the cleverly contrived conspiracy incensed me, and I resolved to show the scoundrel no quarter.

"Well," he said at last, in a tone of defiance, "and after all these wild allegations, what can you do? Surely you do not think that I fear any statement that you can make?"

"You may not fear any statement of mine, but I do not anticipate that you will invite La Gioia to reveal all she knows. The latter might place you in enforced confinement for a few years."

"La Gioia is at liberty to say whatever she likes," he answered. "If she is actually a friend of Beryl's she will, no doubt, assist you; but at present she is her deadliest antagonist. Therefore, if you take my advice, you'll just calm yourself and await another opportunity for revenge at a latter date."

His cool words caused my blood to boil.

"You treat this affair as though it were a matter of little importance, sir!" I cried. "Let me tell you, however, that I have been your victim, and I intend to probe the matter to the bottom and ascertain your motives."

"That you'll never do," he laughed.

"I tell you I will!" I cried. "I am Beryl's husband, and she is no longer defenceless. You have to answer to me!"

"I have answered you by saying that in future you are at liberty to act as you think fit. I merely warn you that La Gioia is no more your friend than she is your wife's."

"You contrived to entrap me into marriage. Why? Answer me that question," I demanded.

"I refuse. You have threatened me with all sorts of pains and penalties, but I defy you!"

From his silver case he took a cigar, and, biting off the end, leisurely lit it. His countenance had changed. Again it was the same grey sinister face that had so long haunted me in my dream—the face of the Tempter.

"Have you finished?" he asked, with mock politeness.

"For the moment, yes," I answered. "But yours is an ill-advised defiance, as you will very soon see."

He burst forth into a peal of strained, unnatural laughter, whereat I turned upon my heel and left him standing there a dark silhouette in the crimson sunset. Blindly I walked on to the house, dressed mechanically, and descended late for dinner. But the Tempter was not in his place; he had been called away to London, it was said, and had been compelled to catch the 07:30 train from Corsham.

I glanced at my watch; it was already 07:35. I had blundered, and had allowed him to slip through my fingers. I bit my lip in mad vexation.

Beryl's beautiful eyes were fixed upon me, and in her face I detected deep anxiety. She looked perfectly charming in a gown of pale pink crêpe-de-chine. Had he sought her before departure, I wondered?

"It's an awful disappointment that he has had to leave," said the baronet's wife. "I endeavoured to persuade him to remain until the morning, but he received a letter by the afternoon post making it imperative that he should return to London. But he says he will be back again either on Monday or Tuesday."

"I do hope he will return," observed some one at the end of the table, and then the subject dropped. When the ladies had left the room Sir Henry remarked—"Queer fellow, Ashwicke—a bit eccentric, I always think. His movements are most erratic—a regular rolling stone."

I embraced that opportunity to inquire regarding his antecedents, but my host appeared to know very little beyond the fact that he was wealthy, good company, a keen sportsman, and moved in a very smart set in town.

"I've known him a couple of years or so; he's a member of my club," he added. "My wife declares that none of the parties are complete without him."

"Do you know his friend, Tattersett—Major Tattersett?"

"No," responded Sir Henry; "never met him." With the others I went along to the drawing-room and found Beryl alone in a cozy corner, obviously awaiting me. She twisted a lace scarf about her shoulders and we strolled out upon the terrace, as was our habit each evening if fine and starlight. When we had gained the further end she suddenly halted, and turning to me said, in a low, husky voice that trembled with emotion—

"Doctor Colkirk, you have deceived me!"

"Deceived you, Miss Wynd?" I exclaimed, taken completely aback by her allegation. "How?"

"I know the truth—a truth that you cannot deny. I—I am your wife."

"I do not seek to deny it," I answered in deep, solemn earnestness, taking her small white hand in mine. "It is true, Beryl, that you are my wife—true also that I love you."

"But it cannot be possible!" she gasped. "I knew that I was a wife, but never dreamed that you were actually my husband."

"And how did you discover it?"

"I was down by the waterside this evening, before dinner, and overheard your conversation with Mr Ashwicke."

"All of it?"

"Yes, all of it. I know that I am your wife;" and she sighed, while her little hand trembled within mine.

"I love you, Beryl," I said, simply and earnestly. "I have known all along that you are my wife, yet I dared not tell you so, being unable to offer sufficient proof of it and unable to convince you of my affection. Yet, in these few weeks that have passed, you have surely seen that I am devoted to you—that I love you with a strange and deeper love than ever man has borne within his heart. A thousand times I have longed to tell you this, but have always feared to do so. The truth is that you are my wife—my adored."

Her hand tightened upon mine, and unable to restrain her emotions further, she burst into tears.

"Tell me, darling," I whispered into her car—"tell me that you will try to love me now that you know the truth. Tell me that you forgive me for keeping the secret until now, for, as I will show you, it was entirely in our mutual interests. We have both been victims of a vile and widespread conspiracy, therefore we must unite our efforts to combat the vengeance of our enemies. Tell me that you will try and love me—nay, that you do love me a little. Give me hope, darling, and let us act together as man and wife."

"But it is so sudden," she faltered. "I hardly know my own feelings."

"You know whether you love me, or whether you hate me," I said, placing my hand around her slim waist and drawing her towards me.

"No," she responded in a low voice, "I do not hate you. How could

I?"

"Then you love me—you really love me, after all!" I cried joyously.

For answer she burst again into a flood of tears, and I, with mad passion, covered her white brow with hot kisses while she clung to me—my love, my wife.

Ah! when I reflect upon the ecstasy of those moments—how I kissed her sweet lips, and she, in return, responded to my tender caresses, how she clung to me as though shrinking in fear from the world about her, how her heart beat quickly in unison with my own, I feel that I cannot properly convey here a sufficient sense of my wild delight. It is enough to say that in those tender moments I knew that I had won the most beautiful and graceful woman I had ever beheld—a woman who was peerless above all—and that she was already my wife. The man who reads this narrative, and whose own love has been reciprocated after long waiting, as mine has been, can alone understand the blissful happiness that came to me and the complete joy that filled my heart.

We stood lost in the ecstasies of each other's love, heedless of time, heedless of those who might discover us, heedless of everything. The remembrance of that hour remains with me to-day like a pleasant dream, a foretaste of the bliss of paradise.

Many were the questions that I asked and answered, many our declarations of affection and of fidelity. Our marriage had been made by false contract on that fateful day, months before, but that night, beneath the shining stars, we exchanged solemn vows before God as man and wife.

I endeavoured to obtain from her some facts regarding Ashwicke and his accomplice, Tattersett, but what she knew seemed very unsatisfactory. I related to her the whole of the curious circumstances of our marriage, just as I have recounted it in the opening chapters of my narrative, seeking neither to suppress nor exaggerate any of the singular incidents.

Then, at last, she made confession—a strange amazing confession which held me dumb.

Chapter Twenty Nine.

Put to the Test.

"I remember very little of the events of that day," my love said, with some reluctance. "I know Ashwicke, he having been a guest here last year, and a frequent visitor at Gloucester Square. With Nora and Sir Henry I returned to London in early May, after wintering in Florence, and one morning at the end of June I met Major Tattersett unexpectedly in the Burlington. He told me that his sister and niece from Scotland were visiting him at his house in Queen's-gate Gardens, and invited me to call and make their acquaintance."

"Had you never been to his house previously?"

"Never. He, however, gave me an invitation to luncheon for the twenty-fourth of July, which I accepted. On arrival I found the Major; his sister and his niece were out shopping, therefore I sat alone awaiting them in the drawing-room, when of a sudden I experienced for the first time that curious sensation of being frozen. I tried to move, but was unable. I cried out for help, but no one came. My limbs were stiff and rigid as though I were struck by paralysis, while the pain was excruciating. I fought against unconsciousness, but my last clear recollection of those agonising moments was of an indistinct, sinister face peering into mine. All then became strangely distorted. The balance of my brain became inverted and I lost my will-power, being absolutely helpless in the hands of those who directed my movements. I could not hold back, for all my actions were mechanical, obeying those around me. I remember being dressed for the wedding, the journey to the church, my meeting with my future husband—whose face, however, I was unable to afterwards recall—the service, and the return. Then came a perfect blank."

"And afterwards?"

"Night had fallen when I returned to my senses, and the strange sensation of intense cold generally left me. I looked around, and, to my amazement, saw the pale moon high in the sky. My head was resting upon something hard, which I gradually made out to be a wooden seat. Then, when I sat up, I became aware of the bewildering truth—that I was lying upon one of the seats in Hyde Park."

"In Hyde Park? And you had been placed there while in a state of unconsciousness?"

"Yes. Upon my finger I found a wedding-ring. Was it possible, I wondered, that I was actually married to some unknown man?"

"You saw nothing of Ashwicke?"

"I saw no one except the maid-servant who showed me into the drawing-room, and cannot in the least account for the strange sensation which held me helpless in the hands of my enemies. I saw the man I married at the church, but so mistily that I did not recognise you when we met again."

"But you knew the house in Queen's-gate Gardens. Did you not afterwards return there, and seek an explanation of Tattersett?"

"On discovering my whereabouts I rose and walked across the park to Gloucester Square. It was then nearly one o'clock in the morning, but Nora was sitting up in anxiety as to what had become of me. I had, however, taken the ring from my finger, and to her told a fictitious story to account for my tardy return. Two days later I returned to the house to which Tattersett had invited me, but on inquiry found, to my amazement, that it was really occupied by a lady named Stentiford, who was abroad, while the man left in charge knew nothing whatever either of the Major or of his sister and niece. I told him how I had visited there two days previously, but he laughed incredulously; and when I asked for the maid-servant who had admitted me, he said that no maid had been left there by Mrs Stentiford. In prosecution of my inquiries I sought to discover the register of my marriage, but, not knowing the parish in which it had taken place, my search at Somerset House was fruitless. They told me that the registers were not made up there until six months or so after the ceremony."

"You did not apply at Doctors' Commons?"

"No," she responded; "I thought the entry would be at Somerset House."

"What previous knowledge had you of the Major?"

"He was a friend of Ashwicke's, who had been introduced to us one night in the stalls at Daly's. He afterwards dined several times at Gloucester Square."

"But Sir Henry does not know him."

"It was while he was away at the Cape."

"Then you have not the faintest idea of the reason of our extraordinary marriage, darling?" I asked, holding her hand. "I have told you all that actually occurred. Can you form no conclusion whatever as to the motive?"

"Absolutely none," she answered. "I am as utterly in the dark as yourself. I cannot understand why you were selected as my husband."

"But you do not regret?" I asked tenderly.

"Regret? No," she repeated, raising her beautiful face to mine, perfect in its loveliness and purity. "I do not regret now, Richard—because I love you." And our lips met again in fervent tenderness.

"It is still an absolute mystery," I observed at last. "We know that we are wedded, but there our knowledge ends."

"We have both been victims of a plot," she responded. "If we could but discern the motive, then we might find some clue to lead us to the truth."

"But there is a woman called La Gioia," I said; and, continuing, explained my presence in the park at Whitton, and the conversation I had overheard between herself and Tattersett.

Her hand, still in mine, trembled perceptibly, and I saw that I had approached a subject distasteful to her.

"Yes," she admitted at last, in a hard, strange voice, "it is true that he wrote making an appointment to meet me in the park that night. I kept it because I wished to ascertain the truth regarding my marriage. But he would tell me nothing; he only urged me to secure my own safety because La Gioia had returned."

"And who is La Gioia?"

"My enemy—my bitterest enemy."

"Can you tell me nothing else?" I asked in a tone of slight reproach.

"I know nothing else. I do not know who or what she is, or where she lives. I only know that she is my unseen evil genius."

"But you have seen her. She called upon you on that evening at Gloucester Square when she assumed the character of your dressmaker, and a few nights ago she was here—in this house."

"Here?" she echoed in alarm. "Impossible!"

Then I related how I had seen her, and how her evil influence had fallen upon me when afterwards I had entered my room.

"The thing is actually beyond belief," she declared. "Do you really think you were not mistaken?"

"Most assuredly I was not. It was the woman who called upon you in London. But you have not told me the reason you were absent from your room that night." She was silent for a few moments, then answered, "I met Tattersett. He demanded that I should meet him, as he wished to speak with me secretly. I did so."

"Why did he wish to see you?"

"In order to prove to me that he had no hand in the tragic affair at Whitton. I had suspected all along that he was responsible for the Colonel's death, and my opinion has not altered. I begged him to tell me the reason of the plot against me, the motive of my marriage, and the identity of my husband. But he refused point-blank, telling me to ask La Gioia, who knew everything."

"Have you no idea of her whereabouts?"

"None whatever."

"If we could but find her," I said, "she might tell us something. Ah! if we could but find her."

My love was trembling. Her heart was filled to overflowing with the mystery of it all. Yet I knew that she loved me—yes, she loved me.

How long we lingered there upon the terrace I know not, but it was late ere we re-entered the drawing-room. Who among those assembled guests would have dreamt the truth—we were man and wife!

As I went upstairs I found a letter lying upon the hall table in the place where the guests' letters were placed. Barton had, I suppose, driven into Corsham and brought with him the mail which would, in the usual course, have been delivered on the following morning. The note was from Hoefer, a couple of awkwardly scribbled lines asking me to come and see him without a moment's delay.

Eager to hear whether the queer old fellow had made any discovery, I departed next morning by the eight o'clock express for London, having left a note with Beryl's maid explaining the cause of my sudden journey, and soon after eleven was seated with the old German in his lofty laboratory. The table was, as usual, filled with various contrivances—bottles of liquids and test-tubes containing fluids of various hues—while before him, as I entered, a small tube containing a bright blue liquid was bubbling over the spirit-lamp, the heat causing the colour to gradually fade.

"Ah, my frient," he said, with his strong accent, holding out his big fat hand encased in a stout leather glove, "I am glad you have come—very glad. It has been a long search, but I haf discovered something, after all. You see these?"—and he indicated his formidable array of retorts and test-tubes. "Well, I have been investigating at Gloucester Square, and have found the affair much more extraordinary than I believed."

"And you have discovered the truth?" I demanded.

"Yes," he responded, turning down the flame of the lamp and bending attentively to the bubbling fluid from which all colour had disappeared while I had been watching. "Shall I relate to you the course of my investigations?"

"Do. I am all attention."

"Well," he said, leaning both elbows upon the table and resting his chin upon his hands, while the tame brown rat ran along the table and scrambled into his pocket, "on the first evening you sought my assistance I knew, from the remote effects which both of us experienced, that the evil influence of that mysterious visitor in black, was due to some unknown neurotic poison. It was for that reason that I was enabled to administer an antidote without making an exact diagnosis. Now, as you are well aware, toxicology is a very strange study. Even common table-salt is a poison, and has caused death. But my own experiments have proved that, although the various narcotic poisons produce but little local change, their remote effects are very remarkable. Certain substances affect certain organs in particular. The remote action of a poison may be said to be due, in every instance, to its absorption into the veins or lymphatics, except when there is a direct continuity of effect traceable from the point where the poison was applied to the point where the remote effect is shown. It is remarkable that the agents which most affect the nervous system do not act at all when applied to the brain or trunks of nerves. Poisonous effects result from absorption of the poisoning body, and absorption implies solution; the more soluble, therefore, the compound is, the more speedy are its effects. Do you follow me?"

"Quite clearly."

"The rapid, remote effect produced on leaving that room made it plain that I must look for some powerful neurotic poison that may be absorbed through the skin," he went on. "With this object I searched microscopically various objects within and without the room, but for a long time was unsuccessful, when, one morning, I made a discovery that upon the white porcelain handle of the door a little colourless liquid had been applied. Greater part of it had disappeared by constant handling, but there was still some remaining on the shaft of the handle, and the microscope showed distinct prism-shaped crystals. All these I secured, and with them have since been experimenting. I found them to be a more deadly poison than any of the known paralysants or hyposthenisants, with an effect of muscular paralysis very similar to that produced by curare, combined with the stiffness about the neck and inability to move the jaws so apparent in symptoms provoked by strychnia. The unknown substance—a most deadly, secret poison, and, as I have since proved, one of those known to the ancients—had been applied to the door-handle on the inside, so that any person in pulling open the door to go out must absorb it in sufficient quantity to prove fatal. Indeed, had it not been for the antidote of chlorine and the mixed oxides of iron which I fortunately hit upon, death must have ensued in the case of each of us.

"To determine exactly what was the poison used was an almost insurmountable task, for I had never met with the substance before;

but, after working diligently all this time, I have found that by treating it with sulphuric acid it underwent no change, yet by adding a fragment of bichromate of potassium a series of blue, violet, purple, and red tints were produced, very similar to those seen in the tests for strychnia. The same results were brought about, also, by peroxide of lead and black oxide of manganese. I dried the skin of a frog and touched it with a drop of solution containing a single one of the tiny crystals, when strong tetantic convulsions ensued and the animal died in ten seconds. At last, however, after many other experiments, the idea occurred to me that it was an alkaloid of some plant unknown in modern toxicology. I was, of course, aware of the action of the calabar bean of the West Coast of Africa, the akazga, the datura seeds of India, and such-like poisons, but this was certainly none of these. It was a substance terribly deadly—the only substance that could strike death through the cuticle—utterly unknown to us, yet the most potent of all secret poisons."

"And how did you determine it at last?"

"By a reference I discovered in an ancient Latin treatise on poisons from the old monastery at Pavia, now in the British Museum. It gave me a clue which ultimately led me to establish it as the alkaloid of the vayana bean. This bean, it appears, was used in the tenth and eleventh centuries by a sect of the despotic Arab mystics called the Fatimites, who had made Cairo their capital, and held rule over Syria as well as the northern coast of Africa. The last Fatimite was, at a later date, dethroned by Saladin, conqueror of the Koords, and who opposed Richard the First of England. The poison, introduced from Egypt into Italy, was known to the old alchemists as the most secret means of ridding one of undesirable acquaintances. Its effect, it was stated, was the most curious of any known drug, because, for the time being, it completely altered the disposition of the individual and caused him to give way to all sorts of curious notions and delusions, while at the same time he would be entirely obedient to the will of any second person. Afterwards came fierce delirium, a sensation as though the lower limbs were frozen, complete loss of power, exhaustion, and death. But in modern toxicology even the name of the vayana was lost.

"My first step, therefore, was to seek assistance of the great botanist who is curator of Kew Gardens, and, after considerable difficulty and many experiments, we both arrived at the conclusion that it was the bean of a small and very rare plant peculiar to the oasis of the Ahir in the south of the Great Sahara. At Kew there was a stunted specimen, but it had never borne fruit, therefore we both searched for any other specimen that might exist in England. We heard of one in the wonderful gardens of La Mortola, near Mentone, and, after diligent inquiries, discovered that a firm of importers in Liverpool had sold a specimen with the beans in pod, which was delivered to a person named Turton, living in Bishop's-wood Road, Highgate, and planted in a small greenhouse there. I have not been idle," he added with a grin. Then, taking from a drawer in the table before him a photograph, he handed it to me, saying, "I have been able to obtain this photograph of Mrs Turton—the lady who purchased the plant in question."

He held it out to me, and in an instant I recognised the face. It was that of the woman who had crept so silently through the rooms at Atworth—La Gioia!

Briefly, I told him all that had transpired on that night, and declared that I recognised her features, whereat he grunted in satisfaction.

"You have asked me to try and solve the mystery, and I have done so. You will find this woman living at a house called 'Fairmead' in the road I have indicated. I have not only established the cause of the phenomena, but I have, at the same time, rediscovered the most extraordinary and deadly substance known in toxicology. As far as the present case is concerned, my work is finished—I have succeeded in making some of the vayana alkaloid. Here it is?" and, taking a small yellow glass tube, securely corked and sealed, he handed it to me.

In the bottom I saw half a grain of tiny white crystals. I knew now why he was wearing gloves in his laboratory.

"And have you seen this woman?" I asked the queer old fellow, whose careful investigations had been crowned with such success. "How did you know, on the following day, that it was La Gioia who had come in the guise of a dressmaker?"

"I have seen her, and I have seen the plant. It is from one of the beans which I secured secretly that I have been able to produce that substance. I knew her by overhearing a conversation between Miss Wynd and her cousin on the following morning."

"And the woman is in ignorance that you know the truth?"

"Entirely. I have finished. It is for you now to act as you think fit."

I expressed admiration for his marvellous patience and ingenuity in solving the mystery, and, when I left, it was with the understanding that, if I required his further assistance he would willingly render it.

Chapter Thirty.

"La Gioia."

On the following afternoon, in response to a telegram I had sent to Beryl, she accompanied me to Highgate to face La Gioia. Now that I had such complete evidence of her attempts to poison, I did not fear her, but was determined to elucidate the mystery. Beryl accompanied me rather reluctantly, declaring that, with such power as the woman held, our lives were not safe; but I resolved to take her by surprise, and to risk all. After leaving Hoefer I had sought an interview with the detective Bullen, and he, by appointment, was in the vicinity of the house in question, accompanied by a couple of plain-clothes subordinates.

We stopped our cab in Hampstead Lane, and descending, found that the Bishop's-wood Road was a semicircular thoroughfare of substantial detached houses, the garden of each abutting upon a cricket-ground in the centre, and each with its usual greenhouse where geraniums were potted and stored in winter. On entering the quiet, highly-respectable crescent, we were not long in discovering a house with the name "Fairmead" inscribed in gilt letters upon the gate, while a little further along my eyes caught sight of two scavengers diligently sweeping the road, and, not far away, Bullen himself was walking with his back turned towards me.

On our summons being responded to I inquired for Mrs Turton, and we were shown into the drawing-room—a rather severely furnished apartment which ran through into the greenhouse wherein stood the rare plant. Hoefer had described it minutely, and while we waited, we both peered into the greenhouse and examined it. The plant standing in the full sunlight was about two feet high, with broad, spreading leaves of a rich, dark green, and grew in an ordinary flower-pot. Half-hidden by the leaves, just as Hoefer had said, we saw some small green pods, long and narrow—the pods of the fatal vayana.

Ere we had time to exchange words the door of the room opened, and there stood before us the tall, dark-robed figure of "La Gioia." Her hard face, pale and expectant, showed in the full light to be that of a woman of perhaps forty, with dark hair, keen, swift eyes, thin cheeks, and bony features—a countenance not exactly ugly, but rather that of a woman whose beauty had prematurely faded owing to the heavy cares upon her.

I was the first to address her, saying, "I think, madam, you are sufficiently well acquainted with both of us not to need any formal introduction."

Her brow contracted and her lips stood apart. Then, without hesitation, I told her my name and that of my companion, while the light died from her careworn face and she stood motionless as one petrified.

"We have come here, to you, to seek the truth of the conspiracy against us—the plot in which you yourself have taken part. We demand to know the reason of the secret attempts you have made upon the lives of both of us."

"I don't understand you," she answered with hauteur.

"To deny it is useless," I said determinedly. "The insidious poison you have used is the vayana, and the only specimen in England bearing fruit is standing there in your greenhouse." And as I uttered those words I closed the door leading beyond, and, locking it, placed the key in my pocket.

Her teeth were firmly set. She glanced at me and tried to deny the allegation, but so utterly was she taken aback by my sudden denunciation that words failed her. A moment later, however, taking several paces forward to where we stood, she cried with a sudden outburst of uncontrollable anger—

"You—Beryl Wynd—I hate you! I swore that you should die, and you shall—you shall!"

But I stepped between them, firm and determined. I saw that this woman was a veritable virago, and that now we had cornered her so neatly she was capable of any crime.

"I demand to know the truth!" I said in a hard, distinct voice.

"You will know nothing from me," she snarled. "That woman has betrayed me!" she added, indicating Beryl.

"Your evil deeds alone have betrayed you," I responded, "and if you decline to tell me anything of your own free will, then perhaps you will make a statement to the police when put upon your trial for attempted murder."

"My trial!" she gasped, turning pale again. "You think to frighten me into telling you something, eh?" she laughed. "Ah! you do not know me."

"I know you sufficiently well to be aware that you are a clever and ingenious woman," I replied. "And in this affair I entertain a belief that our interests may, after all, be mutual."

"How?"

"Tattersett is your enemy, as he is ours." It was a wild shot, but I recollected his words that I had overheard in the park at Whitton. "There has been a conspiracy against myself and this lady here, who is my wife."

"Your wife!" she gasped.

"I have spoken the truth," I said. "I am here to learn the details from you. If, on the other hand, you prefer to preserve the secret of your accomplices, I shall demand your arrest without delay."

She was silent. Then, after further declarations of ignorance, she was driven to desperation by my threats of arrest, and at last said in a hard, husky voice—

"I must first tell you who and what I am. My father was an English merchant, named Turton, who lived in Palermo, and my mother was Italian. Fifteen years ago I was a popular dancer, known throughout Italy as 'La Gioia.' While engaged at La Scala Theatre, in Milan, I met an Englishman named Ashwicke—"

"Ashwicke?" I exclaimed.

"Not the man whom you know as Ashwicke, but another," she responded. "He was interested in the occult sciences, apparently wealthy, and much enamoured of me. In the six months of our courtship I learned to love him madly, and the result was that we were married at the Municipio, in Milan, which stands exactly opposite the entrance to the theatre. A month afterwards, however, he decamped with my jewels and the whole of the money I had saved, leaving behind him, as his only personal possessions, a box containing some rare old vellum books which he had purchased somewhere down in the old Tuscan towns, and of which he had been extremely careful. At first I could not believe that he could have treated me thus, after all his professions of love; but as the weeks passed and he did not return, I slowly realised the truth that I had been duped and deserted. It was then that I made a vow of revenge.

"Ten endless years passed, and, my personal beauty having faded, I was compelled to remain on the stage, accepting menial parts and struggling for bread until, by the death of a cousin, I found myself with sufficient to live upon. Though I had no clue to who my husband was, beyond a name which had most probably been assumed, I nevertheless treasured his books, feeling vaguely that some day they might give me a clue. In those years that went by I spent days and days deciphering the old black letters, and translating from the Latin and Italian. They were nearly all works dealing with the ancient practice of medicine, but one there was dealt with secret poisons. I have it here;" and unlocking a drawer in a rosewood cabinet, she took therefrom a big leather-covered tome, written in Latin upon vellum.

There was an old rusted lock of Florentine workmanship upon it, and the leather was worm-eaten and tattered.

"This contains the secret of the vayana," she went on, opening the ponderous volume before me upon the table. "I discovered that the poison was the only one impossible of detection, and then it occurred to me to prepare it, and with it strike revenge. Well, although I had been in London a dozen times in search of the man I had once loved, I came again and settled down here, determined to spare no effort to discover him. Through four whole years I sought him diligently, when at last I was successful. I discovered who and what he was."

"Who was he?" I inquired.

"The man you know as Major Tattersett. His real name is Ashwicke."

"Tattersett?" gasped Beryl. "And he is your husband?"

"Most certainly," she responded. "I watched him diligently for more than twelve months, and discovered that his career had been a most extraordinary one, and that he was in association with a man named Graham—who sometimes also called himself Ashwicke—and who was one of the most expert and ingenious forgers ever known. Graham was a continental swindler whom the police had for years been endeavouring to arrest, while the man who was my husband was known in criminal circles as 'The Major.' Their operations in England, Belgium, and America were on a most extensive-scale, and in the past eight years or so they have amassed a large fortune, and have succeeded in entering a very respectable circle of society. While keeping watch upon my husband's movements, I found that he, one evening a few months ago, went down to Hounslow, and, unobserved by him, I travelled by the same train. I followed him to Whitton, and watched him meet clandestinely a lady who was one of the guests."

"It was myself?" Beryl exclaimed, standing utterly dumbfounded by these revelations.

"Yes," the woman went on. "I was present at your meeting, although not sufficiently near to overhear your conversation. By your manner, however, I felt confident that you were lovers, and then a fiendish suggestion—one that I now deeply regret—occurred to me, namely to kill you both by secret means. With that object I went to the small rustic bridge by the lake—over which I knew you must pass on your return to the house, both of you having crossed it on your way there—and upon the hand-rail I placed the poison I had prepared. I knew that if you placed your hand upon the rail the poison would at once be absorbed through the skin, and must prove fatal. My calculations were, however, incorrect, for an innocent man fell victim. Colonel Chetwode came down that path, and, unconsciously grasping the rail, received the sting of death, while you and your companion returned by a circuitous route, and did not therefore discover him."

"And is that really the true story of the Colonel's death?" I asked blankly.

"Yes," she answered, her chin upon her breast. "You may denounce me. I am a murderess—a murderess?"

There was a long and awkward pause.

"And can you tell us nothing of our mysterious union and its motive?" I asked her.

"Nothing," she responded, shaking her head. "I would tell you all, if I knew, for you, like myself, have fallen victims in the hands of Tattersett and Graham—only they themselves know the truth. After the tragedy at Whitton I traced Beryl Wynd to Gloucester Square, and, still believing her to have supplanted me in my husband's affections, called there in the guise of a dressmaker, and while your wife was absent from the room managed to write a reply to a fictitious message I had brought her from Graham. I placed the liquid upon the porcelain handle of the door on the inside, so that a person on entering would experience no ill effect, but on pulling open the door to leave would receive the full strength of the deadly vayana. This again proved ineffectual; therefore ascertaining that Graham intended to visit Atworth, I entered there and placed the terrible alkaloid on certain objects in your wife's room—upon her waist-belt, and in the room that had been occupied by him on his previous visit, but which proved to be then occupied by yourself."

"And that accounts for the mysterious attacks which we both experienced!" I observed, amazed at her confession.

"Yes," she replied; "I intended to commit murder. I was unaware that Beryl was your wife, and I have committed an error which I shall regret through all my life, I can only ask your forgiveness—if you really can forgive."

"I have not yet learnt the whole facts—the motive of our marriage,"

I answered. "Can you direct us to either of the men?"

She paused. Then at last answered, "Graham, or the man you know as Ashwicke, is here in this house; he called upon me by appointment this afternoon. If you so desire, I will tell my servant to ask him in."

"But before doing so," cried Beryl, excitedly, "let me first explain my own position! I, too, am not altogether blameless. The story of my parentage, as I have given it to you, Richard, is a fictitious one. I never knew my parents. My earliest recollections were of the Convent of the Sacré Coeur at Brunoy, near Paris, where I spent fourteen years, having as companion, during the latter seven years, Nora Findlay, the daughter of a Scotch ironmaster. Of my own parents the Sisters declared they knew nothing, and as I grew up they constantly tried to persuade me to take the veil. Nora, my best friend, left the convent, returned to England, and two years afterwards married Sir Henry, whereupon she generously offered me a place in her house as companion. She is no relation, but, knowing my susceptibilities, and in order that I should not be looked upon as a paid companion, she gave out that we were cousins—hence I was accepted as such everywhere.

"With Nora I had a pleasant, careless life, until about two years ago I met the Major, unknown to Nora, and afterwards became on friendly terms with a young man, an officer in the guards, who was his friend. Tattersett won a large sum from him at cards; and then I saw, to my dismay, that he had been attracted only by the mild flirtation I had carried on with him, and that he had played in order to please me. The Major increased my dismay by telling me that this young man was the son of a certain woman who was his bitterest enemy—the Italian woman called La Gioia—and that she would seek a terrible revenge upon us both. This was to frighten me. My life having been spent in the convent, I knew very little of the ways of the world, yet I soon saw sufficient of both to know that Tattersett was an expert forger, and that his accomplice Graham was a clever continental thief whom the police had long been wanting. How I called at the house in Queen's-gate Gardens, and afterwards lost control over my own actions, I have already explained. The motive of our marriage is an absolute enigma."

She stood before me white-faced and rigid.

"It is fortunate that Graham is here. Shall we seek the truth from him?" I asked.

"Yes," she responded. "Demand from him the reason of our mysterious union."

La Gioia touched the bell, gave an order to the servant, and, after a few moments of dead silence, Graham stood in the doorway.

Chapter Thirty One.

Conclusion.

"You!" gasped the man, halting quickly in alarm.

"Yes," I said. "Enter, Mr Graham; we wish to speak with you."

"You've betrayed me—curse you!" he cried, turning upon La Gioia. "You've told them the truth?"

The colour had died from his face, and he looked as grey and aged as on the first occasion when we had met and he had tempted me.

"We desire the truth from your own lips," I said determinedly. "I am not here without precautions. The house is surrounded by police, and they will enter at a sign from me if you refuse an explanation—the truth, mind. If you lie you will both be arrested."

"I know nothing," he declared, his countenance dark and sullen.

He made a slight instinctive movement towards his pocket, and I knew that a revolver was there.

"You know the reason of our marriage," I said quickly. "What was it?"

"Speak!" urged La Gioia. "You can only save yourself by telling the truth."

"Save myself!" he cried in a tone of defiance. "You wish to force me to confession—you and this woman! You've acted cleverly. When she invited me here, this afternoon, I did not dream that she had outwitted me."

The woman had, however, made the appointment in ignorance of our intentions, therefore she must have had some other motive. But he was entrapped, and saw no way of escape.

"I have worked diligently all these months, and have solved the mystery of what you really are," I said.

"Then that's sufficient for you, I suppose;" and his thin lips snapped together.

"No, it is not sufficient. To attempt to conceal anything further is useless. I desire from you a statement of the whole truth."

"And condemn myself?"

"You will not condemn yourself if you are perfectly frank with us," I assured him.

There was a long silence. His small eyes darted an evil look at La

Gioia, who stood near him, erect and triumphant. Suddenly he answered, in a tone hard and unnatural—

"If you know all, as you declare, there is little need to say much about my own association with Tattersett. Of the latter the police are well aware that he is one of the most expert forgers in Europe. It was he and I who obtained thirty thousand pounds from the Crédit Lyonnais in Bordeaux, and who, among other little matters of business, tricked Parr's for twenty thousand. At Scotland Yard they have all along suspected us, but have never obtained sufficient evidence to justify arrest. We took very good care of that, for after ten years' partnership we were not likely to blunder." He spoke braggingly, for all thieves seem proud of the extent of their frauds.

"But you want to know about your marriage, eh?" he went on. "Well, to tell the truth, it happened like this. The Major, who had dabbled in the byways of chemistry as a toxicologist, held the secret of a certain most deadly poison—one that was used by the ancients a thousand years ago—and conceived by its means a gigantic plan of defrauding life insurance companies. About that time he accidentally met Miss Wynd, and cultivated her acquaintance because, being extremely handsome, she would be useful as a decoy. The secret marriage was accomplished, but just as the elaborate plan was to be put into operation he made an astounding discovery."

"What was the reason of the marriage?" I inquired breathlessly.

He paused in hesitation.

"Because it was essential that, in close association with us, we should have a doctor of reputation, able to assist when necessary, and give death-certificates for production to the various life insurance companies. You were known to us by repute as a clever but impecunious man, therefore it was decided that you should become our accomplice. With that object Tattersett, accompanied by a young woman, whom he paid to represent herself as Beryl Wynd, went to Doctors' Commons, and petitioned for a special licence. Possession was obtained of the house in Queen's-gate Gardens which I had occupied two years previously under the name of Ashwicke—for we used each other's names just as circumstances required—paying the caretaker a ten-pound note; and, when all was in readiness, you were called and bribed to marry Beryl, who was already there, rendered helpless with unbalanced brain by the deadly vayana. I posed, as you will remember, as Wyndham Wynd, father of the young lady, and, after the marriage, in order to entrap you into becoming our accomplice, tempted you to take her life. You refused, therefore you also fell a victim to a cigarette steeped in a decoction of curare, handed you by the Major, and were sent out of the country, it being our intention, on your return, to threaten you with being a party to a fraudulent marriage, and thus compel you to become our accomplice."

"But this paper which I found beneath her pillow?" And I took from my pocket the sheet of paper with the name of La Gioia upon it.

"It is a note I sent her, on the day before her visit to Queen's-gate Gardens, in order to induce her to come and consult with me. She had evidently carried it in her pocket."

"And this photograph?" I asked, showing him the picture I had found concealed in the Colonel's study.

"We took that picture of her as she lay, apparently dead, for production afterwards to the life insurance company. The Colonel, who was a friend of Tattersett's, must have found it in the latter's room and secured it. It was only because two days after the marriage Sir Henry's wife overheard a conversation between myself and Tattersett, in which you were mentioned, that we were prevented from making our gigantic coup against the life offices. While Beryl was asleep her ladyship found the wedding-ring. Then, knowing your address—for she had seen you with Doctor Raymond—she sought your acquaintance on your return, and, by ingenious questioning, became half convinced that you were actually Beryl's husband. Your friend Raymond was slightly acquainted with her, and had been introduced to Beryl some months before."

"But I cannot see why I should have been specially chosen as victim of this extraordinary plot," my wife exclaimed, her arm linked in mine. "You say that Tattersett made a discovery which caused him to alter his plans. What was it?"

"He discovered a few hours after your marriage that you were his daughter!"

"His daughter—the daughter of that man?" she cried.

"Yes," he answered seriously. "He did not know it, however, until when you were lying insensible after the marriage, he discovered upon your chest the tattoo-mark of the three hearts, which he himself had placed there years before. Then, overcome by remorse, he administered an antidote, placed you upon a seat in Hyde Park, and witched until you recovered consciousness and returned to Gloucester Square. It had before been arranged that an insurance already effected upon you should be claimed. The truth is," he went on, "that

Wyndham Ashwicke, alias Major Tattersett, first married in York the daughter of a cavalry officer, and by her you were born. A year afterwards, however, they separated, your mother died, and you were placed in the convent at Brunoy under the name of Wynd, while your father plunged into a life of dissipation on the Continent which ended in the marriage with this lady, then known as La Gioia."

"It seems incredible?" my love declared. "I cannot believe it?"

"But Nora introduced you as Feo Ashwicke on the first occasion we met after our marriage," I remarked.

"I well remember it. Nora must have discovered the secret of my birth, although, when I questioned her after your departure, she declared that she had only bestowed a fictitious name upon me as a joke."

"Yet Ashwicke was your actual name," I observed.

"You will find the register of your birth in York," interposed Graham. "I have told you the truth."

"I will hear it from my father's own lips," she said.

"Alas!" the grey-haired man answered very gravely, "that is impossible. Your father is dead."

"Dead?" I echoed. "Tattersett dead?"

"Yes; he was found lifeless in his rooms in Piccadilly East yesterday afternoon. His man called me, and discovered upon the table a tiny tube containing some crystals of the secret vayana. He had evidently touched them accidentally with his fingers, and the result was fatal. The police and doctor believe it to be due to natural causes, as I secured the tube and destroyed it before their arrival. The news of the discovery is in the evening papers;" and, taking a copy of the Globe from his pocket, he handed it to me, indicating the paragraph.

I read the four bare lines aloud, both my well-beloved and the dead man's widow standing in rigid silence.

The elucidation of the bewildering mystery and its tragic dénouement held us speechless. It staggered belief.

My explanation to Bullen, or our subsequent conversation, need not be here recounted. Suffice it to say that from that moment, when the truth became apparent, the Major's widow, who had once sought to take both our lives, became our firmest and most intimate friend, while Graham, having expressed regret at his association in the conspiracy, and declared his intention of leading an honest life in future, was allowed to escape abroad, where he still remains.

And Beryl? She is my wife. Ah! that small word, which is

synonymous with peace and happiness. Several years have passed, and I have risen rapidly in my profession—far beyond my deserts, I fear—yet we are still lovers. We are often visitors at Atworth and at Gloucester Square, while there is no more welcome guest at our own table in Harley Street than the ever-erratic Bob Raymond.

The original copy of the ponderous ancient Florentine treatise with its rusty lock, which the Major left in possession of La Gioia, had been presented by the latter to the Bodleian Library at Oxford, where it can now be seen, while Hoefer's re-discovery of the vayana having opened up an entirely new field to toxicologists, the deadly vegetable, like strychnine and atropia, is to-day used as one of the most powerful and valuable medicines, many lives being saved yearly by its administration in infinitesimal doses.

All the bitterness of the past has faded. What more need I say?

To-night as I sit here in my consulting-room, writing down this strange history for you, my friendly reader, my wife lingers beside me, sweet and smiling in white raiment—a dead-white dress that reminds me vividly of that June day long ago when we first met within the church of St. Ann's, Wilton Place, while at her throat is that quaint little charm, the note of interrogation set with diamonds, a relic of her ill-fated mother.

She has bent, and, kissing me tenderly upon the brow, has whispered into my ear that no man and wife in all the world are half as happy as ourselves.